W9-AHF-916

You

Would

Have

Told

Me

Not

To

Also by Christopher Coake

We're in Trouble (stories)

You Came Back

You
Would
Have
Told
Me
Not
To

stories

Christopher Coake

Delphinium Books

YOU WOULD HAVE TOLD ME NOT TO

For information, address DELPHINIUM BOOKS, INC.,
16350 Ventura Boulevard, Suite D
PO Box 803
Encino, CA 91436

Library of Congress Cataloging-in-Publication Data is available
on request.
ISBN 978-1-883285-90-6
20 21 22 LSC 10 9 8 7 6 5 4 3 2 1

First Edition

"That First Time" was originally published in *Granta*
"Waste" was originally published in *Booth*
"Getaway" was originally published in *The Portland Review*
"You Would Have Told Me Not To" was originally published on-
line in *Great Jones Street*

To my mother, Jan Coake, who wrote my stories down
when they first appeared.

Contents

That First Time

Bob Kline was sitting at his computer, reading and then deleting a number of old letters from his soon-to-be ex-wife, Yvonne, when he received an email from a sender he didn't know. Its subject line contained a name—Annabeth Cole—he didn't recognize, either. The email read:

Is this the Bobby Kline who went to Westover High in 1988? If so, I'm sorry to tell you that Annabeth Cole died several months ago. She wanted you to know. If you have any questions, call me. Sorry to bring bad news.

At the bottom of the message was a number and a name: Vicky Jeffords.

Bob stared at the email for a long time, not understanding it at all, his eyes still damp and blurred from the hour he'd spent reading Yvonne's old love letters. In the early days of their marriage her job had kept her traveling, and she'd sent him dozens of them, each one impossibly sweet. *I'm just looking out over the ocean and missing you. I'll be thinking of you as I fall asleep. I heard a song today that reminded me of you.* He tried now to pull his thoughts together.

Annabeth Cole? He was the Bob Kline this Vicky wanted, but as far as he could remember, he'd never gone to school with an Annabeth. He dug for a while in his closet, pulled out his yearbook. He didn't see an Annabeth in his class—or a Vicky, for that matter.

He went to the kitchen of his apartment and opened a can of beer. Then he called the number Vicky had given him. A woman answered after two rings.

"This is Bob Kline," he said. "Vicky? You emailed—?"

"Bobby!" she said. "This is Vicky. Thanks for calling."

Her voice was completely unfamiliar.

"Sure," he said. "Listen—I'm the guy you want, but I have to say I'm a little confused. I don't remember going to school with an Annabeth."

"Annabeth *Cole*."

"Help me out. How did I know her? Did I know *you?*"

After a few seconds of silence, she said, "Not as well as you knew Annabeth. You slept with her once. If that narrows it down any."

He looked up at the ceiling. "I did?"

"She and I went to Oak Park. She met you at a—"

And then Bob knew. "*Annie?*" he said. "Holy shit."

He sat down hard on the couch. Annie. It had been what—eighteen years? He'd forgotten her last name. And if she'd ever told him her full name was Annabeth, he'd forgotten that, too. A picture of her came into his mind: a small, slender girl, long sandy-colored hair, glasses. He'd only known her a week, if that. They *had* slept together, just once, when he was seventeen. He'd never spoken to her again.

He asked, "How?"

"Cancer. Non-Hodgkin's lymphoma."

Vicky told him the story while he stared at the beer can on his knee. She had been Annabeth's—Annie's—best friend since grade school. And Bobby had met Vicky soon after he met Annabeth—did he remember? At the pizza place? He told her he did, but this was mostly a lie. He remembered a girl, sitting across the booth, while he flirted with Annie. A placeholder shape in his memory. Was she tall? Maybe blond?

Vicky told him she had gone to stay with Annabeth in Chicago for the month before Annabeth died. Toward the very end they talked a lot about the old days, and about what to do when Annabeth was gone, and Annabeth had written Bob's name on a list of people who might want to hear the news. Vicky had been tracking everyone down.

"There are a lot of Bob Klines," she said. "You're a hard man to find."

Vicky then told him about the service, three months past. He tried to follow the details, but he was still too stunned, still trying to figure out why he'd gotten the call.

When Vicky was quiet again, he said, "Look, I guess I don't remember Annie and me . . . ending up on the best of terms. Back then."

"I don't either," Vicky said.

"Was she—was she still angry with me?"

It was a stupid question, and he knew it the moment the words were in the air.

Vicky said, "Well, you were her first time."

"Yeah," he said, rubbing a knot at the base of his skull.

"And it was kind of intense. For her. I mean the whole thing. She was pretty messed up, after you dumped her."

"Yeah," he said again.

Vicky said, "Well. She thought you might remember her. And that you'd want to know."

"I do," he said. "Listen, Vicky—"

He could barely believe he was saying this.

"I'm not like I was then. I mean, I was seventeen. She was such a sweet girl. If I could do it over—"

"Hey," Vicky said, "we were kids."

He couldn't even picture the outlines of the girl Vicky had been, but he could see her now, on the other end of the phone: a middle-aged woman with her head in her hand, tired and sad. He wanted to say something else to her, to console her. But while he was thinking of what that might be, she said, "I should go. I'm sorry, Bobby."

When she'd hung up, Bob went to the patio doors and opened the blinds. He lived in an apartment overlooking downtown Indianapolis, fifteen floors up. The sun was setting, and the city lights were coming on, which was more or less the best thing that happened to him anymore, and he liked to keep the appointment. He'd been separated from Yvonne for six months, and hadn't been doing much since but working and then coming home to sit out on his balcony at night, drinking and watching the lights come on, telling himself they'd done the right thing.

His head was pounding now. He decided the circumstances called for a switch from beer to bourbon. For a little impromptu wake.

Bob picked up a bottle and glass from the kitchen, and took them both to the balcony. A helicopter darted overhead. Next door he could hear a lot of people talking, the sound of music playing, jazz. He had classy neighbors on that side.

He finished the bourbon in his glass and tried to find

grief for poor Annie in his swimming head. It was some-where outside of him, but faint, like the music he could just hear through the walls from next door.

Annie Cole. He'd broken her heart. Not on purpose, but all the same he had. He meant all of what he'd said to Vicky—she had been a sweet girl, and he'd been stupidly cruel. When he'd thought of Annie these past eighteen years, it was to wish her a happy life, a good husband, a big yard with kids and dogs. Had she told him she wanted those things? Or had he simply given them to her, in his mind? He couldn't remember.

He lifted his glass, first to the party next door, then to the big glittery mirror-windowed office building across the street, where a few sad souls still worked; in this light he could just see them, ghostlike, through the reflective glass. *To Annie*, he thought. He wasn't a religious man, but for her sake he hoped there was a heaven, someplace far away from loneliness, from sickness, from people like him.

• • •

A week went by. Bob's settlement meeting with Yvonne and her attorney was coming up in another two. As the day pulled closer, he grew more and more impatient, more restless.

He ran his own business, a house-painting compa-ny. As he worked that week, both in his office and bal-anced carefully on his ladder, he found himself think-ing more and more about Annie Cole. He'd been so shocked to hear the news that he'd asked Vicky almost nothing about her. The adult Annabeth. In his head she was still the tiny slip of a girl he'd known for a week in high school; he couldn't picture her as a grown woman, let alone someone pale, bald, suffering. Dying, and then dead.

Then, Bob remembered: he might still have a picture of Annie, packed away in storage. She'd sent one to him, after, and he didn't think he'd ever had the heart to throw it out. When he came home that night, he unlocked his basement storage cage and dug out the box labeled HIGH SCHOOL. He lugged it upstairs and emptied it on the living-room floor. He set aside his diploma, and a bunch of old report cards, all relentlessly unexceptional. For the first time in years he looked at his senior prom picture, taken with Yvonne. In her gown she looked fabulous, proud, older than she was; he, however, looked confused, maybe even a little scared. But, then, he'd been stoned that night.

Scattered on the bottom of the box were several loose photos. Annie's was one of them: a wallet-sized picture, well tattered. In it she leaned against a tree, wearing a baby-blue sweater and a tan skirt. She was smiling shyly, and wasn't wearing her glasses. Her hair fell thick and glossy over her shoulder. On the back of the photo was a girl's handwriting: *To Bobby. I'll never forget. Love, Annie.*

By the time Annie sent him this picture, he had already moved on, and was avoiding her. He set it down on the carpet, right next to the prom photo. And there they were: the triangle Yvonne had never known about.

Bob had already been in love with Yvonne the summer he and Annie met. That was the whole problem. Yvonne, his first girlfriend, the first person he'd slept with. That summer–1988–they'd briefly broken up, while she prepared to leave Indiana for college in Maryland. Bob's folks had just split, and by arrangement he spent the summer in his father's house in little Oak Park, fifty miles from Westover. There Bob had a jumbled basement room with its own bathroom and exterior door. His father worked late a lot, and Bob was in a town he didn't know well, and in which he wouldn't stay past summer's end. Everything, even the ground under his feet, felt impermanent.

He worked part-time in a restaurant, and met a lot of Oak Park kids there. He was a decent-looking guy, and thanks to connected friends back in Westover, he always had pot, so he found himself, that summer, strangely popular. He took advantage. In the month after Yvonne broke things off, he brought three different girls back to his basement room. Why not? He didn't know then whether what he felt was freedom or despair. When he was in his room, smoking a joint, or stripping off the panties of a girl he'd just met, he was able to believe it was freedom.

He'd met Annie at the park, while he was waiting with his friend Leo for their turn at a game of pickup hoops one sweltering June night. Annie sat in the grass next to them with a friend—it must have been Vicky—watching boys she knew on the other team. Who had talked first? Bob couldn't remember. But they'd introduced themselves, chatted, joked.

He looked down at the picture in his hands. He would have noticed Annie's hair first. And then her voice. He remembered it: strangely deep, sly. He remembered her long thin legs, her white tennis shoes. He and Leo got up to play their game, and when he came back twenty minutes later, Annie had left. But she'd written her number on a slip of paper and tucked it beneath his keys.

Bob called her that afternoon, and a couple of nights later they met up at the Pizza King downtown. Annie brought Vicky and he brought Leo. Bob sat next to Annie in the booth. She was wearing a short skirt, and was laughing and wild and flirty, turning in the seat to face him and, once, putting her hand on his knee.

Later that night, down in his basement room, he was shocked when Annie told him it was her first time. *Why me?* he asked her. *You barely know me.*

Annie, curled up beside him on the bed, laughed and blushed, and said, *I feel like I do. Like you're right for me.*

Bob put down the photo. Against whatever judgment he had left, he called Yvonne. She didn't answer. He left her a message: "A friend of mine from high school died. It's thrown me for a loop. I'd really like to see you before next week—"

He realized what he was saying and quickly hung up. Then, without setting down the phone, he dialed Vicky's number.

While her phone rang, he stood out on the balcony. Off to the east a thunderhead had massed; lightning flickered down over the suburbs. If it rained tomorrow, there'd be no painting; he'd have nothing at all to do. The thought filled him with panic.

"Vicky," he said when she answered. "It's Bob Kline."

"Oh! I thought the number looked familiar."

"Is it a bad time? I can let you go."

"No. I'm fine, really. How are you?"

"I don't know," he said. Leaves blew onto his balcony, from someplace in the city that had trees. "I guess I'm a little curious."

He listened to the long silence.

"Is it all right if I ask about her?" he said. "I don't want to put you in a bad spot—"

"No! Ask. Please."

Her voice was strange. Was she crying? He couldn't tell.

He said, "I forgot to ask whether she was happy. I want to know if she—if she was in a good place."

"Yes," Vicky said. "Until she got sick, she was very happy."

"Was she married?"

"Yes."

"Nice guy?"

"Yeah. They were good for each other."

"Kids?"

"No. She wanted them. But no."

Bob stood and leaned against the rough concrete wall of the building. Rain was starting to fall through the glow of the patio light, the drops appearing frozen for an eyeblink.

"What did she do?" he asked.

"She was a lawyer."

He laughed.

"Is that funny?"

"I'm in the middle of a divorce," he said. "Or at the end, I guess I mean. I make a lot of lawyer jokes."

"She was a prosecutor."

"Well, I've steered clear of those, at least," he said, sounding so inane he swallowed a quarter of his drink.

She was quiet on the other end. He said, "Hey, I can let you go. I'm just shooting the shit now."

"It's all right," Vicky said. "I'm—I get a little defensive about her."

"Can I ask another question? Do you mind?"

"Sure."

"Was it–" He ran a hand through his hair. "Did she suffer? Was it bad?"

Another long quiet.

"It was cancer," Vicky said.

"You were with her."

"Yes. Me and Luke and her folks."

"That must have been–"

"It was hard."

He said the next part quickly, meaning every word of it: "I don't know you, or even her, really. But it sounds to me like she was real lucky in her friends."

The line sounded so empty that he had to check the screen on his phone to make sure he hadn't lost the call.

"Thanks," Vicky said at last. A little burble of sound. "It's–it's been rough. I miss her."

Bob wanted to say, I do too–but that would be stupid. Up until a week ago he hadn't missed her at all. But he did, now that he thought about her. He missed the girl touching his knee at the Pizza King. That feeling of invitation.

"Listen," he said. "You said you live in Indy?"

"Yeah."

"You want a drink? I'm just sitting around here thinking about this. If it'll help–I mean if you want to–I'm glad to meet you someplace. To–you know. I'd listen."

He hadn't planned on saying that, but once he had, he hoped dearly Vicky would say yes. But why would she? She didn't know a thing about him except that he'd screwed over her friend in the eleventh grade. He paced back and forth and wondered at his own stupidity.

But then Vicky said, "Sure. Okay."

It turned out she lived not very far from him, out in the neighborhoods to the east, right underneath the lightning and the smudge of rain. She gave him the name of a bar halfway between them.

Bob spent a few minutes in the bathroom, shaving off two days' worth of stubble, looking with dismay at his jowls, scraping white paint from his cuticles, rubbing some gel in his hair. He was thirty-five, but he looked older. He had some gray at his temples. Years working in the sun had done a number on his skin. He was tanned, at least; he didn't look unhealthy. Vicky would be remembering the seventeen-year-old he'd been: long, greasy hair, bloodshot eyes, a wispy goatee. Whatever he was now would have to be an improvement. He put on a nice polo shirt and clean blue jeans and black shoes.

Bob squared himself up in the mirror. After the attention, he still looked just like he felt: lonely, a little drunk, probably on his way to making a mistake.

• • •

Just before Bob walked into the bar, he realized he'd forgotten to ask what Vicky looked like. She hadn't asked him, either.

But it was a Tuesday night and the bar wasn't busy. After his eyes had adjusted to the light, he spotted Vicky right away, sitting at a small table against the outer wall. She was the only woman in the place who looked as though someone close to her had just died: her face was a white, sad oval in the low warm light. Whatever he looked like, she spotted him too, right away; she stood the moment he met her eyes, offering a half-wave.

He'd been trying to remember a blonde, but Vicky was a redhead, her hair in a pixie cut, though her face was a little too round for that to work. She'd dressed in a light-green blouse and black slacks. Work clothes, he thought. On the whole she looked nice, but not done up. Plain, Yvonne would say, in the way she had. The beautiful woman's judgment.

"Bobby," she said.

"Vicky."

Then she smiled at him, crookedly, maybe happy or sad or both at once—and right there he remembered her, sitting across the table from him at the Pizza King. The smile was the key. While Annie flirted with him, Vicky's smile had gone more and more lopsided, tipping through sadness and into panic; her laughter had gotten louder and louder. The best friend getting left behind.

He held out a hand to her, but Vicky shrugged and gave him an embrace instead, quick and clumsy. When they pulled apart, she said, "You haven't changed a bit."

He wanted to protest that.

"I remembered you," he said, "but I wasn't sure I'd recognize you."

Vicky laughed a little. Her cheeks were dotted with freckles, and the low neckline of her blouse showed him more. He didn't remember those, but he liked them.

"So, you want a drink?" she said. "First round's on me."

"Thanks," he said. "Jack and Coke?"

Vicky walked over to the bar and Bob sat at her table. An empty margarita glass stood next to her car keys. Beside her keychain was a small photo album, closed with a clasp. She'd brought pictures of Annie along. Bob wished he had the drink in him already.

Vicky came back with their drinks. She sat and sighed, and said, "Bobby Kline."

"You know," he said, "I go by Bob these days."

"Oh, right. I don't know if I can do that. In my head, you've been Bobby for eighteen years."

"Fair enough. You mind if I keep calling Annabeth Annie?"

Her eyes flickered up. "I guess not."

"And you're Vicky."

"And Vicky I shall remain."

He liked her. Had he expected not to? He lifted his glass, and she followed suit; they clinked rims. "Thanks for this," he said.

"You're buying the next one."

"I will. But I mean meeting me."

She shrugged, smiled her half smile. "I've been spending a lot of time in my head, you know? It's good to be out."

"This your bar?"

"One of them."

"It's nice."

She nodded and took a sip of her drink. "Oh, Bobby," she said. "I don't know if I can do small talk."

Her eyes were very green.

He said, "I guess now that I've got you here, I don't know what to ask."

Vicky said, "I think I can guess. You can't figure out why she wanted me to call you."

He laughed, surprised—that was it all right. "Yeah."

"You weren't the only person I called. The only ex-boyfriend."

"I'd be real sorry if I was."

Vicky kept her eyes on him. She was very good at that.

He said, "I guess for my sake I was kind of hoping I wasn't . . . still important."

Vicky said, "You were the first guy she ever slept with. You never forget your first, right?"

Bob remembered Yvonne, in the back seat of his old Impala, grinning, unbuttoning his jeans, guiding his hand underneath her skirt. *You better be sure,* she'd told him. *This is the big time.*

He'd felt the warm inside of her thigh with wonder and said, *I am absolutely, positively sure.*

"Yeah," he told Vicky. "You never do."

"Annabeth was obsessed with you," Vicky said. "Right from the start, when she talked to you in the park. She was crushed for months, after you dumped her."

It hurt him to hear, but he had no place to hide from it.

"I was an asshole," he said. "I admit it."

"You were a total prick, is what you were."

He kept his eyes on his drink.

"I'm sorry, Vicky. I wish I could have apologized to her. I know that's easy to say, now—"

"So why didn't you?"

"I don't know. I always thought about looking her up, but at a certain point I figured the past is the past, you know?"

He was lying. It had never occurred to him to call Annie, or any of the other women he'd slept with that summer, after Yvonne showed up at his doorstep and said she wanted him back. Sure, he'd treated Annie badly, but Yvonne had come back for him, and once that happened, he couldn't turn around and stare for even a second at where he'd been, what he'd done.

A furrow was deepening between Vicky's eyebrows.

He said, "I don't want to excuse myself, okay? I feel like shit. It's why I called you. I can't stop thinking about how terrible it is that this happened."

"You can't, huh."

"Do you need to tell me off?" he asked. "Would that make it better?"

"No," Vicky said. "It wouldn't."

Bob wished he hadn't called her, that he hadn't come. He took another drink. It had gotten dark, and the rain was coming down hard.

He asked, "Did she hate me?"

Vicky might have been gearing up to it for a while, but after that question, out of nowhere, she dropped her head and began to cry. Not noisily; she ducked her head and tears rolled out of her eyes, and she fumbled for a napkin.

"Hey now," he said.

After a while she shook her head. "She wasn't like that."

"She had to. At least a little."

Vicky jerked her head up. "No! She wanted you to remember! Is that so fucking hard to figure out? She was dying! She shared something really special with you. Maybe she thought you might still have a heart in there, huh?"

Over Vicky's shoulder the bartender was giving them both the eye. Other people were looking, too.

Vicky's voice quavered. "She was the one who told *me* not to hate you—"

Bob stood up. Vicky had started to sound too much like Yvonne, like every phone call he'd taken from her late at night, when she'd had to accuse him of anything and everything, and he'd had to agree.

"I'm sorry. I didn't mean to upset you. I'll go."

Vicky put a hand over her eyes. "You don't have to," she said. "I'm sorry."

"Annie was a good girl. Better than me. I'll always remember her. Okay?"

Vicky didn't say anything, or move her hand. Her shoulders shook. Bob stood at her side for a few seconds, unsure whether to say anything more, or squeeze her shoulder, or what. She still didn't move. Finally he figured he'd done enough damage and he walked out the front door. The heavy rain gave him an excuse to jog the half block to his car, to pile in and drive away as fast as he could.

• • •

Inside his parking garage he didn't get out of the car. He couldn't bring himself to go home yet. What had Vicky said? She'd been in her head too much. That was about right—so had he. If he went inside he'd call Yvonne, he knew it. Better to keep both of his hands on the wheel and maneuver the downtown streets. He had a little too much drink in him, so he stopped at a drive-through for black coffee and sipped it carefully in a drugstore parking lot before taking on the rest of the drive.

He'd lied to Vicky. He'd said he'd always remember Annie. But he couldn't remember everything that happened, at least not in the way Annie had always believed. He remembered meeting her, remembered flirting with her. Remembered taking her to his room.

But the sex, the actual first time Annie had chosen him for—he couldn't remember any of it.

He remembered pulling a handful of beers for the two of them out of his father's refrigerator. He remembered Annie asking him if he had any pot—she said she'd heard that if you got high before you did it, it wouldn't hurt as much. He told her he did have pot, but that it might hurt anyway. *It's okay*, she said. *I'm ready*.

So they smoked for a while, and then made out. He remembered the two of them listening to one of his father's Pink Floyd records, and some hazy other pictures, and not much afterward.

He remembered waking: Annie's head tucked against his shoulder, one of her legs flung across him. They were both hung over, and he took her to a diner on the interstate for coffee, which he found she'd never tried before. She made a face and joked about how sex was easier, the first time. He remembered thinking: Oh. So *they had* done it. They both joked about how much trouble she'd be in, for staying out all night without permission.

It was worth it, she said.

You sure? he asked. *It was all right?*

I'm sure.

He dropped her off down the block from her house. When he got back home, he saw the blood on his sheets, and that was what he remembered most of all: sitting hung over out behind the house, wadding up his sheets into a five-gallon bucket full of bleach and stirring them around with a stick before his father got home, the fumes causing his head to pound.

Annie called him that night, in tears, to tell him she

was grounded for two weeks. She told him she missed him. He remembered being reassuring, but feeling uneasy; she was an emotional girl, acting like he was a boyfriend.

And then a week later Yvonne called him, for the first time in a month. He remembered that call with great clarity; he'd been hoping for it all summer, jumping to his feet whenever the phone rang. *I can't do this,* she told him, crying, while he listened in disbelief. She said, *I can't live without you.*

He told her to come over, and she did. They lay together on his clean sheets, and she said, *Bobby, make love to me,* and if he thought about Annie Cole, or any of the other girls, it was only to hope he hadn't missed cleaning any trace of them out of the room. Yvonne took off his clothes and he took off hers and they cried together, and made love, and in the early morning he said, *I think we ought to get married, as soon as we can.* And she said, *Of course we should. We're meant for each other.* He remembered, and would always remember, kissing her then, his hands cupping her cheeks, while she pressed her entire length against him; afterward she stared into him with her big unblinking brown eyes.

Annie called again two days later, and that was when he'd begun to hurt her. She'd left a message on the machine: how she wanted to see him, how she was thinking about him all the time, how she was worried because he hadn't called. Yvonne was in the shower when he listened, and he was afraid she'd hear, too. He hit the Erase button before the message was over.

Annie left two more messages, her voice growing sadder and sadder. The last time she cried. *I can't understand this,* she said, over and over. He erased it. He'd told himself to call her, to explain, and he was working up the nerve when he came home two days later and found a letter taped to his door.

He tore up the letter without reading it, though he kept the picture that fell out when he'd undone the tape.

After that he never heard from her again. And if he felt bad, thinking of her afterward, well—there was Yvonne, talking about their wedding, the kids they'd have, the names they'd give them.

As Bob drove through the city, he imagined what it would have been like, if he'd chosen differently. If whatever had happened with Annie had made him love her, instead of Yvonne. Annie with her tiny body and her deep laugh. Her long silky hair. What if she'd been less desperate? Would he have liked her more, then? He imagined the two of them going off to IU together. Marrying their sophomore year. Maybe they would have been able to have kids. Maybe they would have had something to talk about, these last five years.

But whatever they would have been, Annie would still have gotten sick and died, and he would have had to watch.

Maybe, he thought—allowing himself the thought despite its poison—it would be better that way: maybe it was better to love someone who died than to see a woman who loved you slowly and surely realize her mistake.

Here was a first he'd never forget: the first time he cheated on Yvonne. This was three years ago. Yvonne was out of town, at her sister's. He'd started a fight just before she got on the plane, and she'd left tight-lipped, furious. He sat at home thinking about what she must be saying to her sister until he couldn't stand it anymore. He walked to a bar downtown and traded drinks with a woman ten years younger than him, who was only weeks away from going off to grad school. At the end of the night they shared a taxi home. While they were parked at the curb, he gave her a look, and she gave it back.

She said, *It's what you think.*

I'm married, he said.

She was twenty-two, blond, impossible. One of the straps of her dress had fallen off her shoulder. *Who am I going to tell? Come on in. We'll have fun.*

He had. They had. He remembered damn near everything.

• • •

Bob tried and tried to avoid it, but after an hour of driving aimlessly he found himself in Yvonne's neighborhood, up in Carmel. Their old neighborhood. She lived in their big condo, behind a gate, and at eight o'clock, after circling the block five times, he gave up and turned the wheel into the entrance. He hadn't seen her in two months. He punched her number into the security box. She answered right away.

"It's me," he said.

"What do you want?"

"To talk to you."

". . . Are you drunk?"

"No," he said. "Five minutes, that's all."

"Bob—"

"Five minutes. I don't even have to come in. We can even do it like this, if you want."

She didn't say anything. But after several seconds the gate buzzed open, and he drove slowly through. He parked in one of the Visitor slots, which, for a moment, made him want to cry.

Yvonne answered the door in a little black dress and heels. Immediately he smelled her perfume; it made him want to reach for her. She'd dyed her hair a dark maroon; the last time he saw her, it was long, but she'd had it cut short. It showed off her neck. He thought she might have lost a little weight, too. Her mouth was pursed, and she didn't look at him, beyond an initial once-over.

"You *are* drunk," she said. "You shouldn't be driving."

"I'm all right. You look great, by the way."

"I'm about to go out."

"A guy?"

She laughed and crossed her arms. "Like I'd tell you?"

He figured that meant no; these days, she would tell him.

"So what do you want?" she asked. "Four minutes, and I've got to go."

Bob peered at her again, trying to see the girl she'd been, the one he'd taken to prom. He could feel her anger swelling while he did.

"I've just been thinking about us," he said. "Trying to make sense out of it."

She laughed, without any humor. "Join the club."

He said, "How did this happen?"

"You told me you didn't love me anymore, is what happened. Remember?"

He ran a hand through his hair. "What if it wasn't true? What if I got it wrong?"

"Well, it's too late for that now," she said, and glanced theatrically at her watch. That was a favorite line of hers, right up there with *Maybe you should have thought of that before you fucked all those girls.*

"I did love you," he said. "I know that, and you do, too."

"And you felt the need to drive over here and tell me?"

"Can I ask you something?"

"Two minutes."

"Would you have done things differently? If you'd known?"

"What—if I knew we'd end up like this?"

"Yes."

She laughed again. "Of course I would have. I *married* you; I didn't think I was taking out a lease. Seriously, Bob. Would *you* have?"

"I don't know if I could have stopped myself," he said. "That's how in love I was."

"I'm leaving," she said. "Right after you."

Yvonne grabbed her purse from the kitchen table and gestured toward the door. She was still beautiful, still smarter and better than him. And Bob was everything she said he was, believed him to be. It was better for them to be apart. Better for her. He knew that.

But Yvonne was so beautiful—spectacular, really, in her dress and good shoes, smelling of flowers, her new hair shimmering around her neck. He couldn't help it.

"Von, are you really going to be mad at me the rest of your life?"

She stared at him.

He said, "If I died tomorrow, would you still hate me?"

Yvonne pressed her lips together and pointed at the door.

"Come on," he said. "Soon it's permanent. Answer me."

For a second he saw something else in her eyes, a moment of—of what? Sadness? Remorse? She still didn't answer him.

His next words surprised him. "Let me kiss you again," he said. "Once more, while I'm still your husband."

"Uh-uh. Absolutely not."

"I don't remember the last time we kissed," he said.

This was true; it had been bothering him. The last one had probably been nothing but a meaningless kiss goodbye, some morning as they left for work. His closed lips against her turning cheek.

She opened the door for him. Her voice still shaking, she said, "Well, I do."

• • •

The next day was a Saturday. It did rain, hard; he spent the entire day in his apartment, trying to keep busy, but in the evening he did what he had told himself he wouldn't do, what he'd spent all day cleaning and puttering around to avoid: he sat on the couch with a drink in one hand and the old pictures—Annie, he and Yvonne at prom—in the other. Both women looking up at the camera, happy, expectant. And him looking dull, stoned. Maybe a little scared. How had that skinny kid in the tux managed to cause so much pain? He looked at Yvonne, eighteen, thrilled to be alive and holding his hands. He turned over Annie's picture and read the inscription again. Why had they trusted him with anything?

His phone buzzed then against his hip; he dug it out. Yvonne, he thought. She'd probably thought up some good lines, or was going to give him the AA speech again.

Instead he saw Vicky Jefford's number on the screen. He told himself, *Don't answer. Do her a favor and never speak to her again.*

But he couldn't help it.

"Bobby," she said. "Thanks for picking up."

"Did you think I wouldn't?"

She sighed. "I wouldn't blame you. Listen. I'm sorry. I went off on you, and I shouldn't have."

"Vicky," he said, touched. "Come on. It was my fault, too."

"This is really hard on me," she said. "I lost my best friend. But I wouldn't want someone calling me on shit I did when I was seventeen, either."

"It's okay," he said. "My soon-to-be ex does all the time."

He thought he heard her lighting a cigarette. She said, "It's just that I feel like I have to honor her, you know? But I'm too unstable to do it right. I don't know why she trusted me with all this. She wouldn't have wanted me to yell at you."

He swirled the bourbon in his glass and looked at the pictures in front of him. He said, "Tell me something I don't know about her. What would she have wanted me to know?"

Vicky was quiet for a while. Then she said, "She would have wanted you to know she was strong. To know she was *tough*. She grew up and put bad guys in jail. She was proud of that."

Another silence, and he knew they were coming to

the end of things. After they hung up, there'd be no reason for either of them to call again. But he didn't want to hang up. Vicky might be crazy, but he liked her voice on the other end of the phone. He thought again of the freckles on her chest, and wondered what kind of a man that made him.

She surprised him. "Hey, Bobby," she said, "do you still get high?"

"What?"

"That was your rep," she said. "You were the Westover guy with the good pot. Annie was all nuts about you, and the first thing I said was, *the pot guy?*"

"Jesus," he said, leaning his head back on the couch. "Yeah, sometimes. But I don't exactly have the supply I used to."

She said, "I've got some. You want to come by? If we're going to talk about Annie—let's talk about Annie."

He sat up and looked at the clock. Was she really inviting him over?

"Vicky, it's late."

"I know. I don't sleep much. Not these days."

• • •

Half an hour later, showered, in a change of clothes and wearing aftershave, a rubber in his wallet (he'd debated it, and here it was), Bob knocked at Vicky's door. She lived in a nice new brownstone townhouse, not two miles from his apartment building. While he waited for her to open the door, he saw a tiger-striped cat watching him from the windowsill, its tail lashing. He tapped a finger against the glass; it fled instantly.

Vicky answered the door. Her eyes were red, a little glassy; she might not have waited for him to light up. "Bobby," she said, with her crooked smile. "Come on in."

She was dressed in a pajama top and cut-off shorts, and was barefoot. One of her ankles was ringed with some kind of tribal tattoo. Her thighs were freckled, too.

He followed her into the townhouse. "Nice place," he said, even though it was a mess. Her living room was full of books, and every surface was dusty. Through an arched doorway he could see a kitchen counter piled with dishes. The air smelled like incense and weed and maybe some kind of Mediterranean food.

"Thanks for calling," he said.

"Thanks for coming," she said. Then she stopped and leaned forward and hugged him, as awkwardly as she had at the bar. She sniffled in his ear. She might be high, but she was still sad, too.

"You want a drink?" she asked. "I've only got wine. Red."

"I'll take some, sure."

Wine and bourbon and weed. He might not survive the coming morning. From the couch, he heard the kitchen faucet come on, water splashing. Music was playing softly from speakers he couldn't see—a woman and an acoustic guitar; he couldn't make out the words. He looked over the walls. Even the spaces that weren't covered by bookshelves had books stacked against them, as high as his chest. He realized he'd not asked what Vicky did for a living.

On the end table, next to his elbow, was a baggie of weed and rolling papers. Beside it was a photograph in a wooden frame. He turned it to get a better look. It showed Vicky—in college, he guessed—and another woman, standing together in bikinis, on a dock someplace blue and tropical.

He stared a few seconds before he recognized the other woman as Annie.

He picked up the photo and peered closely. Annie hadn't remained a skinny little girl. She'd grown up and out—she'd become a knockout, in fact, tanned and curvy. The Vicky next to her—tall, angular, sunburnt across her forehead—seemed to know it, too; she was shrinking into herself, her smile as uncertain as it had been back in Oak Park. She knew she was completely outmatched.

This was the picture Vicky kept out for herself to see.

She came back from the kitchen and handed him a generous glassful of wine. "That's my favorite picture of her," she said.

"She's beautiful."

"Yeah. She always was." Vicky took the photo from him and held it against her chest. "You want to see more pictures?"

Did he? Vicky wanted him to, at least, and he didn't want to disappoint her. "Sure."

Vicky disappeared, then returned with the little photo album he'd seen last night, on the table at the bar.

She sat next to him on the couch and put the album between them, balanced on their knees. He resisted the impulse to put his arm around her shoulders. He hadn't picked up any definitive signs from her, that way, since arriving, and he felt a little sheepish. He wished he hadn't put on aftershave, but if she noticed it, she gave no sign.

She opened the album. "That's us in elementary school," she said.

Looking at the pictures was the strangest thing he'd done in a long time. He turned the pages and watched Annie slowly age, from a little kid with braces into a tomboy, and from there into the skinny long-haired girl he remembered.

In college Annie suddenly blossomed, and not just her body; he saw something in her face that hadn't been there before. She and Vicky toasted the camera with martini glasses. Was it that she seemed calmer? A sudden intuition told him: there was someone on the other side of the camera she liked.

Then on to adulthood. Annie and Vicky sitting at a New Year's party, wearing hats. A man sat next to Annie, smiling at the camera, his hand over hers. An average-looking white guy, thin, with a full beard and glasses.

"Luke?" he said.

"That's him."

Only two pictures in the album didn't have Vicky in them. The first was a wedding picture, in black and white: Annie in her gown, caught in a swirl of activity, at the reception probably—she looked to be on a dance floor, surrounded by blurred bodies. Annie was grinning, eyes and teeth shining, her face turning back to look at the camera over her shoulder. Bob thought of the pictures he had of Yvonne, looking like that, and had to pinch the bridge of his nose.

The second picture—the last one—showed Annie sick. She was sitting on a deep couch, looking up at the camera, a blanket on her lap and a mug in her hands. She was wearing a bulky sweatshirt, but her face and her

drunk. We didn't take home any medals, okay?"

Vicky took a breath and held it. He braced himself for her anger.

But she said, "Tell me about her."

"You know her so much better—"

Vicky's cheeks were scarlet.

"No," she said. "I mean—I mean *during*. When you were . . . together."

"I can't," he said, his mouth dry.

"It's the only way I'll ever know," she said. "Who else could I ask? Luke?"

He thought of Vicky, across the table at the Pizza King, her face just a blur in the background, while Annie touched his knee. He thought of erasing Annie's message, her voice cutting off mid-word.

"Please," Vicky said.

So he took a deep breath and told her what he could. Vicky leaned closer. He told her all the details he could remember: Annie touching his knee. Twining her fingers in his as he drove to his apartment. Murmuring while he kissed her. He hoped this would be enough.

Vicky nodded. She took a drink, her fingers white around her glass. She whispered the next question: "Tell me what it was like?"

Bob wanted to tell her, but he'd reached the limit of his memories.

"It was great," he said anyway.

"How?"

Vicky had closed her eyes, was waiting.

He couldn't remember. He really couldn't.

Then the solution came to him.

Carefully, without using her name, he told Vicky instead about Yvonne—about that first time, after Yvonne came back to him. He told Vicky about a beautiful girl naked beneath the blankets, laughing; about the silky feel of her body; about how she never stopped moving against him, almost like water on a shore. About the surprising strength of her kisses. He told her about the sweet taste of her skin and lips. How, when they were done, she took his hand and kissed his palm, right in the center. How she said, *This is special.*

Vicky's eyes were still closed. She spoke so softly he could barely hear the words: "She really tasted sweet?"

He thought of Yvonne's clean wet hair, smelling of apples; of the vanilla gloss she used to put on her lips.

"Yeah," he said. "She really did."

"I knew it," Vicky said. She was smiling. "I just knew it."

Her Kind of People

It was nine p.m., and the wedding reception she was working was halfway through—the best man was making his toast; all the guests had just groaned at his first joke— and Brooke died a little inside, and all she could think was whether *this* was the night she needed to figure out a way to get fired.

She was near the end of her second summer working as a server at the Cortazar Hotel's restaurant and banquet hall, and for well over a month now she'd been daydreaming longingly about a dramatic exit—one that would blow her life up so spectacularly that she'd have no choice but to move immediately away from Reno, to start over anew in some other city. But dreaming was not the same as doing, was it?

The best man referred to meeting the groom at a fraternity initiation, and a lot of the bros in the room laughed knowingly, and that was when Brooke could stand it no longer; she asked another server, Lin, to cover for her. Lin, maybe spotting the chaos in her eyes, hissed, "Five minutes," and Brooke fled through the doors at the back of the banquet room.

She could just walk away. She ached to.

She lowered her head and walked through the chaos of the kitchen, then out again through a service door, and— as had been the case on each of the last several nights at work—she made herself calm down, to think rationally.

To—once again—perform the math.

The Cortazar and its restaurant had a reputation for elegance—hard to come by, in this town—and it paid good servers time-and-a-half not to screw up family memories. If she quit she would only end up serving at some other place where she'd have no seniority and even less dignity—for instance, at a casino, where she'd wear a miniskirt and heels while delivering cocktails to handsy old men playing slots, as her mother had done for the last twenty years. Brooke was—temporarily, while she tried, somehow, to build savings—not going to college, and so was three years at best from having the degree in business she really wanted. Her car was a peeling, creaking, hand-me-down Volvo that might or might not start if she asked it to, let alone take her to Denver, or Portland, where the rents were higher, where she knew almost no one, and where she'd end up serving anyway.

Brooke exited the hallway into the hotel's south stairwell. There she descended all the way to the bottom, where the stairs dead-ended below street level in a dark concrete well. The staff threw bags of dirty linens down here at the end of every shift, but otherwise no one lingered in the stairway for long—the hotel guests rarely bothered to use the ground-floor door, which exited into one of Reno's shadier downtown alleys.

Brooke lay down on top of the bags in the near darkness. She'd asked Lin for five minutes, but Lin took longer breaks all the time, and Brooke figured she could get away with taking ten. She let herself sink into the soft linens, her feet throbbing, her lower back aching, as though she were an old woman—her mother—already. (When her mother was twenty-three, Brooke had been four; reminding herself that she had it easier didn't make her feel better.) Through the exit door overhead she heard the muted conversations of passersby, the beat of drums from a band playing live outside the casinos across the train tracks, the thrum of Ubers and taxis.

Her phone buzzed. She couldn't look. It was either a text from Lin, urging her to come back already—and screw that—or it was from Kyle.

Her boyfriend, with whom she had now been living for a month.

This arrangement had been completely unexpected. Two months ago, Brooke had lost her roommate of a year (her good friend Maggie, who'd called her to say she'd eloped with a guy from Vegas); this news coincided with being told her rent was about to go up three hundred dollars. She'd been near despair. Rents were suddenly through the roof everywhere in town, if you could find a place at all.

Kyle, though, had room; he was thirty, and made good money selling Jeeps for a dealership, and owned a house northwest of downtown with two bedrooms and a landscaped backyard. He had been incredibly nice and decent with Brooke after Maggie moved out, and finally he'd taken her to dinner and said, reddening, *You know, you could come stay with me.* He'd seen her alarm and added quickly: *Just while you figure out what to do?* She'd held out for as long as she could bear—after all, she and Kyle hadn't even been seeing each other six months—but finally she'd relented. The math was the math. Kyle was only charging her a share of utilities, and she'd had to argue to pay him that. She had a roof over her head and a chance to fill up her bank account—

But god, she hated serving, god, she hated weddings and their speeches and their weird emotional politics, and *god*, she especially hated working them now that, for the first time in her life, she was living with a man . . . one, she knew, who would *really* like it if their arrangement was permanent.

That was the thing. Kyle loved her, had been crazy about her from the start—which baffled her. She was young and broke and always exhausted; what made *her* the answer to his prayers? She had spent too much time tonight distracted, thinking about how Kyle was home—at *his* home—cooking her some kind of elaborate but not-good meal for the end of her shift, and that he was going to stay awake until midnight, or after, and present it to her with all kinds of affection when she walked in the door. Afterwards, he was going to want to have sex. This was all very nice. He was extraordinarily nice. But Brooke was running out of ways to tell him she was tired, that as nice as he was, she sometimes needed to be alone. Or—

Her phone buzzed again. She checked: it *was* Kyle. He'd sent a photo of himself, standing in front of the full-length mirror in the bathroom. He was wearing an apron and nothing else, and he'd turned to the side and stuck out his muscular rear, and pressed a naughty finger to his lips.

She laughed, just a little. Kyle was a good dude.

He'd been introduced to her that way, by her friend Lars: *I know this really good dude you should meet.* Brooke hadn't yet come up with a better description. Kyle was a fundamentally cheerful, decent human, always trying to put a positive spin on everyone's troubles. He was a small-town Northern Californian, blond and leanly muscled, who had spent much of his life playing outside. Their first date was a snowshoeing trip to a peak above Tahoe, and while she was no slouch, Brooke had been amazed at the speed with which he could climb, the way his laughter came out of him as easily as his steaming breath.

But Kyle was also, well . . . limited. He didn't read. He didn't do much besides work and play. His body and his strength and his smiling handsome face made sex with him aesthetically pleasing—but none of it felt particularly *good*, either. It felt kind of like working out. (He was older than her; he'd had several girlfriends before! He'd lived for thirty years! Was he so pretty no one had taught him anything?)

But oftentimes he'd pound barefoot away from the bed and come back bearing cold beers, and she'd watch Netflix on his laptop with him, buried in the crook of his big arm—and that part was really good. He was big and warm and safe and he liked her, accepted her, thought she was smart and funny.

He was lovable, sure.

But that wasn't the same as Brooke loving him, was it?

She was living in his house, and the best she could say was that she enjoyed the quiet moments, sometimes?

She wasn't saying she *couldn't love him*. Just that she *didn't*. At least not yet.

She'd been in love before, with her last boyfriend, Everett (god, the *thought* of him), and that relationship had ended up hurting like hell, and now here was Kyle, sweet Kyle, who wanted to take care of her. She should be happy! But at home, like here at work, she found herself employing, more and more, the same professional, practiced smile.

• • •

Above her, then, Brooke heard the interior door to the stairwell open.

She glanced, startled, at her phone. Was this the maître d', Constancia, coming to look for her? Maybe she was going to get fired, after all.

A single set of footsteps descended slowly to the level of the street: a heavy tread, a man's. A guest, probably. The door to the street opened–*good, good*–but the man didn't go outside. She heard him light a cigarette. Traffic grumbled on the street. The band next door was playing "Funkytown." A tendril of smoke found its way down to her. She supposed she could stand up and scold whoever it was–the hotel was strictly nonsmoking–but she wanted so badly to be alone. So she kept quiet and tried to wait him out.

Then the man spoke, so quietly Brooke almost thought she'd made up the words: "What are you *doing*?"

He had spoken to himself, she realized, but for a second there she'd felt caught out.

Then the stairwell door opened again. A woman called down: "Josh?"

The man said, "Yeah! Down here."

The woman descended the stairs; her heels clacked against each step. "Busted."

The man–Josh–said, "And here I thought I was being discreet."

"I saw you leave," the woman said. "I thought maybe you were avoiding me."

"No, no, I just–"

"I also heard you quit."

"Well, I did! But on special occasions ..."

"Shitty weddings?"

Josh laughed. The woman did, too.

Their laughter was wicked, conspiratorial, and in the dark below, Brooke smiled despite herself. She liked them for their laughter, whoever these people were. She'd heard too many trembling, earnest toasts to love everlasting all summer. These people, though—they seemed like her kind of people.

"I flew two thousand miles for a wedding," Josh said. "I'm across the street from a giant neon clown. I'm a little drunk. When else am I gonna smoke?"

"Ha," the woman said. Just like that, as a word. "What would Sonia say?"

A slight pause, a moment of high tension. Brooke was sure she'd heard it.

"God. She'd strangle me. Then make me watch one of those high school videos. Show me pictures of lungs full of tar."

"Ha," the woman said again. ". . . So can I have one?"

". . . And what would Rich say?"

"Oh, he'd approve," the woman said. "According to him, I'm repressed. Anything I do to show him I have actual desires, he likes to reinforce."

Josh didn't answer. Brooke heard the woman light the cigarette, or accept the light.

"Helen looks happy," Josh said finally. "Have you had a chance to meet Brian yet?"

"No, not really," the woman said. "I just got in this morning." Then, her voice lower: "He looks like such a *tool*."

Josh laughed, deeply, richly. "He talks like one, too. Tried to break my hand when he shook it."

"Helen can sure pick 'em."

Reno was, in the end, a small town; one of the weirdest things about working the weddings and rehearsal dinners was that a lot of the servers ended up knowing the secrets of a lot of the people in the room, and all the lace and fancy toasts and tear-stained cheeks and slow dances to Ed Sheeran couldn't undo that knowledge. Brooke could tell these two that the groom, Brian, was indeed a tool of the first order, a guy who moved a lot of coke through the bar he owned in Midtown, and who harassed women who served for him—like her friend Julia, whose ass he'd felt up while she was changing a tap, and not too long ago, either.

"At least Helen believes in true love," the woman said.

"Karen," the man said. Something in his tone said, *Be careful.* And something was maybe sad, too.

"Josh," the woman—Karen—said, slyly, teasingly.

"Helen told me you weren't coming."

"I only told Helen two days ago."

"And Rich couldn't come?"

"I didn't ask him to come."

"Oh." Josh shut the door to the street, and the stairwell grew quiet and contained, seemed to close around the conversation. Brooke breathed carefully through her nose. "I heard from Danny you two were giving it another try."

Karen said, "We are."

"So . . . he's not—"

"He ended it. He said so, anyway. And we've been in counseling. But the thing is, he's lying. I know he's lying. So I called Helen and said I could make it after all."

"And he didn't object?"

"Not very much. I'd bet a hundred bucks I know what he's doing with his time."

Brooke's phone buzzed, and for a sliver of a second

she thought it might be loud enough for the couple up the steps to hear. Slowly, deliberately, she slid it down between her hip and one of the bags of linen, and in the dark she felt her cheeks burn. *Kyle*, she thought, *hush!*

Or she was being summoned back upstairs. In which case, either now or soon, she was going to be in a world of trouble. Brooke had no way back to the restaurant except up those steps, and if these two didn't finish catching up soon—

She wondered what they'd do if they heard her cough. If she said, suddenly, *Excuse me, folks, but there's someone working down here.*

But she also kind of wanted to hear where this was all going—because the way these two talked to each other, she figured she knew.

And knowing this made her think of Everett, her ex-boyfriend, the boy she thought she'd loved, and what it had been like to see him at a party two weeks ago, and talk to him alone.

"Okay," Karen was saying, "So where's Sonia?"

"She couldn't get away from work."

"Couldn't she?"

"Truly. She also said there was no way in hell she'd fly to Reno for a third wedding. Not for Helen's, anyway." Josh chuckled.

"She didn't mind you going alone?"

"No," Josh said. "Then again, she didn't think you'd be here."

So, Brooke thought, she'd been right.

Brooke heard one of them—Karen, she thought—sit on one of the steps, just above her head. Brooke couldn't see them, of course, but she was close enough to them, to their voices, that she thought she could send her vision hovering up the short distance between her and the man and the woman, felt like she could stand beside them. She wanted to imagine them as beautiful, though of course they probably weren't. Most people weren't. But she was stuck, listening, and so they could be anybody she wanted. Josh, then, was tall and clean-shaven and had short brown hair and kind, sad eyes behind glasses, and wore a beautiful tailored black suit. Karen, she imagined as thin, with long lustrous black hair that curled in just above her shoulders, wearing a vintage cream dress with a flower print, and nude heels.

"This is surreal," Karen said. "It's been ten years since we were in the same room."

"I know," Josh said.

"Saying it out loud makes me feel old."

"You're not old."

"I am, and that means so are you." Then she lifted her voice. "Sit here with me a bit?"

Josh said, "Is that a good idea?"

"Nobody's going to see us. And so what if they do?"

"I can think of a lot of *so whats.*"

"Come on. Everyone assumes it anyway. And, what ... *Jeanine's* going to call Sonia? Or Danny? Please. Just sit."

Brooke heard Josh exhale, then cross the landing and sit beside her. He let out a brief, nervous-sounding laugh that echoed off the concrete.

She said, "Aren't you at least happy to see me?"

"Of course I am." Josh enunciated each word carefully. "I missed you."

They were silent a long while.

"You look really good," Karen said.

"Madame, you're drunk."

Karen's laugh was warm and low. Intimate. "Well, I

thought it when I was sober, too." A pause. "So how are you two doing? Really?"

"I don't know," he said. "I'd have to say not so good."

"I heard a rumor. Is Sonia really–"

"*It's not important.*"

"It's not important," Karen repeated, disbelieving.

"Not to me," he said. "Not really. I just want her to figure it all out."

Karen said, "Christ. You're nicer than I am."

Brooke swore she could hear Josh let out a long breath. "I can't push her. If I do–"

"Stop," Karen said, and her voice had a creak in it. "I'm sorry I asked."

A silence built between them.

Josh said, finally, "I've really missed you."

Then Karen was sniffling, and then crying, and Brooke, down below, closed her eyes.

• • •

For a while Josh was saying soft, concerned things. *Hey now,* he said, and *It's okay,* and *Shh. Tell me what's wrong.*

As though he didn't know.

And instead of worrying about how long it would take Karen to stop crying, and how she might be getting fired here in a few minutes if she couldn't get back upstairs, Brooke remembered instead how *she'd* cried after a party two weeks ago, after talking to Everett, her ex, in the corner of her friend's living room, after listening to him while *he'd* cried. How she'd felt, driving home later, to Kyle's.

And she remembered, too, how it was that she'd come to the party alone–Kyle was away for the weekend, backpacking the remote parts of Yosemite, and she'd been sitting alone in his house, afraid to touch anything, feeling like an intruder there about to be caught. And how, after she decided to go—and after a friend had texted her, *Hey just so you know E's here*—she'd spent extra time picking out a skirt and tights and putting on her makeup while staring at Kyle's speckled bathroom mirror.

How she'd told herself, *I just want to see what it feels like to talk to him again.*

How, when she'd seen Everett, standing in the corner of their friend's living room, looking as always wary and afraid, like an animal ready to flee into the woods, she'd gone right to him without any hesitation at all. How when he'd seen her, he'd straightened. Smiled. How she'd given him the briefest of sideways hugs—and how, even in that tiny window of touch, she'd felt her body welcome him. How twenty minutes later, after catching up, he'd touched her forearm before leaving.

He'd texted her later that night. *It was good to see you. I hope you're OK.*

By then she'd been back in Kyle's house, looking guiltily at her phone, in the middle of a living room that was, somehow, supposed to be hers.

She'd met Everett two years ago, in a photography class at the community college, during her last semester there. She'd been good at photography, according to their professor—it was an elective she'd picked at random; who knew?—and as a result she was often paired with Everett, the class's star. She'd not known what to make of him at first. Everett was short, thin, all elbows and ribs and knees. He had wide brown eyes and a deep voice for his little frame, and when she made smartass comments, he sometimes let out a big guileless blurt of a laugh, and he complimented her photos, pointing out details with his long thin fingers, and when he finally asked her out for a beer, she could tell how afraid he was, which charmed her, made her feel more beautiful, more talented, than she thought she probably was.

After class they got a beer, and then more beers, and talked late into the night, walking downtown up and down the path alongside the river. They sat beside each other on a rock on the banks and took off their shoes and put their feet in the icy water. She'd asked him for a kiss, which made him stammer.

He was a good person—she was sure of that—but Everett was *complicated*. To hang out with him usually meant enduring a grinding intellectual discussion or argument—everything *mattered* to him, always, and he was amazed when it didn't matter so much to others. To her. He was open about being depressed, and when he wasn't having intense conversations, he was often looking inward, brooding, distant. His mother drank heavily and lived in a truly frightening trailer park north of the city, and after Brooke had dated him only a month, the mother got hold of Brooke's number and began calling her, leaving long messages about Everett being a bad son, about how Brooke better not marry him—that Everett would turn on Brooke, just like he had turned on her.

Don't listen, Everett would say to her, bristling. *Why do you do that to yourself?*

It was a good question. The answer was always different:

Sometimes it was the jut of Everett's shoulder blades when he dressed himself beside her bed in the morning. Or the way he couldn't grow hair to connect his mustache and the beard on his chin. The torn and raggedy metal band T-shirts he wore, about which he was possessive and sentimental. The smell of his hair. That he knew how to kiss. The way he looked at the pictures he'd taken, his soft eyes darting from spot to spot on the screen of his laptop, like they were chasing something. The way he'd drum a fingertip on her knee during a movie, until all of her being seemed gathered into the spot he touched.

Because all of these things could and had made her a little dizzy, and she'd begun to wonder whether Everett's crazy mother might end up being in her life a long, long time.

Brooke began to see a new life stretching in front of her, one in which she followed Everett to college in Seattle, and then to a graduate art program—because he was not only good at photography, he was *great* at it, an artist through and through, and of course he'd pursue it; it would be a crime if he didn't.

Everett wanted her to come along. He asked her to. He sent her links to business programs at all of Seattle's colleges.

She put off answering him. She wanted to go, and she didn't. She wanted to keep dating Everett, to spend time with him—but he had come into her life earlier than she'd thought someone like him might or should. She had a *plan*: finish community college, save money for another year or two, then enroll in the university and get her degree. Her mother had married way too young, and though a lot of bad decisions had gone into her mother's life, that was the first and biggest, and her mother talked about it a lot: How she didn't regret Brooke, but she did regret a certain lack of *living*, that she hadn't gotten to be a young woman before becoming a wife and then a single mother, after Brooke's father ran off to Georgia with one of her friends.

Everett liked to take portraits of her. Brooke had never posed naked for him (though he'd asked, a lot), but in every picture he took of her, she seemed naked anyway— the way he saw her, the way he caught her with her guard down, was unsettling. In these photos she thought she looked too young, hesitant, even a little frightened. After a year together, she began to realize she felt naked with Everett all the time.

They began to argue about leaving town. *It hurts that you won't just say yes,* he'd say. *I've made up my mind, but you won't.* It was exhausting. Even when they didn't talk about it, she was tired and wary, knowing that he wanted so much from her. That she was disappointing him, even if he couldn't say it that way.

So one night she heard herself begin to say it aloud: *We need to end this.*

It was awful. Everett cried and begged her not to do it; she cried and told him she had to. It seemed to her that she watched herself do it, and only returned to her skin when it was done, and she was alone, drained, in her apartment. She told herself she was relieved, and a lot of the time it seemed to be true.

Somehow several months passed. Her friends tried to cheer her up, to fix her up. She'd gone on a few aimless dates. She'd told her friends, and the boys she met, that she didn't want anything complicated.

And then her friend Lars had said, *I know this really good dude.*

• • •

Above her, on the stairs, Karen could finally talk again.

"I can't go back in there," she was saying. "I don't want to have to answer any more questions about where Rich is. I don't want to pretend I'm happy for anybody."

Josh didn't answer.

Karen said, "Do I have to get divorced? How does Helen do it? I keep thinking: is this going to be me, in five years?"

Brooke held her breath.

"I know," Josh said. "I hear you."

"I'm scared," she said. "Aren't you?"

"Yes," Josh said. "All the time."

"So can we please just sit here a minute? Just like this?"

". . . Yeah," he said. "Sure."

Brooke should have been worried, for herself; she should have wanted them to stand up and free her. But she had closed her eyes, listening, imagining. She felt as though she was a spirit, hovering next to them. And then Josh said what she was urging him to.

"Here," he said. Brooke heard the rustle of clothing, the scrape of Karen's shoes.

"You're shivering," she said.

"Yeah," he said. "Sorry."

Karen said, "I just wish—"

But she didn't finish.

"Wish what?" Josh said.

She laughed. Sniffled. "I just wish we'd found people who'd love us better."

A long silence, so deep and stretched out that Brooke thought the beating of her own heart might be audible. He'd have to say something in return, wouldn't he?

Or maybe—and when she thought it, she couldn't help but yearn for it—they must be kissing. Maybe that was the only answer worth anything.

But then Josh said, "Hey. It's been a long time. We really need to get back in there."

"You never change," she said. "Do you?"

He didn't answer her then, either.

They stood. Brooke heard the rustle of Karen's dress. "Do I look like I've been crying?"

"You look great."

"Liar. . . . Aren't you coming?"

"You go ahead," he said. "I'll be up in a minute."

The clack of her heels, ascending the stairs. The door clicked open and then shut.

Brooke put a hand over her mouth, and listened as carefully as she could while her phone buzzed again into her hipbone. Above her Josh's breath came and went in long, slow, shaking sighs. He stood and paced the landing. He muttered a few things to himself, and Brooke couldn't hear most of them. But before at last he climbed the stairs, she heard this, clearly:

"I'm so sorry," he whispered.

● ● ●

Before Brooke went back into the dining room she let herself cry—not only because she wanted to, now, but because she was late in returning from break, and it was possible she was going to have to dance to keep her job. And indeed, Constancia the maître d' met her in the hallway to the stairs, furious—but she stopped when she saw Brooke's red eyes. "I'm so sorry," Brooke said—she heard herself say it, amazed—letting her voice rasp. "I shouldn't have checked my messages."

Constancia frowned, but in her kindly way. "Did something happen?"

"I'm fine," Brooke told her, squaring her shoulders, waving away the trauma, forcing all of her body language to scream *Men are the worst.* "Thanks. It's just stupid bullshit. Totally unprofessional. It won't happen again."

"Take another five and get cleaned up," Constancia said. "Do it again, though, and you're gone." Then she walked away, and Brooke felt a little thrill.

The getting away with it.

She went to the bathroom and splashed water on her face, touched up her makeup. She checked her phone. Six texts from Kyle. *Busy night?* he asked, in one. *I miss you,* he said in another. *I hope im not bugging you, just want you to know.* And then: *Babe sorry if im bothering you.*

She didn't answer him. She should want to, she knew.

She shouldn't want a man she loved to worry.

Back in the private dining room she went from table to table, replacing glasses, pouring water, taking away plates, the small of her back and her calves aching again, but she paid them no mind. (Nor Lin, glowering at her from across the floor.) There were a hundred or so people at the reception, sitting at tables and dancing and milling around, and two of them were Josh and Karen. Brooke wanted to see them, to put faces to them. She found an excuse to visit each table. This man, scratching his cheek; this one, folding and refolding his napkin? This woman, with the blond updo and the soft jowls and the bangles on her wrists? The Asian couple slow-dancing to Bon Iver? No. They wouldn't be dancing together, would they? Not after what they'd said?

This man? This one right here?

She said, "How are we doing tonight?" and refilled his water, and he said, "Doing just great, how about you?" and it was *his voice*: this ordinary man, older than she'd imagined—she felt ashamed, somehow, to have imagined him so young and handsome—his cheeks and belly rounded, his temples and trimmed beard gone gray, laugh lines radiating from his light blue eyes, his wedding ring gold and scuffed. She put a fingertip on his shoulder as she left the table.

And knowing where he was, she could then find Karen: again, older than she'd imagined, her black hair streaked with gray, her eyes, like her dress, a beautiful deep green, but soft and sad with drink. She was talking to another woman at a table across the room. The corners of her mouth lined and weary, her hair smelling faintly of cigarette smoke when Brooke bent over her to take her untouched plate. Karen didn't speak, but from behind her Brooke could see exactly where she looked, and it was across the room, right at Josh, who was looking right back, smiling the tiniest bit.

The evening ended. The DJ bade them good night. Everyone clapped once more for Helen and Brian, who took one last, lusty kiss while everyone whooped. The guests left, many of them staggering. Nobody puked, which was a blessing. Josh and Karen both left when Brooke was busy elsewhere, headed upstairs to their separate rooms.

Brooke couldn't help it: she imagined them doing something else. Finding each other again in this big hotel tonight, in this time they had away. Turning to each other in an elevator.

She told herself that if their spouses had been here,

HER KIND OF PEOPLE

if they were real to her, she'd not want this, it was *wrong*
to want this—but they weren't here. Brooke only had
what she'd heard to go on, only that tiny, tiny part. They
hadn't meant to give this part of their lives to her, but they
had, and it filled her. Karen and Josh were older than her
mother and father. She kept thinking about their lives,
lived, all the choices they'd made—and they'd still ended
up sitting alone in a stairwell, sad and afraid.

By the end of her shift it was after midnight, and
she was exhausted, and Kyle was texting her, *Where are
you?? Are you done? When are you coming home?*

She couldn't reply to him, couldn't face him.

The answer—*an* answer—was obvious when it came
to her, and filled her with resolve, made her heart beat
faster, despite the exhaustion of the night. She wasn't
even half the age of the couple on the stairs. She wasn't
married, no matter that she had a man to go home to.

She still had time.

While her car was warming up in the hotel's garage,
she texted Everett.

That he answered immediately was no surprise to
her, but she felt that old thrill anyway when she read his
message: *Just went to bed. What's wrong? Is it urgent?*

She touched the screen of the phone as though it
were his hand in hers.

Yeah, she thought. *It is.*

You Would Have Told Me Not To

I.

Just after midnight, Suzanne stopped for gas on the Indiana-Ohio border. Next to the gas station was a liquor store; without much hesitation, she went inside and bought a handful of miniature whiskey bottles. She drank one in the parking lot, then checked her phone one more time: still no messages—from Abby, Sean, a doctor, anyone. She called the hospital one more time, and received the same runaround: Sean had been admitted, and that was all they'd reveal. She said unkind things and hung up. When she'd gotten her Buick back to speed on the interstate, snow swirled past her windshield in a manner she could only describe as malevolent. The liquor burned her in her belly, and she focused on it, used it as a platform from which she could step back into her best and most rational self.

Fifty more miles of mostly empty highway, though, and she was back to remembering herself and Sean at their worst: what she had sworn she would not do, since her son's girlfriend Abby had called two hours ago, and left a message that he'd had been shot.

She hadn't spoken with Sean since early August, when he had called to tell her he was quitting his graduate program in anthropology. *There* was a reason to want a drink: the last conversation she might ever have had with her only child had been an argument, an ugly one.

From the tone of his voice (too honeyed and placating; he'd learned that trick from his father), and the over-solicitous way he'd asked after Miguel and the bank branch that she managed, she'd known what he was calling to tell her. She began to rage, not only because of Sean's irresponsibility (though, god, definitely because of that), but because of his *predictability*.

Sean told her his reasons—his heart wasn't in it; the work wasn't engaging him—but she filled in the real answers: *You're quitting because grad school asked you to work very hard, and you don't like to. Because I wrote you several large checks last year to make grad school happen, and some part of you takes joy in wasting my money. You're quitting because you know I wanted this for you.*

You're quitting because you asked your father first, and I just know he told you to follow your heart, and your father is full of shit.

She said none of this aloud. What had she expected? She'd been too eager to help him, after all. Too eager for him to make something of himself, too eager to write him the checks, too exultant the night she'd toasted him in front of Abby, calling him "Dr. Sypes."

Finally she couldn't listen to any more. She'd interrupted, and told Sean she was disappointed in him. That he was twenty-seven, and too old to be leaving things like this unfinished. That sooner or later he'd have to make up his mind about who he was. She couldn't decide that for him—

"I never asked you to!" he said. "Jesus, Mom—you're a really awful person, sometimes. You know that?"

He'd hung up, and she had never called him back. They often went weeks without talking, but this last silence had lasted nearly three months.

Abby's message had been frantic, tearful—*Sean's*

been shot, we're going to Riverside Hospital, come quick. She'd not called again, and her phone went right to voicemail. Suzanne had tried calling Sean's father, Rick, in London, but he didn't answer, either. Sean could very well be dead by now, a long pale form beneath a sheet. Suzanne imagined a doctor, tall and serious, wearily stripping off bloodied latex gloves.

No, remember something else. Remember him as a baby again, as fat at birth as he would someday be tall, squalling wetly in her arms, smelling both sweet and obscene, her body turned inside out and given to her to hold.

She had loved him—let no one ever doubt that she had loved him!—but she was someone (*Be honest,* she heard her therapist say) for whom relationships were complicated, and even then, even when he was a baby, the love she'd felt for her boy had been tinged with a bitter doom. *I can't,* she'd thought, feeling him begin to nurse. *I can't do this. I'll ruin him.*

Be honest.

More than once she had thought, *He'll ruin me.*

She could still feel the weight of him, then, the breath trickling out of him, the delicate redness of his skin. How fragile, how impermanent he'd seemed. She could have cut him open with a fingernail.

II.

Sean was not only alive; when Suzanne entered his room an hour and a half later, she found him sitting up and laughing.

Abigail leaned across the bed, her hands clasped on his stomach; in her dazed, puffy face Suzanne saw, at least, some evidence that another human being had been put through hell tonight, too. Sean was drawn–skinnier! He'd lost weight–and his right arm was in a sling. He was pale, his chin coated by several days' stubble. A long brown scribble of dried blood rose from under his gown and ended in a smear below his earlobe.

"Mama!" Sean cried, holding out his free arm. "Mi madre!"

"Baby boy," she said–she heard herself say it–and, helpless, rushed to him, buried her face into the crook of his neck, which was warm and smelled of blood.

• • •

He'd been shot through the biceps, she learned; she trailed a surgeon (not at all the tall white movie star she'd imagined; he was slim, Japanese, and very cheerful) out of the room and got the full report. The bullet had traveled cleanly through the muscle, missing arteries and major nerves–which, the doctor told her, had been the most advantageous path it could have taken.

"It could have missed him!"

"My understanding," the doctor told her, smiling proudly, as though Sean were his own son, "is that Sean was shot protecting his wife. Shielding her, and the baby."

She stopped herself from asking, *His wife? Who's that? And why had they been holding a baby?*

When Suzanne returned to the room, Abby was standing up, and she saw clearly that Abby was pregnant, and well along, too. Oh. And Abby and Sean were both wearing rings on the proper fingers. Oh, again.

Sean was drowsy with painkiller. He smiled up at her, heartbreakingly sweet. "Mama," he said, slurring, "you must be so mad at me."

• • •

Sean was discharged only a couple of hours after her arrival, at four a.m., and Suzanne drove him and Abby home to their apartment. Abby sat in back with Sean, her legs across his, her fingers in his hair, and neither of them said anything about being married, or about Abigail's belly.

"Please," Suzanne said, watching Abby's ring finger in the rearview mirror. "Tell me what happened?"

The shooting, Abby told her, had happened at the bar where Sean was working. (Her son, a bartender!) Sean's shift had ended, and Abby had driven to pick him up—she didn't like him walking so late at night, especially when it was nasty out. The parking lot had mostly been empty, and when she'd gotten out of her car to walk inside the rear door and talk to Sean and her good friend Mikki, she'd heard a man yell at her. He was probably just a drunk, or even a bum, she figured—so she'd hurried to the door, but then the man had run up and pulled on her arm, dug his fingers in—"I'm bruised, I showed the cops"—and she was *sure* she was about to get abducted and raped—

But at the *exact moment* the man grabbed her, Sean opened the door, and saw what was going on, and he'd acted so fast, Abby couldn't even believe it; in an eye-blink—*literally*—Sean had yanked her away from the man and inside. And then he did something dumb—

"But very brave," Sean said, his eyes closed.

"Dumb, but very brave"—Abby pecked wetly at his cheek, then rubbed the kiss away—and then Sean had gone back out into the parking lot, yelling. And right away the guy pulled a gun out of his jacket pocket and pointed it at the door, or Sean—no one knew who he was really aiming at, but it didn't matter—Sean jumped at the door and slammed it, and on the other side Abby heard the gun go off, and part of her died, literally died, and she and Mikki started screaming, and she opened the door even though she knew she shouldn't have, and Sean ran inside, and they locked the door, and that was when they realized he had been shot.

"It's weird," Sean said. His eyes were closed, but his voice was hale and engaged. "Getting shot. I'd just had a bullet go through my arm, and—I don't know, my adrenaline was really going, and I'd had a couple of drinks—sorry, Mom—and I couldn't even figure out where it hurt."

"I was the one who felt it," Abby said. "I felt the blood coming out right under my palm."

"I was pretty numb then."

"I got your blood all over me," Abby said to him, in something like wonder. She'd begun to breathe too hard. Sean twisted to comfort her and groaned with pain, and then Abby was hugging him. "God, Sean, I was so scared—" And he was saying, "I know, baby, I know." In the mirror Suzanne saw them clinging tightly together. Sean was comforting his wife. Then his eyes opened, and met Suzanne's in the mirror.

"So, Ma, we're gonna have a baby."

Abby slapped his chest. "And she has to have a fucking father. You stupid stupid stupid *asshole*."

III.

Sean and Abby lived on the upper floor of a brick duplex not far from the Ohio State campus, up narrow, creaking wooden steps in an unheated stairwell. The inside of their apartment was cluttered with strewn clothes and dirty plates, and smelled of marijuana and garlic. "I would have had it cleaner if we knew you were coming," Abby said, hurriedly, and Suzanne waved her off. For the first time since she'd gotten in her car, she was able to drop into a chair and let her exhaustion roll over her. Now she watched Sean and his wife, trying to understand the strangeness of these new terms.

She had disliked Abby ever since she and Sean had begun dating, and she'd surely made no secret of it to him. She'd never liked any of Sean's girls—he preferred them rebellious and trampy, and dumb enough to think his own rebellions were acts of principle. Abby had always seemed like yet another in that mold: buxom, wide-hipped; she'd studied art, she claimed, but had never finished college. She liked to wear vintage dresses with plunging necklines, and sometimes pulled her dyed-black hair back and to one side, like a waitress on roller skates at a sixties drive-in.

Suzanne had reprimanded some of the young women who worked for her for dressing like this. (Her bank had a dress code, yes, but she couldn't help but think of all these women as clones of Abby; they made her suspicious, weary.) Every time she'd done so, these women had looked at her in tight-lipped betrayal, as though Suzanne had let down all of womankind, doing the work of The Man. Suzanne was so tired of this. She'd been a teenager in the seventies, had worn minidresses that might as well have left her walking around bottomless, but no one had ever had to tell her when to put on a goddamned suit. Sean's generation, she had come to think, were all children who'd never learned how to stop pretending.

Well—neither Sean nor Abby could pretend any longer. Abby was a silly girl, still, and maybe not so smart, but she was pregnant; Suzanne reminded herself that the world had already changed for her. She probably wouldn't listen to Suzanne any more than Suzanne had listened to the older women who'd touched her own pregnant belly and made pronouncements, but even so, Suzanne wanted to take her aside, to tell her—to tell her what?

Your life as you know it is over. Your child might someday quit school in order to get shot outside a bar, no matter what you do and say.

Abby had been putting Sean to bed; now she stood in the kitchen doorway, obviously drained. She looked ten years older, like a mother already, and Suzanne was ashamed. "I put sheets and a blanket on the couch. Can I—?"

"I don't need anything. Please, go to bed."

She was relieved when Abby nodded and obeyed.

Suzanne tried to sleep on the lumpy couch—an old one of hers she'd passed along, now greasy and smelling like an animal—but couldn't. Her brain had taken in too much tonight. Her boy, nearly killed; married; about to be a father!

Suzanne was sure the pregnancy was an accident, as her own had been—Abby and Sean too drunk for caution. Or stoned and forgetful. Or maybe Sean had done what his father had—gone for it, thinking that all would work out for him, if he went ahead and did as he wished.

She felt in her purse for the other little whiskey bottles. She wrapped herself in an afghan and drank them all, one after the other.

Sean was twenty-seven. He'd been with Abby—Suzanne was shocked, when she counted back—well over four years. Long enough to make layers of detritus, to fill a living room with geegaws and a mantelpiece with photos, long enough to decide somehow that this was enough preparation for having a child. Suzanne, however, had spent all of that time thinking of Abby as temporary, yet another thing Sean would tire of and discard.

Sean had dropped out of grad school to be a father. Yes, the timing worked out. He and Abby had conceived, by hook or by crook, and he had chosen a greater responsibility over a lesser one. And in the end he simply hadn't trusted his own mother with the news. She was now only fit to be notified in life-or-death circumstances—and not in the event of simple life.

• • •

Suzanne was woken at noon by Abigail shuffling past her into the kitchen, wearing fuzzy slippers and a silk robe embroidered with a Chinese dragon. Suzanne's head hurt monstrously. All those drinks, on top of dehydration and an empty stomach.

Abby smiled at her. "Hey, do you mind making coffee for Sean? If I smell the beans, I ralph. I wish I was kidding."

Suzanne obliged, even though she very near to ralphing herself.

Sean entered the kitchen as the coffee finished brewing. He sat stiffly in one of the small kitchen chairs, a robe draped across his bare shoulders like a cape, his hair pressed greasily to his head. He had, she saw, a tiny bald spot. His face was gray and grim. She handed him a mug and took one for herself.

"I just looked at it," he said. "I know I shouldn't have. But I had to see it when I wasn't all doped up."

His wound, he meant; for a moment Suzanne thought he meant the baby.

"Was it what you expected?" she said. "And *shouldn't* you be doped up?"

He laughed, held up a rattling vial of pills. "It's gross, and I'm on it. You sleep okay?"

"Your mother had a couple of drinks," she told him, "which she now deeply regrets."

"Drinks?"

"I stopped at a liquor store when I didn't know if you were alive or dead."

"Mother!"

"Desperate times," she said. He laughed, and held out his mug, and she clinked hers against it.

The goodwill in the room was delicate, almost fragile—something like a sleeping infant. She was ashamed that she smelled, that her feet were in mismatched socks. "Sean," she said, "if you wanted . . . you might tell me a little about my grandchild?"

He'd been tugging at the gauze wrapping his bicep. "Yeah, about that!" he said, reddening. "So we decided a while back. It—the whole thing has been complicated. We had a couple of false alarms. We just wanted to get into the second trimester, you know? Not jinx it. We didn't tell anyone."

So Rick hadn't heard yet. Even if Sean was lying, she appreciated the nod toward parental equality. "I suppose I'm just—surprised. You've never—"

"Well, Abby's always wanted kids. I was the straggler. But we're not getting any younger, a lot of our friends are making shitloads of babies—sorry."

"I said more than one bad word on the way over. Come on."

He smiled. "Thanks for coming, by the way."

"Did you think I wouldn't? Sean."

He shrugged. "I know. But thanks."

"You're welcome."

He ran a hand through his hair, his cheeks still gratifyingly flushed. Her own might have been, too.

"So," he said. "Grandma? Maw-maw? What's it going to be?"

"That's a decision your mother will make over another drink."

"Fair enough."

"Sean—" *Be honest.* "I know I don't make it easy, but you still could have told me you were getting married. Or thinking about a baby."

He said it like he was telling a joke: "Oh, you just would have told me not to."

Abby came back to the kitchen from the bathroom, then, looking green. Her arrival saved Suzanne from sputtering. *Of course I wouldn't have said such a thing! I* would *support you, I* always *support you, when have I ever not supported you?*

She rose and poured more coffee. Sean hunched forward, suddenly tense; he knew he'd given offense. And he had; she was furious, not only because of what he'd said, but because the delicate mood had been broken. They could pretend to be a mother and son who loved one another for a minute or two at a time, but in the end they were, simply, themselves.

She had, somehow, raised a child who disliked her.

You would have told me not to. Christ!

Sean's phone buzzed on the tabletop; he frowned at the screen, then answered: "Hi, Pop!"

Suzanne retreated to the living room; she did not

want to hear Rick's voice right now, not even yelping out of a phone. She opened the living-room curtain. It was snowing again, and the asphalt and sidewalks and cars down below were all dusted very prettily white. On the opposite sidewalk a couple was very carefully pushing a stroller. (There were other parents nearby, other children. Good.) On this side of the street, a man was walking slowly down the sidewalk, holding a cell phone to his ear, the other hand shielding his eyes from the snow. He was tall, gangling, half bald; he wore a leather jacket and blue jeans, and she started: he looked so much like Rick that for a moment—

The man was looking right at her. He lowered the phone, his mouth hanging open, exhaling steam. Rick lifted his other hand and waved, every bit as surprised as she was.

IV.

She stood frozen by the window as Rick's footsteps clomped up the stairs. Of course he had come. Of course he had gotten Abby's message—as hysterical, surely, as the one Suzanne had heard—and had dropped everything and rushed for the airport. Money would have been no object, as it would not have been for her. And yet somehow Suzanne had been sure this crisis belonged only to her, that it would never touch Rick, living his breezy life on the other side of the ocean. She was happiest, most days, thinking of her ex-husband as inhabiting another planet: inaccessible, if not lost entirely.

He opened the door without knocking. Abby hugged him fiercely in the doorway, emitting only vowels; his suitcase clattered in the doorframe.

He had his hands on Abby's shoulders, murmuring

in his breezy, chiding Rick-voice about how he'd had to fly across the Atlantic not knowing whether his son was alive or dead, but laughing; Abby had apparently left him a second message, one that he'd only gotten when changing planes in New York; laugh joke laugh joke laugh.

Rick had gotten thinner since she'd seen him last (two years ago, at the funeral of a mutual friend). Fitter, in the same way Sean seemed to have gotten fitter. (She knew how this sort of thing happened—they'd gone on diets and exercised—but she could not comprehend how two men as flighty as the Sypes boys had ever managed.) Rick had shaved his habitual blond beard, though stubble dirtied his chin. She wanted to wipe it off with her thumb. He had many more crow's-feet than she remembered, and age had at least given him the softness of chin that—paradoxically—Sean had come into the world with, and never lost. His hair was long in a way that seemed very English to her. It suited him.

His eyes moved quickly and wincingly past Suzanne to Sean, who had shuffled from the kitchen. Rick lunged for him—but then, seeing his bandage, arrested himself, moved his hands around as though pantomiming the outline of a boy. "Can I—"

Sean consented to be hugged one-armed. "It's okay, it doesn't hurt that bad."

They swayed together. Rick's cheeks were wet. He reached out a hand for Abby and pulled her into the embrace.

"Dear girl," he said. "What a night I bet you had."

Dear girl!

Finally Rick released them and came to Suzanne. "It's good to see you."

She let herself be hugged. His embrace was strong;

he smelled of wet leather and airport bathroom soap and cigarettes. "You look good, Sue," he said, so softly that she doubted Abby and Sean had heard. She'd finished two half-marathons last year; she appreciated the compliment, even if she would have preferred it come from anyone else. Otherwise she might have told him: *No one ever calls me Sue anymore.*

"You, too," she said, and supposed she meant it. She wondered what the name of his latest girlfriend was, how young and beautiful she must be to get him to work on himself as he was working.

He quickly excused himself to the restroom—"I'm close to an emergency, sorry"—which Abigail seemed to find unaccountably lovable and funny, and Suzanne, without prompting, went to the kitchen and put on more coffee.

This latest shock was over, and she could not for the life of her imagine what to do next, except excuse herself and go home. Sean was not going to die; the baby she had not known about was not, suddenly, going to appear. Rick had come a longer distance and would need to stay; she'd surrender the couch and let Sean accept the pampering of his favorite parent.

Yet the thought of leaving made her as sad as she could remember being. She could not imagine a single second of the conversation that would fill her day if she stayed; nevertheless, she remembered laughing with Sean in the kitchen, the pleasure she'd taken in seeing him—because she had, hadn't she?—as a grown man.

For the first time, her son was a man. A husband, a father-to-be. He'd put himself between the baby and a gun! She did not want to look away. Or to leave him in the company of Rick, who—*be honest*—was a terrible influence. No. Her son's change was a gift to her, intentional or not, and she was reluctant to surrender it.

After several minutes she heard, in the other room, Rick's cry of happiness and surprise. He appeared in the doorway to the kitchen.

"Sue!" he said. "We're going to be grandparents!"

Then he sat down at the table, put his head in his hands, and began to weep.

• • •

Exhaustion, he told them when he'd calmed down, only exhaustion, and delayed fear, but he was lying. Rick Sypes was not the crying sort of man. Even when Suzanne had announced she was divorcing him, told him to move his things out of their house, he had nodded, befuddled, and then had done as she asked. She had only seen him weep when Sean was born, and knowing this, in retrospect, had helped her understand her place.

Sean kneaded Rick's shoulder with his good hand. "It's okay, Pop."

"I'm so embarrassed," Rick said, and Suzanne felt for him: yes, he would be. He should be. And yet when he met her eyes, she felt a deeper hurt in them than he was letting on. *Don't ask,* she told herself, *don't get involved.* Every time she felt his eyes searching her out, she turned away.

• • •

She volunteered to make a run for the grocery while Rick caught up with Sean and Abby, and was relieved to leave the apartment, to breathe the cold clean air. At the store she bought two or three meals' worth of food; her mother had insisted she learn how to cook—*Your husband will appreciate it someday! Hah!*—and cooking would keep her busy, and give Abby something less to think about when she had left.

When she returned, Rick was taking a nap; he'd succumbed to jet lag. Sean—bleary-eyed himself, still medicated—told her, "I gave him our sleeping bag and the floor of the study. You can keep the couch."

She unloaded her groceries onto the counter. She'd decided to make a roast, and a couple of casseroles. These things would take time. She hadn't thought much past putting a plate of something he liked in front of the boy: a part of motherhood she'd always liked, despite herself.

"I can get a hotel tonight," she said. "It's no trouble."

"It *is* trouble," he said. "Just stay."

When she hesitated, he jumped to the right conclusion. "Come on, Dad's not so bad these days."

"It's not so easy for me," she said, tightly.

"I know. But listen—I feel bad. I should have told you about the baby and everything—but we weren't getting along, and now I kind of feel like we are?"

He was bashful, maybe doped into truthfulness, dipping his chin like he was a small boy caught fibbing. For the first time in ages this didn't annoy her. She had been so angry at him these past months—ever since he'd graduated college, really. She had been carrying such a weight. What a surprise to hear he'd felt it, too.

"It's just that it's nice to have you here right now," he said. "I'm sorry this—"

She put an arm around his shoulders, careful of his wound. "Shh," she said.

• • •

Suzanne served up pot roast very late in the evening; she'd lost all her own sense of time, but the others didn't seem to mind, and she was pleased, almost luxuriously so, by their response. Even Rick, who seemed to shed his grogginess, his earlier embarrassment, with every bite. "Lordy, Sue—" he said, his mouth full, but then perceived her psychic urgings and did not continue.

Afterward she insisted on doing the dishes. Abby said her goodnights; Sean and his father talked for a long while in Sean's office. She moved from the dishes to a scrubbing of the countertops. She could hear Rick's and Sean's voices through the wall, though separating one from the other wasn't always easy. In a cupboard she found liquor; she sat at the kitchen table with a glass of scotch, eavesdropping not on individual words, but tones, murmurs. Later, water ran and doors shut.

After she'd assumed everyone was asleep, creaking footsteps prefaced Rick's appearance. He was dressed and clean-shaven.

"Oh," he said. "Hello."

"Rick."

He sat down opposite her and nodded at the glass of booze in her hands. "What a fine idea."

"If you can't drink when your son gets himself shot, when can you?"

"I feel left out," Rick said. He tried a charming smile. "I used to be one of the cool kids."

"Neither of us is who we used to be."

He winced. Inside, she did, too, but she pushed the bottle across the table. When he poured himself a glass, she was ashamed to see how little was left. He emptied his glass in one gulp.

"It's good to see you, Sue," he said, massaging his throat. "Among the surprises of the last two days, this one has been pleasant."

She didn't know how to answer, but she was still wrapped in good cheer and exhaustion, and well on toward drunk.

"Tell me how you are, Rick," she said, carefully. "If you'd like."

This seemed to startle him. "You really want to know? Or is this small talk?"

"I'm no good at small talk."

He laughed in agreement. "Tell you what," he said. "There's a bar just down the sidewalk. I was on my way there anyway. Join me. If we're going to talk, I'd rather not whisper."

"Rick."

"Tell me you're not stir crazy in here."

He *would* have noticed a bar. A bar adjacent to the place he had a bed was high on the list of Rick's basic requirements. And yet she *was* grateful for the invitation. She was sick of whispering, and she was reasonably sure she would not be able to sleep. If the price of a little freedom was Rick's company—well, stranger things had been happening.

She said, "I'll get my coat."

• • •

It was, in the end, only a small neighborhood bar, beer-sour and quiet; this was a Monday night, and apart from a few men watching basketball on a hanging television, they were alone. They took a booth with sticky vinyl seats.

"What will you have?" Rick asked her.

"Surprise me."

The bartender was a thin beauty Sean's age, her short red hair mussed and birdy, her bare arms tattooed. Rick, leaning on the bar, flirted shamelessly. From her seat Suzanne could not hear his voice, but she knew too well his teasing laughter, the quick and painless way he had of slipping past your defenses. The bartender turned over her wrist so he could examine one of her tattoos close up. Her look as Rick left was both affronted and fond.

That's how it happens, Suzanne wanted to tell her. *You think they're jokes, you think it's harmless, you like the flattery. And then all of the sudden you've got a baby in you and the joke's on you forever.*

Rick slid a bourbon to her. "A drink for the lovely lady."

"So," she said, "Let's talk about how you burst into tears today. That's a new look for you."

The way he measured his hurt before smiling was not unpleasurable.

"Sue, I'm flattered, but I doubt very seriously that you want to hear about my problems."

She felt herself smiling, too. Talking with Rick had always been a game: exhilarating in small doses. It was only when you played too long that you risked injury.

"What else do we have to talk about?"

"We could talk about *your* problems."

"I don't have any problems."

He seemed to be considering, then discarding, a number of responses.

"All right," he said. "Melanie left me. Only a few weeks ago. I have not—I haven't caught up to that information, yet."

She thought about cruelty: Melanie *who?* But Melanie had been around for a while. Melanie the dentist, divorced, two children in their teens. Sean and Abby had told her how she was good for Rick. *She grounds him,* Abby had said, and Suzanne had wondered how on earth Abby could form an opinion about anyone's grounding.

"I'm sorry to hear it."

"I can't imagine that's true."

"Rick . . ." *Be honest.* "I don't wish you pain."

Maybe he was as surprised to hear that as she was. He gave her a long, appraising look.

"I was . . . a better man with her than I have been with anyone. I think—I think I had convinced myself that this was enough. That I had grown enough for someone to want to keep me around." He swirled the ice in his bourbon. "Hearing I was going to be a grandfather, my first response was—well, it was selfish. I thought, no! I'm getting too old, too fast. I'm running out of time to be good enough to keep." His eyes touched hers. "I know how this must sound to you."

"It's all right."

"Is it?"

"You should have heard the inside of my head on the drive over. Self-reflection doesn't do it justice."

Rick drained his glass and nodded. "He can't be ready for this, can he? Our Sean?"

"You thought it, too?"

"You've met the boy."

She laughed.

Rick said, "I keep reminding myself that when I was Sean's age, Sean was four."

"We weren't ready, either."

"Probably less." Rick shook his head. "If I had

known what I know now, I wouldn't have had the guts to make a child."

"All that optimism."

"Yes! All that optimism. All that blind faith."

"And now we're grandparents."

Rick said, wonderingly, "Sean didn't tell me any of this."

"Me neither."

"You didn't know!"

"Sean tells me nothing."

"Does this happen in other families? This...secrecy?"

Suzanne emptied her glass. "Do we even *qualify* as a family?"

"I don't think we have a choice in the matter." He gave her a quick, sly smile.

When they'd been dating, when Rick was trying hard to get her into bed—which hadn't been a struggle for other men, but which she decided she'd make a struggle in Rick's case—when she'd told him she wasn't sure she trusted him, he'd said: *I can't stop thinking of you. I don't think I've had any choice about you since I laid eyes on you.*

She reminded herself—even though his line had worked—that Rick had started fucking his way across two continents well before she divorced him, that he had certainly made plenty of other choices.

She reminded herself, too, of Miguel back in Indiana, her kind and unsurprising boyfriend. They met twice a week for vegetarian meals; afterward they sat on her couch under a blanket and watched Netflix until they fell asleep. Sweet, calm, maybe-straight Miguel, with whom she'd not had sex in two and a half months.

The bartender, smelling of patchouli, brought them two more bourbons. Suzanne was not aware of either of them having asked. Rick's charm had its benefits.

Rick raised his glass. His eyes, across the rim, were very, very blue.

"You have the look of someone reminiscing," he said.

"I'm going to be a grandmother," she said. "I have a lot more of a past than I know what to do with."

"Ah, Grandma," he said, wonderingly. "I'll drink to that."

"Grandpa," she said and clinked her glass against his.

• • •

Two hours later, they were kissing in the cold, too-bright stairwell. *Don't don't don't*, she'd thought, walking unsteadily out of the bar, and then when they were halfway up the stairs, Rick pressed her against the wall, his hand molded to the small of her back. She should stop him, stop this—but Rick was an excellent kisser, and as they kissed, his hand went to exactly the right spot on her hip, one of those weird erogenous zones he'd been the only man ever to discover.

He had known she wanted to be kissed. He had known how lonely she was. He had always known what she needed, even when she didn't.

The stairs creaked; a car playing booming rap music doppler by.

"Surprise," Rick said at last, his breath warm and boozy against her neck.

"I'm fifty," she said, maybe as a preamble to another point of emphasis, but the whiskey snatched it away.

He laughed and kissed her chin. "Hush. You look amazing."

She almost added, *for a grandmother*, and that was

what she had meant to say, a second before: she didn't *want* to be a grandmother, she didn't know *how* to be a grandmother; she'd never even known how to be a mother, or a wife. She wanted now, with a profound ache, to be twenty, taking Rick to bed for the first time again. She wanted not to know how consequences worked.

He twined his fingers into her hair, used his grip to tilt back her head. She was not twenty. She knew this part. She should hate this part.

She had never, ever, hated this part.

In the living room they waited and waited, hand in hand, panting, staring into the hallway; no light shone from beneath Sean and Abby's door. "They're asleep," Rick whispered. His hand slid down over her ass.

He led her to the couch. The springs squeaked as he eased her back and worked at the button of her jeans. Then he was pushing them down her hips.

"We have to be very quiet," she whispered, as he peeled off her underwear.

He slipped a fingertip into her, hummed. "Hadn't occurred to me."

Was this giddy nihilism what twenty had been like? "You're the worst," she whispered. But why whisper? She could scream, she could cry out. She wanted to do whatever she wanted. She bit Rick's earlobe, hard, until breath hissed out of him; he turned her over, kissed the small of her back, fumbled with his pants. He was panting, strong, aroused—even at her age, she aroused him! And she hadn't been this turned on since—

Then he was inside her, and she was having sex with Rick, the man who'd ruined her life; all these years later, all those lessons learned, and here she was, her cheek abraded against her son's dirty couch, Rick's hands clutching her hips.

She bit her palm to keep from laughing.

• • •

Afterward she dressed quickly while Rick sat naked on the rug, facing the hallway. He and his penis both slouched to the side, exhausted and drunk, at exactly the same angle. "Oh my," he said.

Suzanne excused herself to the bathroom, where she wiped herself clean with a very hot washcloth. She checked the mirror: she was still fifty, gray above her temples, but now carried a lunatic gleam in her eyes. She remembered her college friend Pam leaning across a table at a bar, whispering, *I just got laid in the bathroom,* her eyes looking like just Suzanne's now. *With who?* Suzanne had demanded. *I don't know,* Pam told her, *but he was handsome.* She'd held up a trembling hand, and they both looked at it, hanging in the air between them, until it stilled. Pam's boyfriend had joined them later, and was never the wiser.

Suzanne had just cheated on Miguel.

She called Miguel her boyfriend, after all. He was, by any measure she cared about, a good man. She was attracted to him. He was bookish—a librarian!—and wore patches on the elbows of his jacket. He was a runner, too, in great shape. He had two grown children; she had met and dined with them. She had gone with Miguel once to visit his mother, in a nursing home. *Mamá, this is the woman I was telling you about,* he'd said to his mother, who had leaned forward in her chair, had gravely clasped Suzanne's hands. Suzanne had not told either of her parents about Miguel.

Twice he'd broached the topic of marriage; twice she had told him she wasn't sure marriage suited her.

Do you see anyone else? he had asked.

Of course not, she'd told him. *I'm not like that.*

She thought now of Rick's body, the taste of the skin at his neck. The way she felt when he was looking at her, wanting her.

During their first year together, she had kept a secret tally in a notebook of the number of times they'd slept together. Fifty, sixty—she'd been giddy, clicking her pen, making each mark. No number was too high. And then one night, he'd gotten her pregnant.

Why on earth did you do this? She asked the woman in the mirror, now.

The woman smirked bitterly, and answered as she must: *Because you would have told me not to.*

• • •

When she returned to the living room, Rick was dressed, sitting on the couch with his legs crossed. She sat beside him. Her hands did not shake. He reached over and clasped her knee.

"So," he said.

"I think," she said, "it would be best if we did not talk."

From the back bedroom came a long, clacking snore.

Rick said, "I always wondered if I would be sexually active when I was a grandparent."

She hid her face in her hands. "Oh my god."

"You regret it," he said, not kindly.

"We're divorced. You're terrible. We're terrible for each other."

He sat back; the couch creaked. "Ah." Then he stood,

knees ratcheting audibly. He bent down and kissed the crown of her head. "Sue," he whispered. "I've missed you."

"Dammit, Rick—"

"Come on. It's nice, isn't it? Getting along? Remembering why we used to do this?"

When she didn't answer, he stroked her hair flat to her skull. "Well. It was nice for me." Then he thumped away, too loudly, to Sean's office, and closed the door behind him.

V.

She did not sleep. When Sean and Abby woke up after sunrise, she turned her back to the room and the people creeping through it and kept very still. At some point Rick walked through the room; she could feel his eyes on her humped back like the caress of a finger.

When she heard them all talking in the kitchen, she bolted down the hall, past the closed office door, for the shower, and spent a long time under gratifyingly hot water trying to scrape the previous night from her skin.

She emerged, dressed and scalded, and found the entire apartment seemingly empty. Suzanne was ashamed at her relief. She poured herself coffee and sat at the kitchen table, trying to remember why on earth she'd let Rick kiss her for more than a second.

Abby appeared in the doorway, in her absurd robe, and Suzanne started. "I hope we didn't wake you."

"Oh, no, not at all."

"The guys went out for donuts. There's a bakery down the street. Sean said he needed the air. I don't know about that."

So Rick wasn't ready to see her, either. "He'll always do what he wants."

That seemed to hurt Abby. She sat heavily down. "Do you mind?"

"Of course not."

Though of course she minded; Suzanne wanted nothing more than to sit alone—or, perhaps, to pull a Rick, to sneak away, to vanish, before the consequences arrived.

Abby bit at her lip. "So—can I ask you a personal question?"

Suzanne was sure it would be about Rick, about what they'd done on the squeaking couch. She nodded, but could not speak.

"I'm kind of terrified," Abby said. "About—about everything. I didn't know—" She screwed up her lips. "How old were you? When you had Sean?"

"Twenty-two." Suzanne was still amazed by this. "And scared out of my mind."

Abby seemed surprised; Suzanne supposed she could take that as a point of pride. *You? Scared?*

Honey, you have no idea.

She said, "Did—did Sean ever tell you that he was a . . . a surprise?"

"He told me."

"I hadn't really thought about being a mother," Suzanne said. "I wanted to be a lawyer, I thought, and maybe someday a judge. My father was a judge, and he thought girls should grow up and be wives and have babies, and I wanted to show him he was wrong."

"Oh, wow—"

"No, don't mistake me," Suzanne said, and Abby tensed—she was a girl, Suzanne could not forget that, afraid of her mother-in-law; think of the stories she'd heard, god.

"It wasn't as noble as all that. I was a senior in college, and the boys liked me. I liked to drink all night with the boys." She grimaced. "I liked having–that freedom."

Abby said, "You had Sean anyway."

Suzanne considered her words carefully.

"Rick proposed, when I told him. He was in love with me, he said, and I was dazzled by him. All the girls I knew were. Even so, he had to convince me. Not about him and me–though I suppose he did that, too–but about the idea of us having a family. He told me we'd be perfect, and that we'd have a perfect baby. He made it seem like an adventure. A good story."

Abby said, "Sean always told me you and Rick were a bad match."

Suzanne could have laughed. "We were a terrible match. We had good chemistry" –*Don't think about it!* – "and we make each other laugh, but he was–how do I put this?–Christ, Abby, he cheated on me. A lot."

Like she had cheated on Miguel, last night. Like she had cheated on boys back in college, when she'd had all the freedom she'd just been going on and on about; like she had, more than once, these past years, been the woman with whom a man had done his cheating.

"Yeah," Abby said. "Sean told me. Actually, Rick did." Her eyes met Suzanne's. "He's . . . pretty honest. And sorry. He's told me he's sorry for how he treated you."

Suzanne said, "He's always been sorry."

Abby said, "Sean's . . . a lot like him."

She did not explain what she meant; she did not have to. Suzanne's heart clenched.

"I love Sean," Abby said. "We both make it hard sometimes, but . . . I see a lot of his dad in him."

Suzanne wanted to cry. Wanted to tell her, *That's not how I raised him!* But was that even true? And even if it was, wouldn't saying so be a cruelty? *You'll try and try to make them better than you were, and in the end they'll be—*

Men you come back to? No matter what they do? Men you *choose?*

She reached across the table and took Abby's hands. They were chapped, scratchy.

Abby said, "I love him so much, and we've both done so much work to get here; we've both had to change, and changing is hard. But this feels like I'm gambling. Like, I'm sitting here pregnant, and I'm betting her whole life on her parents having their shit together, and—Christ, I thought I had all this under control, I thought I knew what the dangers were, and then Sean gets *shot—*"

Suzanne said, "I used to have nightmares. Kidnappers, car accidents. Terrible diseases."

"And there's nothing to do about any of it."

"No."

"But if you don't get married, and if you don't have a baby, you only have to worry about yourself."

Careful, Suzanne told herself. *Be so very careful here.*

Suzanne said, "Sean and I have struggled. That's no secret to you. But I don't regret it. I regret the way I raised him, sometimes, but I don't regret having him. I don't regret being a mother."

Say it.

"We fight and we disappoint each other, but the alternative—"

She was about to say, *the alternative would have been worse—*but for a moment, and this moment came to her frequently, like fantasizing about being a billionaire—she envisioned herself in her life without Sean. The life after she had chosen to abort him.

This Suzanne lived in Paris, or Stockholm, or Santiago; she had a boat; she had lovers, new ones, whenever she wished; she knew several languages; she had written a book about her travels. And though some or perhaps all of this was impossible, she saw these images, these refractions of herself, with a terrible, keening nostalgia, if not for the events themselves, then for the person who had once felt herself free to imagine them.

If that version of herself, that other Suzanne, had met Rick in the bar last night, how would things have gone? Would that woman have not been charmed? Would that woman place her hand in the center of Rick's chest and press him backward, instead of kissing him? No. She would have led him to the nearest empty stairwell, too, and consequences be damned.

She could be anything she wanted, and yet, and yet, and yet.

Would that woman have been a better mother to Sean? Would he have told her about the baby he wanted to have? That other, freer woman—would she have been happy for him?

"You can do this," she said, finally—the least dishonest response she knew to give. "You might not think you can, but you can."

Abby said, "I'm really really worried I'll have to do this on my own."

"Are your parents close by?"

"No," Abby said, sorrowfully. "I lost my mom when I was a kid. My dad's in town, but he's—we don't get along."

"I'll help you," Suzanne said. "If that happens."

They heard the door open, down at the sidewalk, and

the voices and heavy footfalls of the men.

Abby said, "Thank you." She stood, bent over Suzanne, and kissed her cheek.

Rick and Sean entered the kitchen then, pushed into the room by a bloom of wintry air from the stairwell—the sort of cold, wet air that seemed to want to get at your secrets. They were laughing and ruddy-cheeked, irresponsibility coded into their genes, into the careless way they stripped off their coats and scarves and boots, in the way their laughter spilled so gaudily out of them.

It was dangerous, that laughter—it struck Suzanne, irrationally and incontrovertibly, as *fertile,* as the sort of substance with which a woman would have to be very careful. Here she was, after all, and here Abby was, the two of them staring at these men, each in her own way in love with and afraid of each of them. And they were here because, once upon a time, Rick had laughed in a bar in Bloomington, Indiana, and she had loved that laugh, wanted more of it, all of it.

Sean hissed, then—he'd been careless with his arm, taking off his coat, and the mood was broken. Suzanne was glad. Abby went to him, cooing and chiding; Rick ducked his chin, guiltily, conditioned by the entire scope of his life to believe he was at fault.

He still hadn't met Suzanne's eyes.

"I can't believe you'd just go out like this," Abby was saying. "The doctor would kill you if he knew."

Sean's smile was exactly as sly as his father's. "He'll only find out if someone tells."

Just like that, Abby was his again; even if they were simply playing at being naughty, she liked the game. She hugged him from behind, burying her face between his shoulder blades. Suzanne risked stealing a glance at

Rick, only to catch him stealing one at her.

Sean said, "So what's been going down here at the homestead?"

"Suzanne's been giving me parenting advice," Abby said, and Suzanne steeled herself for Sean's dismay, for the jokes that would not be jokes.

Sean, though, seemed touched. "Thanks, Mama." He gestured to the room with his good arm. "Mamas, plural."

They sat and ate the donuts. Rick, in the chair next to hers, jounced his knee, drummed his fingers, told too many jokes. He wanted to touch her, she could tell.

She would have to leave them, soon. She would have to go back home to her job and the boyfriend she could certainly no longer keep, and to the rest of the details of the life she had made for herself, which she had been so frantically protecting. She should *want* to go.

Yet leaving seemed unfair. This life, here in the kitchen, was hers, too. Even if she had not, could not, have known it, she had also decided, when she was barely more than a girl, to set this day in motion. Was it so wrong to feel possessive of it now, in all its strangeness?

All of this was hers, all of this was *because* of her.

"Oh," Abby said. "She kicked."

Then everyone was crowding around her—Suzanne, too. Why not? The baby was hers as well, another consequence of her decisions.

Rick's wide hand was on Abby's bare stomach—she'd hiked up her sweater—and he was staring into the corners of the ceiling, all of his wanting in the nerve endings of his palm. Then he was grinning, as he used to, when Sean was inside of Suzanne and they were married.

"Grandma," he said, "your turn."

His hand brushed her hip as they exchanged places.

Abby was standing as though frozen, her stomach on display, eyes slitted in either embarrassment or exaltation, Suzanne could not tell. And there—the baby kicked—and there, Abby's eyes found hers, terrified, and Suzanne might or might not have said softly aloud, "I'm sorry"—

—and if she had, then to whom?

Waste

Right before eight a.m., the new guy shows up at the corner and stands with his back against the bricks of the drugstore, hands in his pockets and not looking anybody in the eye, wearing torn jeans and a dirty down jacket and brand-new work gloves without any creases. He's maybe thirty, got black hair, long and girly in a ponytail. He gives us a look, like he's tough, even though he's just a skinny little guy. A kid. We all stare back.

I say, "Hey queerboy, nobody's buying," and all the guys laugh.

The new guy smiles, except not really, and says, "I'm here to work."

"The fuck you are," Davey says.

The new guy says, "Harvey told me to be here. I'm Jimmy."

Nobody says his name back.

He shrugs, lights a cigarette, and stands off to the side. All of us are quiet, then.

See, we hate it when new guys show up. And this one? He's too pretty, too young, too raw. All of us are sure Harvey's got a thing for little prettyboys just like this one.

But then I start thinking about how the only reason any of us got this work in the first place is because Harvey found us somewhere in this city, crying in our beer, or looking like we were about to knock off a liquor store. And then he sat beside us at the bar, or pulled up beside us at the curb in his big shiny black Mercedes and said *Hello*, and then he offered to buy us a meal, and while we were sitting across from him at the diner feeling warm food hit our stomachs for the first time in who knows how long, he'd talk for a while about Jesus—the real Jesus, not Jesús next to me who I know jacks off in the bathroom during breaks—and by the time he was done, *you* figured *you'd* join any church in the fucking world if it meant Harv would promise you another breakfast like the one in your belly.

I'm thinking, one time it was *you* showing up for the first time at the pickup corner, even though you were sure, deep down, this was going to be one more joke the world played on you; *you* thinking, *If the fat man in his big car shows up and takes you down an alley and whips it out, will you do it, will you do it to eat?*

Maybe that's why Jimmy's now leaning against the wall and smiling, just a little. Because he's seeing what we all saw, once: not that alley, but a bunch of men, ready to work. A job.

I can't help but watch him. There's something about the kid, someone he reminds me of. Hurts my head to think about it.

The kid keeps his chin tucked to his chest. It's late November and cold. I wonder, not for the first time, why I'm so dumb I had to bottom out in Indianapolis, and not, I don't know, Miami, or San Diego, or Houston.

A few minutes after eight Harvey pulls up, not in his Mercedes, but a U-Haul. He climbs out of the cab dressed as he always is, in a black suit and white shirt and no tie and shiny black shoes. He's real pale, Harv, and has the sort of big bald unlined baby face that makes his age impossible to figure. He likes to look you right in the eye, it's something to do with all the Good News he's carrying around.

He says, "Have to go for a drive today, boys."

Most of the jobs he gives us we can walk to; his church farms us out to businesses that need cheap strong backs. In summer we do a lot of weeding and mowing. In winter we mostly do interior work—though a lot of that is off the books. Most of us have learned a trade, but not a one of us is licensed, and none of us pays any taxes—none of us wants to, and more than one of us is afraid to put his name on any form, ever. Harvey follows God's law, but he's a little more flexible about man's. As long as he pays us—and he does—not a one of us will ask any questions.

Even so, the U-Haul is bad news. No one wants to ride squeezed shoulder-to-shoulder in that cold box.

Harv rubs his gloved hands together and smiles real big at new kid and says, "Good to see you, James."

The kid smiles back and says, "Morning, Mr. Pecte," like we're all in first grade, and Davey mutters "Jesus H. Christ" under his breath.

When we're sitting in the back of the U-Haul, all of us trying to brace against the swaying walls, I say to the kid, "Got your nose jammed pretty far up Harv's ass there, son."

Davey laughs, then, but weird-like. Davey's the only friend I got in this town, by which I mean he's the only guy I know who'd back me up if some punk gives me shit at a bar. He's my age—fifty or so—bald, big drooping mustache smells bad up close, his left eye milk-white.

"What's your problem?" I ask.

"You called him *son*," Davey says.

[96]

"So?"

"Poor kid looks just like you, Mickey."

The kid glances at me with horror, and then stares down at his boots. He doesn't want any part of this.

Neither do I. "Fuck you," I say to Davey.

But here's the thing: from the start I didn't like the kid's looks, but now I see it. He does look like me, or, I guess, like I used to look, back when I was thirty and had hair and was paying taxes and not getting tossed around in the back of a U-Haul. He's got a long face, dark hair, black eyes, a lump of a nose.

"Well now," Davey says, getting into it. "Where you from, Jimmy?"

Jimmy looks trapped. He's gotta work with us all day, though, which means he has to play. "Reno."

"Oh!" Davey says, and Jesús and the other guys say it too, because they all know: I lived there for a year, about thirty years back.

Davey's laughing fit to bust a pipe. "Oh, we got a situation here, Jimmy. Mick's told us all about the fine ladies of Reno. Yes he has."

Now everyone's laughing—but something clicks in the kid's eyes.

I say to him, "Will you shut these assholes up? Am I your goddamned pops?"

"Fuck if I know," Jimmy says. He's got the good sense to make it sound like a joke: "Never met the prick."

And the whole truck is rocking, now, all the dudes are laughing so hard. I shut up, and the kid shuts up, but I sneak looks at him, and he's thinking hard about it, and now, Christ, so am I.

"Yo, do you even know his name?" Jesús asks.

"Never got told," Jimmy says.

I wish I could tell you life is more fair than this. But I know better. I don't believe in Harvey's God of love and light—not even for a second—but I do believe in luck. Specifically, I believe in bad luck, and I know for damn sure I possess more than a normal share. Every man in this truck would say the same.

Even Jimmy, the kid from Reno who looks like me.

And every man in this truck would also tell you, based on hard experience, that bad luck gets passed on in the genes.

• • •

After half an hour the truck stops, and then Harvey opens up the gate and lets us out into the razor-bright sunshine and shows us the job.

Right away we can see it's going to be a lucrative week. But Christ, this isn't gonna be a cakewalk where we paint offices in a strip mall. This one is going to hurt.

We're looking at an old brick building, four stories high, a quarter of a block wide, on a side street I don't even begin to recognize. Its windows are covered by metal shutters, every floor. A broken plastic sign hangs over our heads, and it says: —ARD'S GYM. Bernard's? Leonard's? Howard's?—that part of the sign's been busted in with rocks. The building's got neighbors just like it on either side, both boarded up. One of them was a liquor store, and the other place used to be a salon; the sign above its windows just says NAILS. The bunch of us are white and spic—Harvey has never seemed real eager to bring his Jesus to the blacks—but we're deep in the 'hood now, row houses on the other side of the street, and everywhere I see dudes peeping out windows at us, and at Harvey in his good overcoat and suit and his shiny little shoes, and I start to wonder if maybe part of our job today is going to be working as Harv's bodyguards.

Harvey takes a giant keychain out of his overcoat pocket, smiling his crazy smile, and goes to work on the padlock and chain looped through the handles of the front door.

I tell Jesús, "Man."

Jesús nods toward the new guy—leaning against the truck, looking around and seeing the same shitpile the rest of us are seeing—and puts his hand on my shoulder and whispers, "Sons are a blessing."

"Screw you."

Harvey pushes the door open, and says, "All righty!" and we go inside.

The smell! The place reeks of piss, like old wet alkie, and underneath it all some chemical smell or exotic mold, scratching at the back of my throat. It's not quite the smell of cooking meth, but it's in the neighborhood.

Harvey unlocks the window shutters, lets in the light. We follow him, covering our noses. The ground floor is mostly open space. We're standing next to what was once a greeter's desk, but the rest of the floor is covered in trash: rolls of old carpet, smashed glass and furniture, bottles and cans and filth. The flooring is hardwood and half pulled up, with a rotted liner and then concrete underneath. Off in the far corners are open plastic buckets, full of dark liquid, and some stacked metal drums.

Next to the door Harvey's got a wheelbarrow full of hard hats and tools—crowbars and shovels and rolls of plastic leaf bags. He's also rented a propane salamander. Next to that is an open carton full of brand-new dark brown Carhartt overalls, too, and that gets our motors running, let me tell you.

"This, gentlemen," he says, "is the new home of the Ecstatic Life Church, East Side. Your job is to get it ready for God to move in."

The church, he tells us, has been saving up for years in order to expand into this, one of Indy's poorest and most disadvantaged neighborhoods. They bought the building for a song, because of how much work it needs.

He tells us the place needs to be gutted, all four floors, top to bottom. Trash removed, flooring stripped, walls torn all the way down to framing—though it looks like some enterprising citizens have already scavenged a lot of the copper pipe and wire, when they weren't pissing in those buckets. It's up to us to finish the job, chew through this place like maggots, take it down to bone.

Harvey says, "Then, alas, the city is going to need us to show we used licensed electricians and plumbers and so on, but in a few months we'll have you back to paint and finish."

Alas!

Still. Harvey's offering us a lot of steady work here. That's why none of us is ever going to care that this place might not have officially sold yet, and probably hasn't even been officially inspected, and if we strip the place down first, and Harvey and the seller and their appraiser come to an agreement that it came this way, he won't have to pay pros for removal of lead and asbestos. He's slick, Harv. We know his game.

We put on hard hats with headlamps and follow Harv to the back, to a loading dock and receiving bay. He lifts the shrieking corrugated door and outside in the alley is a semi-trailer, empty and waiting.

"There you go," Harv tells us. "I'll drop off sandwiches and coffee at lunchtime."

He bounces on his feet, rubs his hands. And that's our cue. "Grab a shovel, dirtbag," I say to Jimmy. "Here we go."

But he's already moving, he's got a crowbar in his hand, like he can't even hear my voice.

• • •

We work hard, all day, and the job's exactly as bad as I suspected. We're doing one floor at a time. The top three floors are jammed full of trash and old furniture. The fourth floor we can barely enter, and it stinks worse than the others. We spend all day on the ground floor, swinging our crowbars, ripping up strips of flooring.

I don't say anything to Jimmy all day, and he says nothing to me.

Five o'clock, we pile into the U-Haul and Harvey drives us back to the corner. And from there I walk a few blocks home.

I live in an old hotel, one that's been converted into apartments. I got a corner room for four hundred a month, and it's the nicest place I've lived in for maybe seven, eight years?—ever since I was shacked up with a gal on the west side: Doreen, fat, but she cooked for me.

Usually Harv's good for about six hundred bucks' worth of work a month. I wash dishes some weekends at this all-night pancake house down on Claremont, that picks me up some more, qualifies me for food stamps. I know a guy lets me hang drywall every now and then, when Harvey's work thins out. I get by.

My apartment is one room and a closet of a bathroom. Shower and a sink so close to the can I sit sideways. I got a coffeepot and three cups and two plates and some silverware. I got a mattress and box springs and a change of sheets. I got a little TV picks up sports; I like to watch the Pacers and Colts when I can.

My room is extra-small, which is why it's cheaper. I got one half-width window, and a card table beside it, so I sit there and blow my smoke outside.

Past the parking lot is a Sam's Club, and past that is a long curving overpass rising up to meet the interstate. After dark I sit at my table and read sometimes—mystery books—and smoke up. Then I like to watch the headlights turn into a streaky light show as they climb the overpass.

And yeah, I get it, I know what this sounds like: sad old loser sitting at his table, watching the pretty lights go somewhere else.

But I've been in much worse places. I used to drink a lot. A few years back I was living on the streets after a girlfriend threw me out. I woke up one morning under an overpass like the one out my window, and I'd been beaten so bad I couldn't open one eye, and I still can't remember it happening. Only pain and running. I had blood all over me, too—way too much to be mine. I cleaned myself up in a bus station bathroom, and I was stumbling down the sidewalk trying to figure out what I'd do next when Harvey drove by for the first time. He bought me breakfast, kept pouring coffee. When I wouldn't go to the hospital, he paid for me to live a week in a motel, and that was when I started to dry myself out. When I was ready again, healed up, Harvey got me work. I spent the next year waiting for the cops to come for me, for whatever it was I'd done. But they never did.

So yeah, I like my little table and my little apartment, and I like Harvey's cash money. I like the lock on my door.

This is what I am and what I have.

Now here's this kid. This kid, whose life has been shitty enough to bring him to the same goddamned corner, looking at me, seeing something he shouldn't.

I strip and I shower the scum and stink off my skin and out of my hair. And when I'm scrubbed raw, I sit back in my chair and eat a sandwich. Then I roll a joint and smoke until I don't hurt so much.

Outside on the interstate all the headlights gleam and smear. It's nice. Because wherever all those people are going, it's the fuck away from me.

• • •

Next day, eight o'clock, we meet at the corner again, load up in the truck. I barely make it in time. When I rolled out of bed, I drank a whole pot of bad coffee and popped some speed, and yes, I know, I'm stripping the gears on my transmission, but once we get this job done and the money's in my pocket, I can maybe take a few days off.

I'm not a kid anymore, though, and my hands shake. When I get to the corner the guys are waiting. Davey's there looking rough, too.

But then Jimmy shows up—back for more? I'm surprised, I guess—and when Harv shows up in the truck he climbs in and sits next to me. He's holding a travel mug full of coffee, wearing the same clothes as yesterday. He doesn't smell bad, though, he's living someplace he gets to shower.

"Morning," he says, as the truck rumbles to life.

I don't answer him. Jesús lets out his little bark of a laugh.

The kid has to have heard this, but he acts like he hasn't. "Reno, huh?"

I say, "Yeah. For a year or so. I was moving all over then."

"I was born there." He looks at me sideways. "Nineteen eighty-two."

I don't answer. I was there in '80, '81.

"Come on, man," he says, finally. "No harm in asking. I mean, what are the odds?"

I can feel everyone's eyes touching me like little fingers.

"Jesus, kid, shut it."

He tenses, then says. "All right. Suit yourself."

By the time the door rattles open and we climb out, I feel weak and brittle, and everyone else goes in the building but Jimmy, who hangs back, until it's just him and me on the dirty sidewalk getting slapped by the dirty cold wind. I can almost see the words he's going to say before he says them.

The poor sap grew up not knowing his father—he's lucky, I could tell him, really lucky—but of course he's got to ask.

"My mother's name was Marie. Marie Boone?"

I try to bring whatever's left of the junkyard dog in me to my eyes. That used to do it.

And you know what? Jimmy stares back. Hands in his pockets, beanpole-skinny, stupid ponytail, and he looks me in the eye, he gives me the dog right back.

"Never heard of her," I say.

Then I move past him, grab a pair of gloves and a crowbar, and I start breaking shit apart as fast as my head will let me.

• • •

Marie. Marie. I don't know a Marie.

I did, though, know a Mary. Was her last name Boone? Did she live in Reno? Or Portland? Or Boise? Or Colorado Springs?

I been to all those places and more. I left Sacramento when I was seventeen, worked construction all over the west until I was twenty. Spent ten years in St. Louis when I got tired of moving. Finally did get married there, but only for a couple of years, to Helen, and she wanted a baby and that's when I left.

I'm not a bad-looking guy—even now, at my age. I've had my share of women and I'm not done yet. But not once have I ever wanted kids.

I'm no genius, but I know what I got in me; I know what my grandpop did to my dad; I know what my dad was like, all too well. It's in me, too. I blacked Helen's eye one night after a bender. Sprained her wrist another time and didn't remember doing it.

She wanted a kid! More of me on this earth. Jesus.

I've wasted my time. That's pretty goddamned clear. But the best thing I've ever done, I figure, is always wear a rubber. I'm a hero only to the kids I never made.

Mary. I remember Mary.

She worked at a Dairy Queen across from a drive-in theater. And the drive-in theater was in Sparks, Nevada, right next door to Reno. I was on a crew building a bank down the street. I went to the Dairy Queen every day for lunch that summer. Mary was what, sixteen, seventeen? I remember. She drove a big Impala; I liked that she drove herself places. She had dark hair and big dark eyes, and a husky voice; she sounded like she smoked, but she didn't. She was a virgin and had the body of a pinup girl, and the first time I unbuttoned her blouse, out on a pic-nic in a grove of aspen trees, my breath caught and I told her it wasn't fair, keeping all that hidden.

You think I don't know? she told me. Gave me a wicked smile when she said it.

She said, *What if I've been saving it for someone special?*

• • •

Today we got three of us working the downstairs and three of us working the next floor up, where they used to have a ballet studio—the walls are lined with broken mirrors—and which is packed half full with old furniture and a bunch of sealed fifty-gallon drums, heavy enough that they might as well be full of cement. No power, freight elevator don't work, so me and Davey have been grunting the drums down the steps to the loading dock.

Right at the bottom of the stairwell, we lose our grip on one.

The drum rolls down the last two steps, and when it hits bottom, one of the sides caves in, probably rusted, and this—this *shit* starts pouring out of it, something that looks, so help me, like the butterscotch topping at Dairy Queen. It oozes out in a slow pool, and it doesn't smell like butterscotch, but then again it kind of does, and also—Christ, it smells like sweet, burning rubber, and we all back away from it, and then we're coughing and our eyes are watering, and all of us are running for the door.

I call Harvey from the pay phone on the sidewalk. There's an awful coating on the inside of my mouth.

Harvey shows up twenty minutes later, takes one look at us, and walks inside the gym. He lasts only a few seconds, then comes out gagging, a handkerchief over his mouth, his face red like an inflating balloon.

He walks away from us, down the sidewalk, to talk on

his cell phone in his happy-Jesus pipsqueak voice.

"Here it comes," says Davey.

"What do you mean?" I ask.

"Sooner or later he was gonna fuck us, and this is it."

After a long discussion with whoever, god maybe, Harvey walks back and claps his hands together. "I've got twenty extra dollars, right now, for the man who goes in and tells me how many of those drums there are."

After a few seconds Jimmy raises his hand.

"Shit," I say, right as Davey does.

The kid looks at us, real quick, then strips off his shirt, right there on the sidewalk, even though it's what, maybe twenty degrees out? He wraps his flannel around his face like he's a desperado about to rob a stagecoach. Under his shirt his skin is gray-white and his ribs are sticking out. It hurts, watching his ribs, the way his pants are tied around his waist with heavy twine.

He sees me watching and gives me a thumbs-up. There's a little *fuck you* in it. Then he walks inside.

He's gone long enough for me to imagine him in there choking to death. To imagine Harvey giving someone else the kid's twenty to go and bring him out. And then that guy keeling over, and so on and so on.

But Jimmy comes back out, after nearly a half hour. His eyes are red and weeping. He unwraps the shirt from around his chin and slides it back on. Bends over and coughs and spits.

"Sixty-four drums," he says. "Most up on the fourth floor. They'd locked them up."

It's almost funny.

Before Harvey and his church made whatever shady deal it took to get this place, someone else made an even shadier one. A factory somewhere in town ended up with a vat of goop they didn't want, and—I just know it—hired a bunch of dumb luckless dudes like us to shovel it into drums, and then they found a place to hide it: an old gym in one of the worst neighborhoods in Indianapolis, a place that would stay shuttered for decades. I can see it: a truck pulls up in the middle of the night, a bunch of guys load pallets onto the elevator, jam them into the up- stairs room, padlock the door, and walk away whistling and coughing and counting their money.

I wonder what their lungs look like now.

Harvey shakes his head, looks up at the fourth-floor windows behind their metal shutters, then walks down the sidewalk and makes calls again, one after another. He doesn't often get all pissy, Harvey, but today he's cold and paying us to stand around and worry about poi- son, and his lips get wet and his cheeks get red, and when he looks back at us, his eyes are angry puffy slits.

"All right," he says, when he finally comes back to us. "I will pay double-time to any man wants to work overnight. Has to be tonight. I found a place that'll take these drums if we can get them onto a truck by sunup."

Double time: One-sixty for a night's work.

Jimmy raises his hand. Jesús and Davey and a guy named Jack.

And I surprise myself. I don't need the money. Not this bad. But once I know the kid's gonna show, then it's like I can't stand the thought of letting him know I didn't.

I raise my hand.

Jimmy looks at me, unsurprised, like I'm confessing.

• • •

Eight at night and I'm standing back at the corner. The

kid's there, and Davey, and Jesús. Rick's a no-show, talked to his baby mama and thought better of it, I guess. Jesús has a big, bulging satchel with him. He says, "Look what Santa brought for you good boys and girls."

He unzips the satchel. It's full of gas masks.

"I got a cousin works at an army surplus," Jesús says. "These are a rental. Twenty bucks for the night, and they got to be clean when they go back. You break it you buy it, yeah?"

Hell yes we pay the twenty. Even the kid, though you can tell he's thinking about how he doesn't want to. Counting every penny, like a man trying to blow town as soon as possible. His eyes are still pink from the afternoon.

Harvey doesn't come for us. Instead it's a big semi that pulls up to the curb. A guy hops out, big black dude, both fat and strong, like a power lifter. "You the guys?" he asks.

"What do you think?" Davey says.

The guy gives Davey a long look and then walks around to the back of the trailer and unlocks the gate and opens it. "Get in."

Davey's got a cell phone, and as we ride in the big trailer he opens it, and his face is green and glowy in the light, and his breath shows up as a fog, like he's smoking. The ride's better than in the U-Haul, but Christ it's scary in there, with all the space around us, and I expect at any time for the truck to stop and the gate to open on an empty field with holes already dug in it, and our driver holding a gun.

"Mick," says the kid.

"Not now."

"Come on." He taps my hand with something metal.

"Take some and pass it on."

A flask.

I uncap it. Whiskey. I shouldn't. But given what we're about to do, why not? I can't turn it down. I take a good swallow and then cap it and pass it across to Jesús. Davey opens his phone and they both bend their heads over the flask, and then lift their eyes to the kid, and Davey says, "Jimmy, you're a saint."

"It ain't much," Jimmy says. "Kill it."

The flask makes two circles, and we sit in the dark, booze lighting up our bellies.

The question I've been asking myself all day, since we talked this morning, comes out of me then.

"You said *was?*"

"What?"

"When you were talking about your mom. You said her name *was*. Like she's—"

"She's dead," he says. "About ten years now."

"Sorry to hear that."

I think of my Mary in the warm summer heat, and I really am.

"Yeah," Jimmy says.

"She was sick?"

He tells us the story, back in the rocking, creaking trailer. And even in the dark you can feel everybody's eyes straining to make the kid out, watching him take shape.

• • •

Is my Mary his Marie? If so, I got to add her to the list.

My friend Louie from Florida is on it. He drilled into a live wire.

This kid, Ben I played cards with on Wednesday

nights in St. Louis, stopped showing up and we found out he had AIDS, basically he crawled off to die by himself.

A woman I knew here in Indy, Tanya, she got her throat cut in her car, that was how we found out she was hooking.

Guy worked with us for a while, Pete, the old-fashioned way, the best way: went to sleep and his heart gave out.

Jimmy tells his story and I feel tired, old and tired well past the way I ought to feel, starting a double shift. His mom was working as a cocktail waitress, and met a guy, a customer, and married him. A real piece of work, a long-haul trucker. And this guy, the stepfather, after a few years of practice, he beat Marie to death when Jimmy was eighteen years old. Jimmy was the one who found her. She'd been dead a couple of days; her boss called him to go check on her. The stepfather was already on the run, and got shot down by cops on the side of the interstate outside of San Antonio.

Just about the worst, most sordid little story there is.

If Mary got knocked up, if it was me who did it—

I told her when we met that I was going to leave at the end of that summer. She laughed about it, I remember that. *We'll just have to enjoy the time we've got,* she said.

But I left a few weeks early, a friend called me from Portland, said he had a good job, and—

I was nineteen. I got the call at seven at night, and they needed me the next morning, so I drank some coffee, popped a couple uppers, and hit the road.

I didn't call her. I didn't leave her a way to call me.

I never told her I loved her, because I didn't. I never promised her anything, I never left any kind of mess she wouldn't get over; I figured she'd go back to school in the fall, surprise her prom date with some moves I taught her, then head off to college . . .

That's where I want to see her now: where she's always been, whenever I happened to remember her. In college. Walking to football games, holding hands with some future doctor.

Sitting in class, raising her hand to answer a question, hair tied back in a long black ponytail, and whenever she's called on, she's always got the answer, she's always smiling, she's always right.

• • •

Our driver finally stops. We hear the dude's boots as he walks around to the gate and lifts it up. He's pulled around in back of the old gym, the dock lit up by a single street lamp. Pissy little snowflakes are falling through the light.

"Right," he says. "Harv says you all gonna fill the truck and tell me when it's full. I call him, he comes and picks you up." He waves a cell phone at us like it's Harvey himself. Then he unlocks the back door of the gym.

The stink rolls out right away, burnt sugar and chemical hell.

Jesús hands us our gas masks. The driver watches us fit them on each other, then goes and sits in the cab.

We have to use Davey's cell phone to find our way through the first floor, over to the generator Harv rolled in a couple days ago. We fire it up. We've only got one big lamp on the first floor; we're going to have to do the upstairs work with headlamps. We start the propane salamander, and as it spits out its tongue of flame, I wonder if the fumes around us are going to explode. But they don't. The drum we dropped earlier is still lying on its side in a mound of scaled-over goo. Three floors up are over sixty more drums. Each of them weighs a couple of hundred pounds at least.

What are we doing here?

The mask smells like aluminum filings and rubber and the gummy taste of my mouth, and yeah, a little residual bit of the chemical stink, and even though it's freezing, I've already got trickles of sweat sliding coldly down my cheekbones. My breath's coming too fast in my ears.

I ask Jesús how long these masks are good for. "My cousin didn't say," he says, eyes wide behind his plastic goggle lenses.

It's Jimmy who gets us moving. He taps me on the shoulder. "We gonna work, or we gonna work?"

That's the question, isn't it? We follow his lead. We work.

• • •

We take a break at two in the morning. We've managed only to load a little more than twenty of the drums onto the truck. We're outside, smoking, leaning against the brick wall of the gym, sweat starting to freeze and stiffen our coveralls. Maybe the mask is working, I dunno, but after four hours my throat feels like someone stuck a wire brush down through it to my lungs. All of us are coughing and spitting.

We're going more slowly than we wanted to—every hour, we have to run outside and rip off the masks, and back-alley air and cigarette smoke never tasted so sweet.

Jimmy figured out a system: Two guys walk a drum to the top of the stairs. Jimmy's rigged ramps out of old sheets of plywood down each of the flights, so we can slide the drums down instead of walking them, using a kind of harness made of a web of old nylon straps. Took a while to get it set up, but now we can get a drum downstairs in ten minutes, while the next team gets another ready at the top of the stairs. It's gonna be tight. But we're gonna get it done.

I'm standing next to Jimmy, and I hear myself start talking.

"You work hard," I tell him. "Sorry we give you shit."

He hacks and spits onto the street. "Doesn't bother me."

"Yeah, well, you don't got to prove you're tough anymore. Somebody gives you a problem, don't think you got to be quiet about it." I spit, too. My lungs ache.

"Thanks," he says.

"Sure."

And that's when I ask him: "What was she like? Your mom?"

You can see him thinking about what to say. Like this is some other dark and sticky and poisonous air he doesn't want to breathe.

He says, "You know, I don't know enough about her. I always thought I did, but now she's dead, I know I didn't."

I remember Mary's dark hair pulled up off her neck, I remember sitting next to her at the Dairy Queen when her shift was done, and the way, when I held her, she smelled like sweat and ice cream. She used to tell me knock-knock jokes as we sat in the back of my truck. The cornier the better. And here, for the first time in thirty years, I can hear her laugh, and it's like she's standing right next to me.

"Was she funny?" I ask.

"Why?"

"Was she?"

He says, "Maybe when I was little. I don't know." It kills him to say this. "We didn't always get along. When I was older."

I want to tell him, she was funny. And pretty. She was a real girl—a real woman. But can I bring myself to say that? *Your mom was something else, before you came along.*

Before she met me.

"Better get back to it," I say.

"Yeah." Before he puts on his mask, he says, "She really liked music. We had a lot of records. Simon and Garfunkel, ABBA." The kid smiles. "She liked Dolly Parton. She tried to teach me to dance once, to Dolly fucking Parton."

"Sounds like she was a good woman," I say.

He looks at me for a long time.

"She had it rough," he says, then puts on his mask, and without waiting, walks back inside.

• • •

At four in the morning I start to lose my concentration. Maybe the mask isn't working; maybe I'm breathing too much of this poison. Every muscle I have is screaming at me. I know it's true of the other guys, too.

Even so, we've starting joking at each other, clowning, except we're wearing the masks and no one can understand a thing anyone else is saying, so we're just barking and growling and cussing all the drums. Maybe it's because Jimmy's so serious, and I don't want to think about what I'm thinking about, but I'm shouting louder than anybody.

I know this feeling. Oh god do I know it.

It's spending the last of your money because you know you can't pay rent no matter what. It's ordering another round of drinks after everyone knows they have to go home. It's knowing you're going to a bar to drink all of a goddamned paycheck.

It's—

It's looking into a woman's eyes, right when you're about to blow.

The shit is killing us. It's eating at our lungs, putting cancer in us. It has to be.

The worst thing is that it's all our fault that we're here. This is all on *us*. No one held a gun to our heads when we were twelve and said, Y*ou do everything in your power to make sure you clean up toxic waste when you're fifty*. No. This is ours. Me, Davey, Jesús, Jimmy—this is each of us reaping what we've sowed.

But do you know what it's like, to have gone this far down? To see the End out there? When you're speeding toward a brick wall the size of the world, and there's no time to stop? Why not yell and take your hands off the wheel?

I'm here to tell you, there's a joy in it. A pure laughing joy.

And that's me, standing with my hands on my hips, cussing and laughing into my mask, right in front of the loading dock, the night air freezing on my skin. I'm looking out at the street, not paying attention, when someone hits me from behind, takes me down into a pile of old plastic sheeting like a linebacker.

It's hard to tell what's going on, behind my mask, but under the plastic is something hard and edgy that gouges at my ribs and makes me scream, and someone's on top of me, and a bright light in my eyes.

I pull myself to my elbows. Jimmy's lying on top of me, struggling up, too, and I punch him in the ear before I can even think, and he goes down, holding up his hands, and then Davey's got his arms around me, saying "Easy, easy, hoss!" And he's showing me: a drum got loose, rolled free down the ramp we made at the last flight, aimed right at the backs of my legs. Jimmy tackled me out of the way—or that drum would have pushed me out of the dock and then landed on me. Or steamrolled me flat on its way.

Jimmy's crouched against the wall of the dock. He's trying to look tough about it, but I staggered him.

I'm both sorry to my bones and a little proud that the kid took it.

We walk outside, pull off our masks. The stray drum is lodged against the wheels of the trailer, intact, so there's a miracle. Everyone looks a little guilty, a little spooked. Davey, Jesús, they're both breathing hard, bug-eyed. They were the ones lost control of the drum. And Jimmy just happened to be there, watching out for me.

But I'm the guy at fault. I was the numbnuts not paying attention.

"How hard did I get you?" I ask.

Jimmy touches a hand to his jaw.

"Pretty good right," he says. He's crying. The tears are leaving filthy tracks down his cheeks.

"I owe you," I say.

"Why start now?" he says.

• • •

And then, suddenly, impossibly, we're done. The sky's getting light when we roll the last drum to the stairs, and we wedge it through the doorway and down and down and down, across plywood ramps gone sticky and cracked. It doesn't go easy. This last drum is dented, and gets wedged up against a step. My gas mask fogs up and something pings in my elbow and I get one more cut, to add to the dozen I've already gotten, and a squashed and pulsing thumb. It's me and Jimmy, and he's taking the downstairs position, and technically that's the harder one, but my back is screaming and we have to rest at every landing and Jimmy says nothing, and I'm grateful, and when he's got the whole weight of the drum on his knees and calves I do my best, thinking, *don't let it fall, don't let it fall, don't let it fall on the kid.*

And then we're in the clear. Davey and Jesús roll it down the ramp and across the floor to the truck. It's the last one, so I half-expect it to disintegrate, give us another hour's work scooping butterscotch into Hefty bags.

But it rolls like a good little poison drum all the way to the truck, and we shut it in, and the big-armed driver comes around, stinking of pot, and padlocks the truck shut, and walks back to the cab and gets in. He drives off without a word. *Thank you, too, sir.*

We watch him ease the trailer around the corner and away. Where to, who knows. Some landfill. Or to a junkyard, a big lot full of abandoned trailers, their identification stripped, the manifests shredded. Twenty years from now another bunch of men are going to get told, *Hey assholes, guess what we found*—and by then maybe those drums will have rotted through.

I say a little prayer for them, and wonder if twenty years ago someone unloading these drums here said one for me.

After ten minutes Harvey drives up in his big car. He gets out, beaming. "Miracle workers," he tells us. He opens a leather case and hands us each stacks of bills from inside. I count mine. Two hundred bucks. Same as all the others, and more than he'd promised.

"I threw in a bonus for hazard pay," Harv says.

He won't go away until we thank him, and Jimmy's smart enough to know it. "Yeah, thanks a bunch, Harv. Real generous."

"I won't expect you all at the corner for a couple of days," he says. "You boys go get some rest. I've got a couple of cabs coming for you now."

I think, not for the first time, about how much other money Harvey's got in his leather case, and what I might get with it, and whether that money—to say nothing of the sheer joy I'd get from popping Harvey's head off his shoulders and riding around the city in his big car— would be worth the rest of my life in prison.

I think, not for the first time, that prison's probably inevitable.

And here, again, is that giddiness. The any- thing's-possible feeling. The thought that if I'm going to go out, I should go out with the biggest possible bang.

For the first time, Harvey might see it in me. In all of us.

He shuts the case, drops it in his car. "Well, good- night, boys." Moving a little too fast, he drops himself behind the wheel and starts the engine, and his big Mer- cedes slides away down the alley like a submarine sink- ing slowly into deep water.

"One of these days," Jesús says, when he's gone.

"Yeah," Davey says.

"I want a drink," Jimmy says.

Who knows why I say what I do? "Come with me," I tell him.

He thinks it over, and then he does.

• • •

We take one of Harvey's cabs to my apartment. The cab- bie must have got a big wad of cash up front, because we stink like alien fucking life. He keeps his window cracked and lights a cigarette.

"Where you living?" I ask Jimmy.

"Guy I know. He's got a couch. Need my own place." Jimmy taps his wallet. "This helps."

"Was it worth it?"

Jimmy shakes his head. "Shit, man, you tell me."

"I don't know. Might never breathe right again."

"I think we probably killed ourselves tonight," Jim- my says, softly. "Just in slow motion."

The cabbie's listening to some kind of jump jazz that makes it hard to feel too sad. Cold air comes into the cab like long strips of sharp metal.

"You're a smart guy," I say. "You know how to work. Why are you even here?"

"That's my business," Jimmy says.

And that's code, code Jimmy's earned the right to use with me, with any of us. Not one guy on our crew has ever spelled it out for anyone else. You learn a guy's story over time, at work, when he wants to tell you. Davey, Jesús, af- ter all our time together? They don't know about Helen, about the overpass and the blood on my hands.

I should leave it alone.

"I can keep my mouth shut," I say. "Whatever you're dealing with."

Jimmy smirks. "What are you, my dad?"

For a minute, driving along like this, the sun pink in the sky, jazz on the radio, our work done, I can just about imagine saying, *Yeah*.

• • •

We're in my apartment twenty minutes later, carrying bags of fast-food breakfast and a bottle of Jack I bought at the liquor store down the sidewalk. It's been a while since I let myself bring one to my place, but Jimmy doesn't need to know that. I pull out a chair for Jimmy at the card table, and he sits in it, looks out the window into the parking lot, looks up at the ceiling, the shelves, my little unmade bed and its puddle of blanket. He asks me how much I pay in rent. I tell him.

"You gotta apply?" he asks.

"Not if you know people, and you can drop five hundred up front. You want, I could put in a word."

He nods, and I can tell he asked to be polite.

Because really he's going to leave. He's probably going to save up for a few more weeks, days maybe, and then skip town. Find another couch, or a YMCA, start over. And I guess maybe he's running—we've had a few on the crew like that—and if he's running, he already took a risk with us, with me. Telling us where he's from, his mother's name.

If I was him, I'd clear out as soon as I could buy a bus ticket. That's the smart move.

I open the bottle and pour into a couple Dixie cups. He nods and we touch cups together and then drink. He downs it in one gulp, and I think, *Jesus, kid.* But then I drink mine, too.

He takes a bite of McMuffin and nods. He pulls a bag of weed out of his jacket pocket and puts it on the table, raises his eyebrows. And I will not say no to weed.

We eat and drink and smoke, saying nothing for a long time. I have no idea what to say. When I speak I tend to make problems, and even though I can see him getting agitated, impatient, I want him to understand this, to know that this is a good time, a nice moment; and look at me, an old man wanting to explain something to a kid, wanting to give him something more lasting than booze. It's terrifying, this feeling.

Finally—maybe because a lot of the bottle is gone—he says, "Mom told me my dad worked construction. That he was a fling. Said he never even knew she was pregnant. He'd blown town."

"What else?" I ask, before I can stop myself. My head feels light, and I tell myself, *Careful now.*

"That he was handsome. A charmer, she said. 'Trouble.' She always told me I looked like him."

"Trouble."

"What do you think?" he asks. "Come on, man, no one else is here. It's not like I'd try and shake you down for money."

He's right. No one else would know. What would it cost me to say yes?

Nothing, part of me says.

Everything, says another. Because if I really am his dad, he might stay. And how would that be better for him? What could he see in the next ten years of my life that would do him a single goddamned bit of good? When have I ever been any good for anybody?

I think of the way his shoulder blades looked yesterday, when he came out after counting the drums. The way he drinks, which is familiar.

And I think about Marie. About the boy's mother.

"You'd be the sort of kid I'd want," I say. "But I can't be the guy."

"Bullshit."

"I checked. I was in Reno in '83. It don't add up."

His face falls, and watching it breaks my heart.

He thinks he wants the truth. But I know different. He thinks knowing it will change something in him. I get it. But what he really wants is something I can't give him no matter what, which is his life to do over. Neither of us is getting that, and I don't want to be the one to tell him. I don't want to watch him figure it out.

At least he's young. At least he's got time to pull himself upright. A chance.

"I owe you for today," I say. I look him in the eye for as long as I can bear it. "I wish I had more to give."

He stares past me, out the window. I think I see Mary in his dark eyes, in the gloss of his hair. His ear is red and swollen, where I hit him.

"I don't know what I was expecting," he says. He stands, gathers up his jacket and keys. He's already stiff from the work, and limps on his way to the door.

"Take care of yourself, Mick," he says.

"You too," I tell him.

I don't know if he meant it, but I did.

• • •

When he's gone, I lock the door and sit in my chair and pour from that bottle, once and then again and again.

And before too long, here's Mary. Mary who is Marie.

She's walking beside me, we're walking along a thin dirt trail, and when we get to an aspen grove she likes, we put down a blanket and sit, and she unpacks peanut butter and jelly sandwiches, and a bag of potato chips that she has folded over very precisely and closed with a clothespin, and two bottles of beer. There are ants, I remember. I keep reaching over to pluck them off her shins and knees and the white tops of her feet. It's summertime and beads of sweat are on her upper lip and her dark hair is stuck to her forehead in strands.

As I'm unbuttoning her shirt she says to me, *I don't do this . . . this kind of thing.*

And I say, *It's okay, I do.*

She laughs, and for the first time I see something a little naughty in her, to go along with the part of her that's sweet. Finding that out about a woman has never done me any favors.

It's like she's right here, right in front of me. I wish I could make myself say I'm sorry, but I can't.

She says to me, *Will it hurt?*

I shake the blanket free of ants and then lay her down on top of it.

I can't lie to you, I say, and kiss the sweat off her lip. *It probably will.*

This Will Come as a Surprise to You

I.

On a Tuesday afternoon at the end of March, Lisa Purcell was running behind, trying to complete several errands with her son Liam, who was not yet two. She needed to buy groceries, and she also had to pick up a picture she was having mounted and framed (Lisa had been promising her mother a good portrait of the family for months, now, and she'd meant to have it done for Christmas, but here it was, already spring). She'd first taken Liam to story hour at her library, which he loved, but he'd thrown a tantrum when it was time to leave. The tantrums were infrequent, but becoming more common, and they mortified her. Lisa had only recently stopped breastfeeding him, and she couldn't help but feel that his objections—to, it seemed, every single one of her ideas—felt almost vengeful, as though they were going through a terrible breakup. He didn't like going down for naps, either, but at least it helped if she drove him places, slowly, with calm music playing—as she was doing now, piloting their Subaru down the side streets of northeast Indianapolis, exhausted, Chopin's Nocturnes on the stereo.

When she arrived at the framing shop in the neighborhood of Broad Ripple, the owner apologized and told her they needed another hour, so Lisa drove to a nearby coffee shop, a homey place she and Liam had been several times before, with big stuffed chairs and old jazz playing softly in the background and the smell of roasting coffee baked into the wallpaper. She was wearing baggy sweat-pants, oversize sunglasses, and a ball cap, and Liam was drowsing in the stroller. Lisa allowed herself the small hope that she might actually sneak in a little rest, too.

A man coming out of the coffee shop held the door open for them. He was tall and thin, and had red hair streaked with gray and pulled back into a ponytail, and a thick orangish beard. He wore a black windbreaker and faded blue jeans. A numbness went through her, all the way to the tips of her fingers. "Here you go," he said, his voice deep, and his eyes slid past her and down to Liam in his stroller. She said "Thank you," as a reflex; it came out pinched, simpering. A little girl's voice. She pushed the stroller quickly past the man, into the coffee shop, and the door swung shut behind her, tinkling a little bell. She turned, bracing herself, only to see the man walk away, past the front window, hands in his pockets. He had a limp. Did he turn and look into the window, just for a moment?

She pushed Liam right into the bathroom—he was still asleep, thank Christ—and locked the door behind her and sat on the toilet seat and waited for her breathing to slow. She was much heavier now at thirty-five than she had been at twenty-two; her usual ash-blond hair was dyed auburn and cut short, and mostly tucked under her cap. She figured she'd changed too much; she'd been pushing a child in a stroller; maybe that was why the man, whose name was Keith, hadn't recognized her, the woman to whom he'd once been married.

• • •

When she'd composed herself, and checked once more on Liam–asleep, his face soft and sweetly round–she made herself go out into the shop again.

Keith was not there, and she nearly exclaimed aloud with relief.

The barista was a beautiful college-age girl, half her hair shaved down to the scalp, wearing an old gray tank top, one with the Rolling Stones' lurid lips and tongue printed on the front. Lisa made her voice cheerful and ordered a drink. "That man who was in here a while ago," she asked, "with the red hair? Is his name Rich?"

She'd made the name up on the spot. Why? He'd been right in front of her. His voice had been the same.

"Oh, no," the girl said. "That's Keith. He has a shop around the corner. He's in here twice a day."

"He looks just like someone I know."

The girl smiled in a way Lisa didn't like. Too fondly. "Right? He probably gets it a lot. That hair."

Lisa thanked her, took her cup of tea, and left.

Keith was not on the sidewalk, waiting. She strapped Liam into his car seat–he whimpered and twisted without waking–and then she stowed his stroller in the back, sure when she'd shut the gate that she'd turn to see Keith approaching them. She then drove around the block, her hands steady on the wheel, a thin trickle of sweat tracing the length of her spine.

"Go home?" Liam asked, from behind her.

"It's okay," she said, in the Mommy-voice that was so natural to her now. Soothing, light, touched with laughter. "Hush now, it's okay."

Her phone had connected to the car and begun playing the Nocturnes again—but now they only deepened her unease. She'd studied and performed many of them, back when she'd been a music student. Before she had to leave school.

Right away she spotted which shop was Keith's—a small red one-story house, with *Big Red Guitars – Repairs – Sales* painted ornately on a sign in the front yard.

Lisa barely remembered to pick up her framed picture. She parked and went into the shop hurriedly, Liam contorting and wailing in her arms; she paid for the picture while he twined his fingers painfully into her hair, performing for the older woman behind the counter, who cooed and smiled said, over and over, "It's all right, little guy, it's all right."

• • •

Lisa had been married to Keith for four years.

She had eloped with him when she was eighteen (driven by Keith away from her parents' house, and her cloistered life there, in the middle of the night), and had left him (driven away from their little house in Bloomington while Keith had been out, by a friend she'd finally summoned the courage to call for help) when she was twenty-three. That had been in 2005. She had not seen Keith in person since a meeting with their attorneys to finalize the divorce later that same year.

In 2008—the same year she'd gotten engaged to her husband Rudy—Keith had emailed her, to tell her he was now sober. He explained that he'd wrecked his truck while driving drunk, and nearly died. He wrote that the experience had finally opened his eyes to the way he'd been behaving and living. He then went into a lengthy apology for the way he'd treated her during the marriage.

Her reply had been terse: *Don't contact me again.* After sending it she'd immediately changed her email address.

Lisa had not heard from him since. She'd spent those years trying not to think about him, either. Shortly after she married Rudy, they had moved to Atlanta, where the insurance company that employed him had a big branch office. The move had been just fine with Lisa; she was, then, still estranged from her parents—leaving Keith had not resulted in Lisa returning to the Pentecostal church she loathed, and they judged her plenty—and being several states away from Keith pleased her more than she ever let on to Rudy, for whom the move had been more difficult.

They had lived in Atlanta for nine years, and made a life there she liked a great deal. Lisa had settled in, found good friends, gotten a job teaching music at a suburban elementary school. She told almost no one in Atlanta about her first marriage, and certainly nothing about what it had been like for her. "A youthful mistake," she said, when anyone asked.

Rudy kept rising up the ladder at work, which provided them with a lot of money, but eventually produced a problem: he would have to move back to Indianapolis if he wanted another promotion, one it seemed the company would inevitably offer him. When he finally explained this to Lisa, they had one of their only real arguments. Rudy missed life in Indiana: his family, his good friends from college. Lisa didn't. She didn't want to change jobs. She didn't want to make new friends. And—especially—she didn't want to go back to the state where her other life had been lived.

As they hashed this out, Lisa found out she was pregnant—a complete surprise, after their many years of trying and failing. She'd been overjoyed . . . and her arguments for staying put were immediately weakened. When they'd been actively trying to conceive, the plan had always been for Lisa to stop working for the first years of the child's life. And she had recently reconciled, painfully but more or less happily, with her mother, after her father died of a sudden heart attack. In Indianapolis they would be able to raise the baby far closer to his grandparents (all three of whom lived within two hours of the city), and she'd not be working, anyway. . .

It made too much sense; the money Rudy could make was too good. They had the child's future to think of. So she acquiesced.

They moved to Indianapolis in 2018, when Liam was not quite a year old. They bought a lovely white-brick split-level near Butler University, a house too large for the three of them. Even now they were still furnishing it. Lisa wanted to love it, and told Rudy she did, but it was too cold and damp in winter, and the floors echoed and creaked and made her feel skittish, and somehow watched, when she was home in it all day.

Lisa had few connections to Keith anymore, but she knew from old friends that he'd lived in Indianapolis for several years. She'd told herself that being nervous about sharing a city with him was silly. He had, after all, respected her wishes, and kept his distance. Indy wasn't as big a city as Atlanta, but it was big enough. Keith could live his life and she could live hers. They would never see each other, except by some fluke. (And if she braced herself, now and then, walking into public spaces, into restaurants and grocery stores, she could tell herself, *Don't be silly,* her interior voice calm and singsong, matching the one she used with her son. *The bad man won't be here.*)

Well. Now the fluke had occurred. Now Lisa knew she lived only a couple of miles from Keith's business, that she had been sharing one of her favorite neighborhoods with him. She had even gone several times into the coffee shop where he was a regular. How many times had they just missed each other?

Lisa thought about all this as she shopped for groceries, Liam pointing out colorful boxes from his seat in the cart, protesting when she didn't stop to hand them to him. All the while she talked to him, gently, chidingly. "No, no," she said. "We're not getting that today." Thinking: She only knew where Keith *worked.* Where did he *live?* Did he shop for groceries at this same Kroger?

She loaded the groceries into the car. She strapped Liam into his car seat. "Mama no," he said, grumpily.

She'd ducked under Keith's outstretched arm, as she pushed by him. They had almost touched.

As she drove them home, she remembered a night toward the end of her marriage to Keith. That evening she had tried to go outside, to meet her friend Ramona, who had been worried about her, and who had just pulled into the driveway outside her and Keith's little rental house, tucked against a thick dark woods outside Bloomington. *I want to talk to you,* Ramona had said on the phone. *Alone.* It had been nearly ten, and by then Keith, as he had been almost every night for over two years, was very drunk, and when Lisa had seen Ramona's headlights and gotten up to leave, Keith had come into the kitchen. *Where are you going?* he asked. He was smiling, and for a moment she felt a small hope—because maybe tonight she was going to get Good Keith, maybe she could actually do what she'd said she would, maybe the night would be okay.

To go out for a little with Ramona, she told him.

What for? he asked. She remembered that his long hair was down around his shoulders, and that he was holding a beer can, that he was barefoot. He'd been playing his guitar in the garage and the house still rang with the music. His eyes were gleaming and half-lidded. *Just to go get a late dinner,* she said, and even now she could hear the wheedling tone in her voice, her attempt to keep Good Keith on the line. *Just to catch up. I don't ever see her, because she works so late.*

But his eyes went cold anyway. He looked at Lisa, for too long, and then out at the driveway. He said, *I don't trust that girl. She's always talking shit about me.* Even though Ramona *was* there to talk about Keith, about her worries, Lisa said *No, no, she's not like that,* in the same way she said everything then: in a tiny, pinched voice. *She's nice,* she said. She walked toward the door but he stood in front of it. He barred it with his arm.

You better just stay home with me, he said, laughing, incredulous that she'd ever thought she might leave, but his eyes were still angry, and she heard the edge in his voice. *Why don't I have a talk with her and tell her you're busy,* he said. She tried to protest, but he said, *I work a lot, too, you know, and I don't see you making this kind of time for me.*

Sit down.

And she obeyed. That was what she did, then. She sat in a kitchen chair as Keith opened the door and walked down the steps and began to chat up Ramona, leaning toward her window, his voice full of laughter, telling her some story about why Lisa wasn't up to it, wasn't feeling well, just *couldn't* tonight. The white oval of Ramona's face was framed in the windshield, looking past Keith, at her. *Wave at her,* Lisa urged herself. *Say something.*

But she didn't, and Ramona left. She and her husband wouldn't drive Lisa away from her marriage for another several months.

Keith came back into the kitchen. He sat heavily across from her. When he spoke, his voice shook.

Tell me, he said, *why the fuck do I even bother with someone who treats me like you do?*

• • •

Lisa spent the rest of the afternoon at home, playing with Liam on the living-room floor, pushing a truck—he loved trucks—back and forth along the roads on his play mat. She taught him, tried to teach him, how to stop: for the bear wanting to cross the street, for the silly floppy-necked giraffe, for the little red car. "Crash!" Liam said, a lot, and once smashed her fingers before she could pull them away.

"Don't hurt Mommy, okay?" she asked him, with more fervor than she'd intended.

Liam was supposed to be able to understand many more words than he could say. She worried all the time about the cues he took from her, the parts of herself she let out by accident.

"You have to be nice to girls," she told him.

"Crashed Mommy's finger," he said, firmly.

"Mommy's a girl," she said, and Liam laughed, as though she had suggested they go ride an elephant. She made herself laugh along with him.

When Rudy came home, she did not tell him about seeing Keith.

She'd texted earlier, and asked Rudy to bring home takeout. They ate dinner at the table, the two of them trading snippets of conversation and sneaking bites of falafel in between trying to feed Liam. She asked Rudy about his day, in part to head off any questions about her own. Liam deigned to eat, which was a relief at least. She tried not to feel jealous when he behaved angelically for Rudy, as though he'd never been obstructionist for a moment in his little life.

All throughout dinner Lisa felt Rudy watching her, warily; no matter how hard she tried, she had always been completely transparent in her moods. Still she said nothing. Rudy knew all about her first marriage. If she were to tell him about seeing Keith, he would only try to soothe her, and she didn't want to be soothed. She wanted what had happened not to have happened at all.

She wanted her younger self, the one that had felt so obedient, so trapped, to say and do everything her older self could.

After dinner she gave Liam a bath—he loved baths, once he was in the water, and she loved his delighted splashing—and then she put him to bed. She read to him while he fell asleep. She rubbed circles between his shoulder blades. When his eyelids finally fluttered closed, she whispered, "Mommy was very frightened today. Did you know? Could you tell?" It was nice to say it, to someone who would ask no questions.

He didn't stir. She watched him until he was uncurled and limp in sleep. She loved watching him become helpless again. She could pretend he was still a baby, needing her utterly. She thought, not for the first time, and not without great sadness, that before she knew it, he would be a little boy, and then a man. He'd probably be like his father. She hoped so.

Keith had really loved his own mother. Had idolized her. Once he'd been a baby, too.

Downstairs, she sat on the couch beside Rudy with a glass of wine; they turned on the baby monitor, and then an old episode of *Parks and Rec*, their favorite. Her limbs were heavy, but her brain was awhirl.

She felt Rudy's concern build and build—he didn't laugh once at the television, and neither did she—and finally break.

"Is something wrong?" he asked her gently. "Did anything happen today?"

"Long day with the kid," she said, trying not to redden. She let out a dramatic sigh. "He's a handful now. That's all."

Rudy put his hand over hers.

To not tell him was cruel, she thought; he would worry. He always worried. But she said nothing.

• • •

As was his habit, Rudy soon fell asleep, his T-shirt pulled up over his ever-expanding belly. Ordinarily she would have made them both get up and go to bed then. While he snored, though, she took out her laptop and searched for Keith's name more thoroughly than she usually let herself.

Within an hour she'd learned a lot.

Keith's guitar shop, for instance, had been in business for a little over four years; it had an Instagram page and its own YouTube channel.

He had been profiled in a neighborhood newspaper two years ago, and the article was still online. In it Keith talked about how he'd learned to repair guitars on his own, and that acquiring those skills had helped *provide his life some focus, after he'd gotten sober. (I was a real mess before then,* he said, *and not a very good person.)* He had a covers band—of course he had a band—and she'd seen its name before, on posters in Broad Ripple restaurants and shops. He'd gotten to sell John Mellencamp a guitar recently, *which had been a real thrill.* Once a year the shop hosted a benefit playathon—several local guitarists jammed on the sidewalk outside his shop for twelve straight hours, most recently to support migrant families at the Mexican border. In the photo accompanying the article, Keith wore a T-shirt that said *#resist.*

The thumbnails of the shop's YouTube videos showed Keith holding the shop's guitars and smiling gently, right at the camera. She didn't dare watch one here, Rudy asleep beside her.

She was most shocked by Keith's Facebook page. His profile picture was a selfie, taken by the woman whose face was pressed cheek-to-cheek with his. They were outside, by a beach somewhere, maybe. The woman was olive-skinned, and wearing big sunglasses, and had long, curly dark hair, blown by the wind. She was holding up a hand to the camera, showing off an engagement ring. The picture was only a month old.

The woman had been tagged in the picture—her name was Gaby Hargreaves. Her Facebook profile was private, but a quick search revealed that she owned a bakery in Carmel.

Lisa spent a long time looking at the photo. Gaby was smiling, a beautiful, smirking kind of smile.

Keith, looking older than his thirty-five years might suggest, was also smiling, but he wasn't wearing sunglasses, and though it had been a long time since she'd looked at him closely, she could tell he was happy, too.

The corners of his eyes pulled down, and they were a little red. At first she wondered if he was drinking again,
but then she realized: he might have been crying.

Lisa closed her computer. She turned off the television.

After a long moment she pulled Rudy up from the
couch, and the two of them prepared for bed, whispering, considerate of one another and their sleeping child
as they moved through their big, dark house.

• • •

Over the next several days Lisa kept thinking back to
that picture: Keith and Gaby Hargreaves and her engagement ring and her smile.

It shouldn't have been a surprise. Of course there
had been other women in Keith's life. When Lisa had
been newly separated, living with Ramona and Steve in
their basement spare room in Indianapolis, she'd often
tortured herself, thinking of Keith with others. That was
part of the horror of it, when she let herself remember
those days: she'd still wanted Keith back sometimes,
after she left. She'd spent valuable months hoping that
her departure would, at last, shake sense into him. She'd
wanted the mesmerizing, sweet boy with whom she'd
eloped—for whom she'd left her parents and their church,
for whom she'd been *disowned!*—to return, to reclaim
her, and their marriage. To apologize. *To change.* She'd
lain awake at night, rigid with humiliation, knowing that
Keith was in Bloomington drowning his anger and disap-
pointment not only in more booze, but also in the wom-
en he'd been sleeping with on the side for the last year,
the ones he kept calling her now, drunk and slurring, to

remind her about. (He always phoned in the early hours of the morning, when he knew she wouldn't answer. He left her long voicemails, describing his conquests: *You know what I did tonight? I screwed a girl on the hood of her car. She really wanted me to. I barely had to ask. Just wanted you to know I'm doing fine over here. Just fine, Lisa.*)

Keith was handsome and talented, and he could be very charming. He was, it seemed, still sober. He wouldn't be alone forever.

When she had wondered—and of course she had— about the women he'd known since, she had also had to wonder what things had been like for them. How Keith treated them. And, of course, she hoped he wouldn't treat them badly—but she could get angry, sick-to-her-stomach angry, thinking that these strange women had the benefit of his sobriety, his kindness.

When she was angry like that, Lisa would imagine him having to admit what he'd done.

A woman might fall for him, things might start to get serious, and then Keith—sober, repentant Keith—would have to tell that woman about his first marriage. About getting divorced. Wouldn't he?

What happened? the woman might ask.

She left me, he might say.

She had to leave me, he might say.

She left me because I was a drunk and I cheated on her all the time and I belittled her and made her feel like it was her fault. Because I shouted at her and made her do things she didn't want to. Because I sabotaged her and distracted her until she had to drop out of school.

Because I ruined her life.

(*Almost,* she corrected herself. Lisa would look at

Liam, playing on the floor, running on his chubby legs after his ball, or pursing his lips as he pushed the right-size blocks into the right-size holes, or thumping across the floor to her in order to hug her leg and beam into her face. Her little boy, changing and growing in her care. Or she'd look over at Rudy, singing off-key country songs while flipping burgers on the stove, or bending over to kiss the part on Liam's scalp. She was *here*, wasn't she? She had rebuilt herself from wreckage. She had *chosen* this.

Almost ruined my life.)

She imagined Keith saying: *I abused her for three years, so she left me.*

These words were all true. They should be said.

But would Keith have the guts to say them?

In her fantasies, he did. The woman he'd told would listen and say, *Thank you for your honesty.*

Then she would stand up and leave him, too.

"Why wish this on him?" Ramona had asked her, back when they'd still talked on the phone. It was the only time Lisa had ever admitted these fantasies aloud. "He got himself right, didn't he?"

"He *hurt* me," Lisa had said. "Every day I remember that hurt. I want him to hurt, too."

"Maybe he does," Ramona had said. She had cradled Lisa while she sobbed, as they drove her away. And now she was defending him? "If he really got sober—"

"Well, I *hope* he does," Lisa had said, surprised by the richness, the rightness of the words coming out of her. "So he's changed. Good for him. But I still hope he feels guilty for the rest of his life. What happened has to cost him something, doesn't it? Don't I get to think that?"

Ramona had dropped it, but even so Lisa had sensed her disapproval. And that had made her angry, too. A couple of therapists, Ramona—they all came around to the topic of forgiveness after a while. *Why carry this anger?* Lisa never let these conversations continue.

Almost no network connected her to Keith anymore, but she'd always assumed she would *know* if he tried to marry, somehow—and when the years passed and he never did, a part of her had assumed (and god, how silly this seemed now) that his past was, in fact, the obstacle that had prevented him. That, maybe, he felt too guilty or ashamed to marry someone else. Or that no woman would have him, damaged as he was.

But now a woman *had.* Gaby Hargreaves had said yes. Had held up her ring to a camera, joyful and happy.

Lisa worried for her, this woman who loved Keith. Keith, who was sober, who was changed—but who still played in Broad Ripple bars with his band on weekend nights, in close proximity to all his favorite temptations. Keith, who caused baristas with half-shaved heads and pretty bare shoulders to smile to themselves when they said his name.

Keith, who'd once thrown a beer can past her head, against the wall.

Keith, who'd given her herpes when she didn't even know what that *was.*

Keith, who'd gotten sober only when she was gone from him, after he'd almost died, and not because of all the times she'd begged him, for her sake, to stop.

One afternoon, during Liam's nap, she visited the website for Gaby Hargreaves's pastry shop. At the top was a link: *Contact Me.* It led to an email form, where you could inquire about bulk orders and catering.

I'd love to hear from you! No request is too big!

II.

Dear Gaby,
 I know this will come as a surprise to you. I'm sorry.
It was the afternoon of the next day, a week after she'd seen Keith, and Liam was asleep, and instead of spending her two hours cleaning, as the house so sorely required, Lisa had opened her laptop on the couch and created a document. Then she began to type.
 My name is Lisa Purcell. I'm a stranger to you. I want you to know I don't bear you any ill will. I was once married to Keith.
 I don't know what he's like now. But—
Liam whimpered through the monitor beside the table, and she stopped. Waited.
Looked at what she'd written.
Why was it so hard to say?
My time with Keith was pretty bad, she wrote.
No. Be direct.
He was abusive to me throughout much of our marriage, she wrote.
That read like a business letter. Or a statement in front of a judge.
Just say what happened.
 I eloped with him during our last year in high school. I was eighteen and had grown up very religious. He was the only boy I'd ever even kissed. My parents forbade me to see him, but I did anyway, in secret, for months. I was crazy for him. Finally he asked me to run away with him, and I did. We got married at a courthouse in

Bloomington, and when my parents found out, they cut me out of their lives.

It all felt like a big adventure. All I knew about love was from novels and television. I certainly didn't learn it from my parents. I threw everything into loving Keith. It felt like life and death, like he was the only one on Earth who knew who I was. He told me everything would be OK, that he would take care of me, and I believed him. I had to. I had a scholarship to IU to study piano but no money of my own, and no support. I was so proud that a school like that had accepted me, and I was proud to have a husband I'd chosen over everything else.

When I started school Keith worked in a warehouse to pay our bills. It was fun at first. But when school got harder and harder for me, he felt neglected. Jealous, I think, that I had to give it all my time. He started drinking a lot. I know he's sober now but back then he would burn through a six-pack of beer at night and even more on weekends. Friends he worked with would buy it for him and then he got a fake ID. He had a band, like now, and they played parties and even some bars and he would come home late—

Say it.

I was a virgin when I met Keith. I didn't know anything about sex. At first things were fine. But he wanted sex all the time when we were married, and I would get so tired at school, and just didn't have the energy, and he always wanted it more than I did anyway. Especially when he was drinking. We fought a lot, and then after a while he started cheating on me, with girls he met at shows. Once I found out, he yelled at me and blamed me. I was his wife, and if I didn't give it to him, what was he supposed to do? He told me it was because I was spend-

ing so much time in school. Because I was too tired to go out and see his band play. And when I did go out I would see these girls he knew looking at me

Her throat tightened.

And sometimes he would come home

How could she write this?

Waking up to the sound of Keith's truck in the driveway outside their little rental house. Pretending to be asleep when he came into their bedroom. His laugh, which had grown cold and mocking. *You're not fooling anyone.* His mouth on hers, tasting of beer and cigarettes.

Keith saying, *Come on, I need it.*

Laughing, pinning her wrists over her head, and going fast and rough, and though he'd never hit her, on those nights it always felt like he was finding a way to hurt her anyway, to punish her for wanting him so little, and she couldn't bear to keep her eyes open, to see what was in his face, and afterward she would curl away from him in the bed, abraded and aching.

He was her husband. He paid their rent. She'd left her entire life behind for him. She didn't know how to write down what that felt like: loving him and being so afraid of him. Giving up a life to be with him, and then discovering she was an entirely different kind of trapped.

Believing him when he told her she was at fault for all of it.

She typed, *Maybe he's changed now. I hope he's good to you.*

But even if he is, doesn't all of this still matter?

• • •

Rudy was growing more and more worried about her.

He was extra solicitous with her, in the evenings. He wasn't the type of man who expected her to do all the parenting, and when he came home, even when he was tired, he changed out of his suit and splashed water on his face and took his turn helping out with Liam, indefatigably cheerful, his ankles still indented from his socks.

Even so, she felt his concern like a weight. It was difficult for him to bring things up with her; his nature was to watch, to wait her out.

"Let me help you," he'd say, taking a squirming Liam from her arms, and she knew he meant the larger thing, the bigger sadness in her.

He had no idea how much of an oppression that kindness could be. And she couldn't blame him. That kindness, his patience, had drawn her to him.

Rudy had, from the very start, been the stable one; she'd been only two years past Keith when they met, and she was still figuring out who she was, suspicious and snappish with men who showed an interest. She'd gone back to school by then—at Ball State, for a music education degree. (She'd told herself she had to make sure she was employable—she'd never be trapped without money again if she could help it—but all the same she ached every time she talked to one of the music majors at BSU. A pianist there, a very nice boy, had even asked her out, and she'd shut him down immediately.) Rudy was the older brother of one of her roommates; they met at a party in her own apartment. He was thirty to her twenty-five, and had a job, was clearly sane and calm. He was a former high school lineman, big and broad, but careful—she'd liked the way he moved through the crowded kitchen toward her, his eyes charting a route, always waiting for others to clear the path.

He didn't drink, either. He never had, and still didn't. She liked that, too.

On their third date she'd finally told Rudy about Keith, and his eyes had glistened. She'd grilled him about his past anyway, and found out he was still good friends with two of his ex-girlfriends. (One of them even came to their wedding.)

Lisa had made him wait six months before she took him into her bed. He'd finally had to say to her, *Look. If you don't want me, you don't want me. But please tell me you know I'm not him. If I am, at all, I'd want to know.*

She had insisted: *You are not. You are not at all like him.* She'd been ashamed, finally, by her instinct toward self-preservation.

But no matter how hard she tried to pretend it didn't exist, what had happened to her was like a permanent muscle inside, always ready to tense.

She hadn't seen Keith, then, in two and a half years, and he was still with her, all the time. She'd lain beside Rudy, after their first time, and it had been nice, but even then she'd thought about Keith, about the difference.

Now, in their home together, caring for their little boy, thirteen years after her divorce, what had changed? Keith was in her mind. Rudy's worry was draped around her shoulders.

She'd told Rudy before how alone she felt now that they were back in Indiana. Her friends from Ball State all lived elsewhere. Ramona and Steve were in Seattle with two children of their own. Rudy's parents lived an hour south of town, and they were kind people, but they only talked about Liam; she and her mother-in-law had never figured out how to talk below the surface. Her own mother was two hours away in Fort Wayne, and devoted, still, to her church. Lisa knew some other moms from visits to a nearby park, and from the library, but only distantly. She'd met a couple of them for coffee, but no real friendship had yet stuck. Same with some of Rudy's colleagues and colleagues' wives, the people with whom they went out to dinner, if rarely, and whom she liked even more rarely.

"I'm feeling ground down," she told Rudy, finally. Something mostly true. "It's just me and the kid, all day. I'm feeling stuck."

More so since seeing Keith. She found herself less and less willing to leave the house. When she took Liam to swing at the park, when she shopped at different stores, she imagined Keith, seeing her, limping closer.

It wasn't just that she didn't want to see him—she didn't want *Liam* to see him, either; she didn't want Keith to see or talk to her little boy.

She didn't want Liam to see her afraid.

She and Rudy were sitting on the couch. Rudy put his arm over her shoulders, and she felt his relief. He resolved conflicts professionally. All he needed was enough material to form a plan. "How can I help?"

She said, "I need more time to myself on weekends."

Rudy agreed, eagerly, as though he'd imagined something far worse. Was this what it felt like, she wondered, to cheat on him? To lie, to deflect, to obsess? To focus her mind somewhere far in the past?

Rudy came home the next day and told her, proudly, that he'd done her one better. He'd negotiated two Mondays a month working from home. He would need to be at his computer in the mornings, but she could have those afternoons to herself. He wanted her to have them. He told her he wanted to carry more of the burden. She needed to get out more.

Lisa thought right away about what she might do with that time, and shoved the idea quickly down. She hugged Rudy, tried to be present for him. She thanked him for his consideration—and she meant it; she was inordinately touched—and his big arm tightened around her.

She told herself, *Let it go.*

• • •

The next day, however, during Liam's nap, her resolve failed.

She watched one of Keith's videos, hunched over her laptop at the dining room table. In the video, he sat on a stuffed chair, facing the camera, an electric guitar on his lap. "Howdy, folks," he said, "It's Big Red himself, from Big Red Guitars, back to tell you about another one of our fabulous vintage instruments."

Big Red? Jesus Christ.

Keith was smiling, friendly. She was repulsed—but, at the same time, she saw in him the old Keith, the long-haired boy who'd introduced himself to her in her high school music class, after she'd moved to the district and knew no one. The popular, handsome, witty boy who made everyone laugh.

Hey there, he'd said, sitting beside her on the risers before class. *You must be the shy new girl.*

I'm not shy, she'd said, blushing. It was a lie. *I just haven't made any friends yet.*

Keith had laughed, as though she'd told a joke.

You've made one now, he said, and held out his hand.

Keith went on to talk about the Les Paul he held, and then he played it. While he talked, she found herself leaning forward to listen to his voice. It was a little thicker, raspier, than she recalled. He was thicker, too–he'd not gained as much weight as she had, but he had a middle, now. His voice was happy, enthused: a salesman's. Now and then he looked up at the camera and smiled or winked or made a goofy face. He seemed entirely harmless. Trustworthy.

She might have bought it, except:

His playing was beautiful. He'd gotten much better, over the years.

He played "The Rain Song," which was an old favorite of hers. Of *theirs*. Keith had been the first person to play it for her, in his car, when they were dating. That was how they spent time together, in high school; after her parents had gone to sleep, she'd sneak out to meet him, and Keith would drive her out far into the countryside in his truck, and they would park beside cornfields and make out, and he would play music for her from his thick folder of CDs, their faces lit up red by the dashboard's glow. She knew hymns and Christian bands, but none of what Keith played for her: Pink Floyd, Nirvana, Weezer, Led Zeppelin. Elton John and Ben Folds–pianists who'd amazed her. What gifts he was giving her, she'd thought. She'd especially loved the faraway, excited look he got, listening to music he loved.

It wasn't so different from the way he looked when he kissed her, when she undressed for him for the first time.

He'd wanted to learn "The Rain Song." She'd helped him. She'd always been able to learn music quickly, by ear; Keith never could. That had been a secret shame of hers, back then: they had bonded over music, and he had introduced her to much that she loved, but–and she knew this especially when she was in music school, surrounded by brilliance—he was an average musician at best. He liked to perform but not to practice. She had been far better.

Listening to Keith play it now, though—with such skill, such evidence of devotion, surrounded by the instruments he loved—made her nearly sick with fury.

This was a song they'd once made love to.

This was music he'd given time to.

He still had music.

Now that she was out of the classroom, Lisa barely played the piano at all. She'd had a used piano in Atlanta, but not now. (She and Rudy had talked about where one might go in the new house, but pretending she'd have time to play during Liam's first years was foolish, and she'd always told Rudy she could wait.)

And yes, these were her decisions, but—

On the video Keith was talking again. It was a special instrument, he was saying, and a special song. Then he invited his viewers to come on down to the shop and see it for themselves.

• • •

Dear Gaby, she wrote that night, when Rudy and Liam were asleep. *Do you like the way Keith plays guitar? Do you play an instrument? I fell in love with him over music. He'd play songs for me on the guitar. We learned to play songs together. Maybe you're the same.*

She wrote, *I dropped out of the music school at Indiana when he and I were married. I was really good. People used to tell me I could be a professional classical pianist.*

She wrote, *When he was drinking and sleeping around, I couldn't sleep, and I was always distracted. My grades fell too low one semester and they took away my scholarship. I was too ashamed to say why to anybody. A professor said to me,* Where's your heart? Because it's not in your music. *He said it to shame me and it worked. Keith had already trained me.*

We had a fight about it. He told me, It's not my fault if you couldn't cut it. *I think he was happy. That it proved some point about us both.*

After that I spent a year working in a video store to help us make rent. A lot of the money I made went into his booze. I'd cry every day, because I didn't think I had a future anymore. I didn't have a piano at home, but Keith had his guitars everywhere.

I went back to school after the divorce and learned how to teach music to children. I was too ashamed to try to be a musician again, and some of that is on me, but a lot of it is on Keith and what happened and what I believed about myself after our time together.

I like teaching. I like children. I have a little boy of my own. But sometimes I teach a kid to play Good King Wenceslaus for the twentieth time and I want to scream, I used to be able to play Chopin and Schumann and Lizst—

Through the monitor she heard Liam begin to laugh and babble. She looked at what she'd just written, and erased the last paragraph. She wiped her eyes, closed the laptop, and then went to Liam's room, where her son was standing in his crib, anxious for the sight of her, eyes alight.

• • •

That Saturday, she and Rudy woke up and had breakfast and then played together with Liam as usual, but at ten o'clock, when Liam brought her several books to read, Rudy told her, "Mommy, why don't you go have some time to yourself? Do something fun."

And here. This was what she'd asked for.

Liam beamed. "Fun!" he crowed.

"That's right," Rudy said, picking him up and swinging him upside down while he shrieked. "Mommy's going to go bye-bye for a bit, and you and I are going to go to the park."

This set Liam off, though—he did not at *all* want Mommy to go bye-bye, and by the time she was ready to go out, he was squirming in Rudy's arms, red-faced, screaming after her, *"Mommy! Mommy!"*

"I'll bring back lunch," she said, to Rudy, and he nodded, his lips held close to Liam's scalp, letting her boy wail into his chest, and the sound of it, of being needed so much, almost broke her resolve.

"Take your time," Rudy said, swaying. "We'll be okay."

• • •

Lisa did what she knew she would do, without Liam along. She drove the Subaru for the first time in weeks to Broad Ripple, toward the block where Keith had his shop. "What are you doing?" she asked herself aloud, since Liam wasn't with her. "What in the hell is Mommy doing?"

She was wearing her sunglasses and cap again.

A parking space was open in front of the guitar shop. She took it, nose in. The sun was out and gleaming off the store's front windows, but the door was propped open. A man crossed the doorway and she tensed—but he wasn't Keith. She cracked her window, and heard the sound of an acoustic guitar being played, and played well, from inside.

Go inside. Ask him to his face how he treats her.

Then she thought that maybe Keith could see out the windows, that he was looking at her right now, and she wouldn't even know.

She pulled out of her parking space. She drove through the neighborhoods, away from Broad Ripple. She realized she was being careful, as though Liam were in the back seat, and then she told herself she didn't have to. She was alone, and could do what she wished. She sped up, driving north, into the suburbs.

• • •

Gaby Hargreaves's bakery was called Rise. It was located in a strip mall in Carmel, but a nice new one, just off 116th. The shop was between a yoga studio and a place that sold fine yarn and knitting supplies. Gaby had chosen her location well, even if her sign and storefront were fairly modest. (Lisa couldn't help but think that Keith's sign, on his shop, was flashier.) She parked at a space near the door and checked her phone, to make sure Rudy and Liam weren't having emergencies.

Nothing. Rudy was, still, giving her the space and time he'd promised.

Lisa had decided on the drive up that she would only look at the place. Today her only goal was to see—

well, what it was like. Maybe–maybe–she would catch a glimpse of Gaby herself. If she saw the woman, in the flesh, maybe then she'd know what to do.

Ramona had called her once, near the end of Lisa's marriage. "I'm worried about you," she'd said. "You look like a ghost these days."

She'd looked in the mirror that night, and saw what Ramona told her was there: her hollow eyes, her sallow skin, her lank hair. That night, from the pay phone outside the video store where she worked, she'd called Ramona back, and–her voice cracking–had asked, "Can I talk to you sometime? Alone?"

If Lisa saw Gaby Hargreaves, how would she seem? Alive, or partly dead?

Lisa decided to walk past the shop on the sidewalk, and take a look through the door. If no one was inside, she'd think about going in. For all she knew, Gaby wouldn't, herself, be working. Maybe then Lisa could just go in and talk with an employee. Ask her if it was a nice place to work. She was just about to unlock her door and get out when the door to the bakery opened.

And here was Keith, walking out, holding a box of pastries and a coffee cup. He was wearing jeans and a green T-shirt, and his hair was loose and wavy around his shoulders. He stopped in front of the window and held up his cup to someone inside. He stuck out his tongue. Then he turned and walked right toward her Subaru, limping, smiling, squinting in the sun. She froze, her hands gripping the steering wheel. He stopped and opened the hatch of the black SUV parked end-in beside her, then slid the pastry box into it. She watched him do this, only a few feet away. He shut the hatch and walked past her and opened his door, carefully, to avoid hitting hers. If he glanced at her, it was only for a second or so. She was wearing her big sunglasses. He got in and shut the door, and then drove away.

After a long minute, so did she, shaken.

She only just remembered to stop at a sandwich shop on the way home, for the lunch she'd promised Rudy.

• • •

That night, after Liam was asleep, just as she reached to turn off the lamp, Rudy put a hand on her shoulder. She startled, and Rudy apologized, his hand still on her back, and she knew what he was going to ask.

"Any chance you want to fool around?" he murmured, hesitantly, as though it would offend her. He stroked her arm from her shoulder to her elbow, which made her shiver. "It's been a while."

It had. Two months and change. Since before seeing Keith again.

Rudy was a good man. He was trying. And because of this, and because she was still swimming in guilt from that afternoon's expedition, she turned, put her hands on his big cheeks, and kissed him. His mouth tasted of toothpaste. She told herself: *Want this.* He slid his hands under the waistband of her pajamas. She told herself: *This man loves you and you love this man. This is what wives do.*

No. *This is what people who love each other do.*

Quietly—the bedframe creaked—they got up and made a nest on the floor out of their comforter and pillows. She could see in his face, hear in his breath, how eager he was, how much he'd missed her, even before she slid off his boxers. She climbed atop him. Being above him, seeing him so hopeful, his eyes bright with desire, helped. "Shh, shhhh," she kept saying, rocking, and for a moment, just a sliver of a moment, she found herself transported in a way she hadn't been, in a long time—

From somewhere else in the house came a loud bang and the sound of shattering glass, and she gasped. She threw herself off Rudy and gathered the comforter over her waist. From down the hall, and through the monitor, Liam began to cry, his voice eerily doubled.

She was holding Liam in his bedroom, bouncing him on her hip, when Rudy returned from downstairs to tell her a picture had fallen off the wall in the guest room below their bedroom. He'd swept up the broken glass.

"Nothing serious," he said, and he laughed and touched her shoulders, her back, while Liam fell back asleep in her arms. "I wonder what could have knocked it loose?"

She made herself laugh, too. Made herself lean against him.

Rudy would want to start again, when Liam was asleep, and she would let him—because otherwise how could she tell him that when she'd heard the noise, all she could think of was Keith, slamming the door, knocking over a glass in their darkened kitchen, and then his footsteps, approaching the bed?

III.

The next day, during her free time in the afternoon, Lisa sat in a coffee shop she'd never been to, one she'd chosen at random several neighborhoods away. She opened her laptop, and then the document which, by now, was running to several pages. Remembering Keith leaving the bakery, waving, sticking out his tongue through the window. How happy he'd been.

She remembered his limp. He'd almost lost that leg when he crashed his truck. He'd written this to her, in his email of apology, all those years ago. He'd nearly died of blood loss and infection during surgery. He'd gone into rehab afterward.

Lisa wrote about all the times he'd driven her places, drunk, when she didn't have a license. The time he yelled at her for bringing a stray home, and how heartbroken she'd been when he gave the dog away without asking. The times—many of them—that he'd told her she was cruel to him, because she didn't believe in his dreams.

She wrote about the night he broke the glass.

She wrote, *He is in my mind when I am alone with my husband.*

She wrote, *I have so many more stories. And if I don't tell you, who do I tell?*

What do I do with them?

Monday was Rudy's first day working at home, and in midmorning, after he'd emerged from his office, she told him, "I'm going to go out for a little bit, okay?" But not before letting Liam watch *Thomas*—and, while he did, printing out the document she'd been writing—ten pages' worth, now—and putting it in a manila envelope.

"Sure thing," Rudy said. Liam was in his lap, reaching down to turn the page of his board book.

Lisa drove peacefully, obeying the speed limit, as though the letter in her purse were contraband. She listened to Schumann, the Concerto in A Minor, which she had, in a long-ago life, devoted many hours to performing as perfectly as she could. She still loved it. Listening to it made her cry without fail.

At eleven Lisa parked her car in front of Rise. She checked her phone for emergencies, but she had no messages. Breathing fast, her fingertips numb, she walked up to the door, and saw through the window that the place was empty of customers.

She took a deep breath and pushed open the door. A bell tinkled her arrival.

Gaby Hargreaves was standing behind the counter, wearing an apron and boxing up cupcakes.

She smiled at Lisa. "Give me just a sec," she said, in a low throaty voice.

"Sure," Lisa said.

She stood in front of the display case. The air smelled pleasantly of yeast and sugar. The space was small, with room for only a couple of tables by the front window, each with a small vase of daisies as a centerpiece. Speakers behind the counter were playing Stevie Wonder.

Lisa stole looks at Gaby, finishing her boxing. She was pretty. Not beautiful, but pretty. She was a little taller than Lisa—most people were—but she was rounded in the way Lisa was, and that surprised her; she'd assumed Keith would have proposed to someone—well, *flashier*. Gaby's hair was pulled into a messy bun, and she wore glasses with pointed rims. Her lipstick was bright red. Her apron was the same color. She was wearing the high-waisted mom jeans that were cool again, somehow. In the one photo Lisa had seen of her, her eyes had been hidden behind sunglasses. Real Gaby's eyes were wide and dark. Italian, maybe.

Gaby turned and put plastic gloves on her hands. "Okay. Now what can I get for you?"

"I'm sorry," Lisa said, and made herself look down at the case. "I've never been in here before."

Gaby pursed her lips. "A first-timer! All right. I can let you try a sample of something if you want. So long as you promise to come back again." Her voice was deep and had a little bit of snap to it. New York, maybe, or Boston.

Lisa liked her. Yes, the woman was a pro, was making a new customer feel good, but she had gravity. She seemed—well, *kind.*

"What do you recommend?"

"Sweet or savory?"

"Sweet."

"My croissants are good. I've got this one"—she was pointing with a pair of plastic tongs, inside the case—"with a ganache in it, and this one with Nutella, and this one with raspberry jam."

Lisa could barely focus. "Ganache. And—I need something for my little guy. He's home with my husband. So something for him, too."

Gaby chuckled as she bent to the case. "Getting some me-time?"

". . . Yeah."

"I remember it well."

Lisa said, "You have kids?"

"Practically adults, now." She handed Lisa the croissant in a small bag. "Oldest is eighteen, youngest is sixteen. Driving." She shook her head. "They were babies just yesterday."

"You must have been so young," Lisa said, trying to keep up, to imagine Keith interacting with children.

"Seventeen when I had my boy," Gaby said. "Barely older than my little girl is now. How I kept us all alive with that little sense is a mystery to me. How old is yours?"

"Just twenty months."

Gaby shook her head. "You must be *tired.*"

Lisa could only nod.

Gaby pointed out various other treats with her tongs. They settled on a big oatmeal cookie for Liam, and a loaf of cinnamon bread for Rudy to use for his breakfasts. Lisa could feel Gaby's eyes on her as she picked. "I'm gonna throw in a couple extra cookies for your boy," Gaby said, and then, when she protested, "No, my pleasure—"

The phone rang, then. "Jeez Louise," she said. "Hang on just a sec."

Gaby walked to a phone on the wall and asked the caller to hold. "Oh, hey, baby," she said. "I got a customer. Can I call back? Well—yeah, Okay. Okay. Thursday's fine. I can get Mona to cover if that's the only time we can do it."

Keith. Keith was on the phone.

Gaby returned, shaking her head, smiling. "Sorry. Guess who's getting married in a few weeks?" She pointed to herself with her thumbs. "Lots to plan. At least I'm not doing the cake."

Lisa made herself say, "Oh! Congratulations."

"Thanks! Wasn't sure it was ever going to happen to me again. But here I am, picking out tablecloths."

Gaby turned the digital screen around instead of saying the price of purchase aloud. Lisa paid with her debit card.

And here, without her even trying, was her opportunity.

"Same with me," Lisa said. "I mean, I'm on my second."

Lisa again felt Gaby's eyes linger on her face as she added a tip on the screen.

"How long?" Gaby asked.

"Thirteen years," Lisa said, and the shame of what she was doing, Rudy at home and oblivious, closed her throat to a pinhole.

Gaby nodded. "I was alone with my kids for twelve years," she said. "Their dad, he was bad news. The guys I tried after weren't much better. But then, finally, the right one came along."

"My first husband was . . . I was sure I wouldn't marry again, either."

Gaby smiled. "It's going okay?"

"Yes," Lisa said, and then more firmly, "*Yes.*"

Then she asked, "Your fiancé . . . he's good with the kids?"

"He is. None of his own. So he's learning. My oldest likes him. They're in a band together. They make unholy noise, but that's how they bonded, so I can't really mind." Gaby smiled, deeply, at the very thought of it.

Lisa forced herself to smile, too.

Gaby said, "You know, it's okay if you sit for a bit. I hope you don't mind me saying, but you look run off your feet."

Lisa nodded mutely. She sat at one of the tables by the front windows, and felt as though she'd floated there.

"You want a coffee or a tea or something?" Gaby asked.

Lisa said, "I'd love some tea." She opened her purse, but Gaby waved her away. "No, no, on me." Behind the counter, she poured hot water out of a carafe.

Lisa watched Gaby move at her work, replaying her words. She seemed all right, didn't she? She seemed happy enough.

Gaby turned and looked at her, hesitant, as though she was trying to say something hard, too.

Lisa had a thought: It wasn't out of the realm of possibility, was it, that Gaby had seen her picture? She'd been assuming all this time that Keith hadn't told Gaby about her.

But what if he *had?*

Gaby came from behind the counter and handed her a Styrofoam cup with a teabag steeping in it. "Nothing fancy," she said and then sat down opposite Lisa and stretched out her legs. She was wearing bright blue clogs. "Slow afternoon. And I do not believe I've asked your name."

"Margie," Lisa said. Her mother's name.

Gaby raised an eyebrow. "I'm Gaby. Pleased."

Lisa remembered she'd just paid with a debit card. Her name had been on the screen. "Same," she said, tightly.

Gaby said, "Are you working?"

"No. We made a deal, I'd stay home for a few years—" She realized Gaby had probably worked and raised two children alone, a baby herself, and her shame rose up again. "I'm a teacher. Was a teacher."

Gaby nodded, as though that added up, and Lisa realized she hadn't bothered to disguise what she did, either.

"Can I ask how you met?" Lisa asked. "You and your fiancé."

Gaby's eyes flickered up. "Well. Brace yourself. We met in AA."

"Oh."

"No, no—It's okay. Took a lot of work to get in that room, and a lot of work to stay there. For me and for him both. I don't mind saying so."

Lisa nodded.

Gaby said, "We were friends for a long time. That was part of it. We did a lot of talking. Propping each other up. We had to figure out who we were, and it took us a while."

"And he's . . . good to you?"

"He is." Gaby said, carefully, "We both have stuff behind us that's hard to look at. And we screwed up with each other a few times, too. But that's what makes it good, now. We have this joke, that we grew up together."

She smiled. Ruefully, Lisa thought. But happy. She met Lisa's eyes.

"I should be going," Lisa said. "I've kept you."

"You really haven't. Mondays are slow. I don't mind the company."

Gaby stood. She put a hand on Lisa's shoulder as she passed, then returned with a plastic lid for her tea. "I hope you come back. Maybe bring the little guy next time?"

Lisa said, "I'll do my best."

"Okay," Gaby said. "Margie, right?"

"Right."

"Margie. Nice to have met you. You take care, now."

• • •

Lisa drove home, emptied out.

Inside her house she gave Liam one of the cookies. She showed Rudy the bag of cinnamon bread, and his eyes lit up, and he gave her a thumbs-up from flat on the floor, where Liam sat cross-legged beside him, breaking the cookie into bits and cackling.

"Where'd you go?" he asked.

"Just out for a drive," she said. Her voice chirpy, and not quite her own.

He didn't ask her about where she'd bought their treats. "Did you get enough time?"

She sat on the couch beside them. Liam rose and toddled to her and handed her a chunk of cookie, moistened from his mouth.

"Thank you, sweetie," she said. "That's very kind."

She said, to Rudy, "I think so. I think so for today."

• • •

Over the next weeks she still thought about Gaby, about Keith. Of course she did. She shredded the letter she'd printed, but she moved the document from her computer onto a memory stick and locked it away in a desk. She no longer felt the need to add to it.

It wasn't that she was no longer angry; she was. When she brought up memories, she could still feel it: that cavernous part of her where it all echoed. The time she had lost, and the hurt that had been done to her. She still avoided taking Liam to the parts of Broad Ripple next to Keith's shop, and sometimes, still, she imagined seeing Keith—any tall man's shape, coming around a corner, could pierce her through.

That would probably always happen, she supposed. And of course, knowing this could make her angry.

But less so. A little less so.

She told Rudy she thought it was time for a piano, and he used his new upper-management money to buy her a good one. She sat at it with Liam, and sometimes alone, where the sight of her own hands on the keys could freeze her in place, in memory.

Weeks passed. A month. Summer came. She checked Facebook in July, and Keith's profile picture had been replaced again; this time it was a black-and-white photo of him at the altar, lifting Gaby's veil, the two of them in profile. They both looked very much in love. The picture had 52 likes and hearts and amazed faces clustered beneath it.

Congratulations, she thought, then folded down the screen on their happiness.

• • •

Back in May, a couple of weeks after she went to meet Gaby, Keith had messaged her, via Facebook.

The subject line read, *I'm sorry to bother you.*

Dear Lisa,

I'm sorry to write you like this. I have respected your wishes all these years. I wouldn't be emailing you at all, except something strange happened recently and I can't shake it.

So, she thought. Gaby *had* recognized her, after all.

I think I saw you a few weeks ago. I was coming out of Maxim's coffee shop in Broad Ripple, and (maybe) you were walking in. You had on a hat and sunglasses and a blue sweatshirt and you were pushing a stroller. I held the door open.

I don't know exactly what you look like these days (though I did hear you had a baby, and congratulations). But this person just <u>seemed</u> like you. She walked like you do. And I got the feeling she'd seen me too and that I'd surprised her. She looked angry, to be honest. Scared. I didn't stick around, so maybe I was scared too.

You've been on my mind a lot lately and maybe that's part of it. I'm getting married again. Her name is Gaby. She's a good woman, someone I've known a long time, and I want to make her happy. These days I've been thinking a lot about you and me and the man I was back then.

If it wasn't you, I'm so sorry. I'll just chalk it up to my conscience. It wouldn't be the first time.

Either way, I just want you to know that, if you ever wanted to, or if it helped, I'd be happy to see you and sit down and talk a little. I won't ever be able to apologize enough for the way I treated you, but I can always try.

I hope you're doing ok. I just want you to know how much I wish for you to be happy these days. I know I don't have any right to. But I hope your life has become a happy one. I really do.

Take care. Keith.

• • •

She'd read Keith's message again. And again. And again.

That night she'd opened a reply and typed:

Keith,

I'm afraid it wasn't me you saw.

And in a way, that would be perfect, wouldn't it? He'd done some of her work for her, after all, invoking his conscience. Claim innocence. Let him wonder who he'd seen. Let him think his mind was capable of conjuring her when he felt guilty. That way, even if he was better, now, even if he was good to Gaby, she could be sure she'd always be in the corner of his vision, watching. Didn't he deserve that?

But that approach also seemed, well, cruel.

She thought of Gaby, smiling, talking about the man she was marrying. She thought about how lost in her own mind she'd been, these last weeks.

Lisa began to delete what she'd written. Then she stopped, halfway through.

She saw what was left.

She didn't send the email, but she saved it as a draft. And in the weeks and months thereafter she thought, sometimes, about what might come next, if she opened it back up and wrote any more.

Keith,
I'm afraid it was.

Getaway

I.

After he nearly flunked out of Oregon State during the spring semester of his freshman year—the same semester, as it happened, that he was cited for possession of marijuana outside a house party—Kevin's mother informed him that many changes were going to have to be made, if he expected her to pay for any more of his education.

She knew this would come as a blow to him—was he *listening?*—but he was not allowed to spend the summer in his apartment in Corvallis. She paid his rent; she had a say. She did not feel she could trust him to live by himself. To make responsible adult decisions.

Was he listening?

"Yeah," he said. "Sure, Mom."

They were sitting opposite one another at the kitchen table in their house—her house—in the Sacramento suburbs. His mother's hands were folded on the tile tabletop. She took a deep breath and told him: she'd arranged a job for him for the summer. She had made a mistake, she was now sure, in letting him slide by without one for so long. He had become too *privileged*.

So on Monday, she told him, she was going to drive him to the little town of Hidalgo, high in the Sierra Nevada, where Kevin would work for her brother Barry at the lodge he owned and operated. Barry needed a handyman, and had agreed to take Kevin on.

Kevin was on probation with her, basically. She would receive regular reports on his behavior. She and her brother were very close, and Kevin should not forget that. Was he listening?

"Yes," he said.

The *problem*—she told him, beginning to cry—was that she'd always forgiven him too easily. That was her mistake. Yes, it was.

"I forgave your father too much," she said. "And look what happened. I'm tired of forgiveness. I'm so tired of people *dumping* on me for being *kind*."

He could no longer contain himself. "Mom, come on, it was just weed."

"This is when people apologize, Kevin. This is when people who were raised the right way apologize to their mothers."

He took a deep, steadying breath. "I'm sorry. Again."

"Again?" she said. "Try being sorry *once*."

• • •

The following Monday, when Kevin's mother had, at last, left the Pine Bough Lodge's office, Kevin's uncle Barry rose from behind his desk and walked past Kevin (who sat, slumped and chastened, in one of the knotty-pine log chairs positioned in front of it). He pushed apart two slats of the blinds that covered the window overlooking the parking lot.

"What's she doing?" Kevin asked.

"Well," Barry said, "she's sitting behind the wheel and crying."

Barry was a couple of years older than Kevin's mother—forty-two—but he looked younger. He was trim and ruddy-faced, and other than a receding hairline and a small, round belly, he could pass for thirty.

"Now she's leaving," Barry said. "And now she's gone."

He returned to his desk. "You make my sister cry a lot, kid."

"I was stupid," Kevin said.

Barry did not seem angry with him. Kevin could never recall Barry being angry. His uncle had always radiated serenity, contentment. He'd worked in investment banking for ten years, and when he'd made enough money, he retired and bought Pine Bough: twelve cabins and a main building containing a restaurant and bar on the shore of a small Sierra lake, which in the mornings provided glassy reflections of alpenglow on the jagged peaks that rose above it to the west. His cabins were usually full; his restaurant got by. He hiked and skied and drove a nice truck and had deep smile lines at the corners of his eyes.

He was long divorced; Kevin barely remembered his aunt Kat. ("Never get married," Barry had told Kevin, the summer before. "Don't fall into that trap. Especially a good-looking kid like you.")

"How long you been getting high?"

When Kevin didn't answer, Barry opened his desk drawer and pulled out a sandwich bag full of weed.

"Oh, wow," Kevin said.

Barry laughed. "Oh wow is right. It's good, too. I know the grower."

"Does Mom know?"

"Oh, she used to. But after your dad . . ."

Kevin's father wasn't just an alcoholic; he was a *drunk*, now living in a small town in North Dakota with a trashy girlfriend. He'd been in jail a couple of times.

Kevin reminded himself that he'd worried for his mother when he'd been arrested. That he had known right away that what he'd done would hurt her. That he wasn't a *complete* shithead.

"Look. I do have a lot of work for you to do here," Barry said. "But this isn't prison. Get high or don't, I don't care. Just do the work, and let's get your mother through this summer without any scars. She deserves that."

Barry took a jangly ring of keys from a nail by the door and led Kevin on a tour of the lodge. He showed him the cabins, the storage and tool sheds, the kitchen and walk-in cooler in the restaurant. He showed Kevin the docks, located past Cabin 12, and the ten rowboats roped to them, and the boathouse that held racks of canoes, and the little sandy beach past the docks, and all the trash cans that needed emptying twice per day, three times on weekends. Barry's own house, a larger cabin tucked back in the woods on the other side of the wide parking lot.

Then Barry took Kevin to the cabin where he'd be staying all summer, far out along the northern curve of the lake, nestled at the edge of the pines. The cabin was a small square, barely big enough to hold its contents: a Formica tabletop bolted to the wall; a mini-fridge, hot-plate, and sink; a television atop a wooden crate, and a ladder leading to a narrow loft bed. The cabin had two windows, a bathroom only big enough for a toilet and a shower, and a flat platform roof accessible through a hatch above the loft. The whole place was smaller than Kevin's bedroom in his Corvallis apartment.

Barry told Kevin he would always need to be on the grounds. Kevin would have to keep his phone charged and turned on at all times; guests would have his number, and text him for help after-hours. Guests invariably had problems with their heaters or TVs or internet. Kevin would have to fix whatever he could, and rouse Barry if he could not.

The key to this job, Barry explained to him—they stood on the shore of the lake—was that people didn't only come to the lodge to get away from their jobs. They came here to pretend to be entirely different people. To get away from their real selves for a while. To be talented fishermen or generous parents or loving newlyweds. Barry's job—now Kevin's job—was to figure out who a guest was pretending to be, and to reflect that person back to them, without letting on that anyone was pretending at all.

Barry stood at Kevin's side, looking out across the lake. A family spread across two canoes was paddling in sloppy circles. A child's laugh skipped and clattered across the water. "That's the key to making people happy," Barry said. "And making our guests happy is job number one."

Kevin believed him. This was because, at the moment, he was very happy himself.

• • •

That night his girlfriend Monica called him from Seattle. When he'd been cited for possession, she'd been cited for underage drinking. They had walked out of a house party, arguing, and hadn't noticed the two campus cops heading up the walk. Kevin had been holding a lit joint in one hand, had been gesturing at Monica with it. Monica had been drunk, screaming that he was a giant asshole.

"God, I miss you," Monica said, when he answered.

He and Monica didn't have much in common. She didn't like parties and acting stupid, and Kevin did, kind of. She was very smart and focused, and if someone (like Kevin) pushed her too far, she could summon an enormous, disturbing rage. He, on the other hand, got bad grades and never raised his voice.

The problem with them—one of many—was that Kevin had been thinking of breaking up with Monica when they'd gotten into trouble.

Three factors had stopped him from doing so. The first was Monica's unwavering loyalty to him; she insisted on defending him to her parents and friends, even though they blamed him for her troubles. He was touched that she saw something in him worth fighting for, a better self he could become, even if he wasn't exactly sure what that was.

The second reason was that the sex was great. Monica was beautiful—vibrant and blond and rosy-cheeked. Looking at her, being with her—her body and her smell and the noises she made when he was inside of her—mesmerized him. It went both ways, too; she pounced on him whenever they were alone. It was hard to have a conversation—like, say, about the future of their relationship—before things got physical.

The third reason? He was, simply, too afraid to do it.

He wondered sometimes if he would ever break up with Monica. He worried that they would get married and have children, and he would still feel this way.

"I miss you, too," he told her.

"This *sucks*," she said. "I'm stuck inside all day." Her very Christian parents had responded harshly to her drinking, and had denied her the use of a car for the summer. "They're also making me see a counselor."

Kevin decided not to tell her that he had his own little cabin, that he would spend all day tomorrow waist-deep in a cool mountain lake, replacing dock planks. "It's pretty lame here, too."

"Wrong. I looked it up. It's *gorgeous* there."

"Dude, it's super boring."

"At least tell me there are no girls."

"A couple waitresses," he said. Several, actually, and a lot of them looked to be his age. One, a small, thin brunette, had given him The Look earlier, he was pretty sure.

Then, as though she could hear his thoughts, Monica was crying.

He could picture her sobbing into a pillow so her parents wouldn't hear. Her family's McMansion, with its view of Mt. Rainier out the dining-room windows, was one of those houses big enough to swallow any noise, but inside of which you never wanted to speak above a whisper. He tried to soothe her. He took his phone up the ladder onto the roof of his cabin and watched the sunset sparkle gold and garnet on the waves of the lake. He told her he hated being away from her. He told her, as he had many times before, that he loved her.

II.

Kevin settled quickly and easily into the work. He'd never had a job before, and was surprised to discover that this one wasn't really that hard. He spent his days hammering nails into loose planks, and resetting the Wi-Fi routers, and changing letters on the roadside sign, and driving the lodge van to Hidalgo's one supermarket in order to pick up supplies for the restaurant. Talking to guests, asking after them, laughing at their jokes.

His nights were mostly free; his phone buzzed only every now and then—usually guests wanting someone to bring buckets of ice or bottles of wine to their cabins from the bar. The guests—almost all of them middle-aged rich white people, *his* people—tipped him well, and by the end of his first week Kevin had amassed a hefty roll of cash even apart from what Barry paid him. (Which was also cash, and sometimes also weed.) After the sun set, he climbed to the roof of his cabin and, wearing a hiker's headlamp, read tattered paperback mysteries from the lodge's little library. Sometimes he'd roll a joint and recline on the roof under a woolen blanket and watch the stars wheel.

He assured his mother, in answer to her frequent texts, that he was working very hard, and learning a great deal.

• • •

On Kevin's first Friday, Barry texted him to come to Cabin 12—the biggest and most luxurious, standing a little apart from the others. All week it had been empty, but today a new black BMW was parked in front, still ticking from the climb up the pass. Barry was standing in the doorway beside a man his age, tall and olive-skinned and curly-haired, wearing a black tracksuit.

"Kevin! Meet Gene Mathers," Barry said. "He's my personal guest this weekend. You'll see him a lot this summer."

"Pleased to meet you," Kevin said, and shook Gene's hand. Gene's grip was strong, and he smiled in a way that suggested he was used to charming people professionally.

"I hear this idiot's your uncle," Gene said.

"True on all counts," Kevin said, and both men exchanged a look, as though Kevin had lived up to an expectation that had been communicated in advance.

"Gene and I went to college together," Barry said. "Take care of whatever he wants, day or night."

"I won't be any trouble, I promise," Gene said, and winked.

A woman walked around the corner of the cabin, returning from the lakeshore. She was tall, almost as tall as Gene, and had long blond hair pulled into a ponytail, and wore giant starlet sunglasses and cutoff shorts. She might be, Kevin thought, only a little older than he himself was. She was barefoot, and held a pair of gold sandals by their straps.

"Babe, this is Kevin," Gene said to her. "He's going to take care of us this weekend. Kevin, this is Lara."

She smiled—a quick twitch of her lips, a kind of masterpiece of not giving a shit. "Excuse me," she said, and walked past them into the cabin, touching Gene on the elbow as she did so. The complicated smell of her perfume lingered.

Barry kept talking, telling him about how he and Gene had met as roommates at San Diego State, how Gene was now a pharmaceutical rep, always traveling. Kevin was half listening when Lara came back out, dressed in a black bikini, a towel wrapped around her hips. She was one of the most perfectly formed women Kevin had ever seen. He couldn't help but watch her walk down the path again to the little sandy beach. Gene and Barry watched her, too. Kevin got the feeling, standing with them, that watching her was all right to do. That Lara's bikini and walk were a kind of performance for the three of them.

She dropped her towel and dove into the lake, perfectly.

Later that night, Kevin smoked behind the restaurant with a couple of guys on the staff he had gotten to know—a host named Luis, who in the off-season studied engineering at Fresno State, and Paulie, a thin white kid who lived in town, studying meth.

Luis asked him, "So you met Clean Gene?"

"That's what we call him?"

"He's up here every other weekend," Paulie said. "Different girl each time, all of them hot as fuck."

Kevin tried to think of women more beautiful than Lara, but they were all actresses.

"He tips big," Luis said.

"Dude's a baller," Paulie said, admiringly, and tossed his butt into the can of sand beside the dumpster. Luis rolled his eyes.

An hour later Kevin received a text. *Gene here. Come by?*

Gene opened the door before Kevin's knock. He was wearing an unbuttoned Hawaiian shirt and swim trunks. He smiled his smile and handed Kevin a wad of bills and a slip of notepaper. "Here's our dinner order, and we need a bottle of good scotch from the bar. Do you know your scotch?"

"Not yet."

Gene grinned. "Macallan 12. Accept no substitutes."

He'd given Kevin two hundred dollars, even though he'd ordered only sandwiches to accompany the liquor. Kevin walked to the restaurant and gave the money and the order to Luis in the kitchen. "Clean fucking Gene," Luis said.

Ten minutes later Kevin wheeled a cart with the meals and the bottle of scotch down the sidewalk to Cabin 12. The moon was up, and the wind, dropping from the mountains, lifted goosebumps on his bare arms.

Lara answered the door, wearing a bathrobe. She did not seem to recognize him, but she was smiling, dazzlingly. Kevin handed her the dinner tray and the bottle. He began to dig in the pockets of his shorts for the change, which was well over a hundred dollars.

"Keep it!" Gene called, from inside the cabin, and laughed. Lara laughed, too. Kevin tried to catch a glimpse of Gene, but she shut the door too quickly.

They were still laughing as he walked away.

III.

The next night, Kevin was relaxing on the roof, nearly dozing, when a voice summoned him to the edge. Luis and the dark-haired waitress—Denise was her name; Kevin had asked—stood below. Luis held up a six-pack of beer. "You coming or what?"

Kevin walked with them—and several other members of the lodge's staff, ten in all—along a narrow path through the chilly dark, to a cove on the far shore. From there, the lodge seemed far smaller and more distant than it really was. Kevin could not see the mountain that rose at his back, but he felt its cold, its sinister gravity. The staffers gave each other shit as they settled into the sand, popping the beers and starting a fire in a sandy pit covered with a fine wire mesh. Some of them stripped down to their shorts and went for a quick swim. Denise removed her sweatshirt, revealing a bikini top and the wink of a belly button ring, and pointed at him. "You have to swim. Tradition."

He pulled off his shirt and followed her—all of them—off the edge of a big rock that ramped out over the lake. He hung briefly in darkness, and then was submerged. The water was deep, and freezing, and all around him he heard the others mumbling and cursing, then laughing. The moon was behind clouds, and he couldn't see who swam near him. A foot brushed his calf beneath the surface. He thought he heard Denise laughing. Then everyone splashed for shore.

He dropped shivering by the fire; Denise sat cross-legged beside him, a towel wrapped around her shoulders. Her legs were long and lean, still dotted with drops of lake water; her calves flexed as she dug her feet into the sand.

"I'm Kevin, by the way," he said.

"I know," she said. "We all know. You're Barry's nephew." But she offered a hand anyway, cold and sandy, and he shook it.

They talked for a long time, the fire drying their hair, tightening their skin. Denise was from here in Hidalgo, and was about to be a sophomore at UNLV. She wanted to teach elementary school. This was her second summer working at the restaurant. She hated her parents and couldn't wait for school to start again.

"Tell me about it," he said.

Kevin was aware of Luis and Paulie and others giving them space, watching them. Denise must have been aware, too, but she didn't seem to care. She lowered her voice so no one could hear and spent a while telling him stories: who was cool, who wasn't. Who was currently hooking up and who wasn't. Her favorite put-down was *boring*—Vegas had ruined her, she said—and she had decided the word applied to everyone at the lodge.

"Please never let me be boring," she said. "That's my biggest fear."

"You are anything but boring," he said.

Her eyes glittered with firelight. "Are you? I can't decide. You don't say much. Tell me something so I know."

"I've been arrested," he said, which was almost true.

"Wow. Okay. For what?"

The thought of it, he could tell, excited her, scared her a little. She leaned forward. The straps of her bikini top fell away from the hollows of her collarbone.

Assault, he thought about saying. A fight over a woman.

"Possession," he said, his bluff called.

"Oooohhh. Possession of *what?*"

• • •

Once Kevin opened the door of his cabin and invited Denise inside, she turned and held out her arms to him, as though she wanted him to lift her off the ground—but then she was kissing him, and touching him, and pulling at his clothes.

Her skin was very hot, and she tasted of lake water: like clean dark stone.

And after half an hour, just like that: he'd slept with someone who wasn't his girlfriend—the girlfriend he was, now, trying very hard not to think about.

Once they'd caught their breath, he invited Denise up the hatch, onto the roof, and they sat there naked under his blanket, sharing a joint.

After a long silence, Denise said, "All right, who is she?"

"Jesus," he said. "How'd you know?"

"Oh, come on. Everyone here's got someone somewhere else."

"Do you?"

"No. I mean, I *did*. I cut him loose before summer started." She swung her legs across his. "Tell me about her."

"I don't know if—"

"You won't offend me. Come on—it's not like we just got married."

So Kevin found himself telling her. About how Monica was being punished for the summer, made to feel as though she were fifteen again. Stuck at home while he had been sent here, with nothing to do but make him feel guilty, whether she meant to or not.

"Do you love her?"

He told her he wasn't sure, even though he'd said he did to Monica.

"Bad move," she said. "I've had guys do that to me. It's as bad as cheating, in my opinion. Saying you love her when you don't."

"Ouch."

"Well, it is. Would you want someone doing it to you?"

No. No he wouldn't.

"I'm not trying to judge. Like, I'm here, too, right? I'm not trying to get you to dump your chick." She took a long hit and passed him the joint. "Though it doesn't sound like you two are happy."

"Maybe."

"Maybe," she said, imitating his voice as a cavemannish grunt. "Just don't do it because of me."

She said that, but then she lifted his hand and uncurled his fingers and kissed the center of his palm. Touched her tongue to it. Her dark eyes lifted to his.

In the morning, he decided, he would call Monica and tell her they were done. Because now that he had done this, things would have to be over between them.

But when the sun rose, after Denise hurriedly gathered her clothes and bade him a laughing farewell before returning home to shower, he sat down and made himself coffee on his little hotpot and didn't call Monica.

And when Monica texted him after she woke up—as she always did—and asked, *How are you? I miss you,* he responded with, *Doing great! Miss you too,* and took a shower, a little stunned at the memory of Denise's body, and how it had displaced Monica's in his imagination; stunned at his own behavior; stunned at how little guilt he felt.

When Denise knocked on his door later that night— and again and again, on many other subsequent nights— he kept inviting her in.

IV.

By July, Kevin had developed a deep tan.

And he had learned many things: How to replace a broken toilet. How to patch the bottom of a canoe. How to chase raccoons out of the storage shed. How to change the oil in the lodge's van.

He'd learned about people: How to guide drunken guests back to their cabins from the bar when it closed. How not to be sarcastic to guests he found rude and wanted to tell off. How to suggest to guests being noisy at two in the morning that they might want to take their fun inside. How to tell Barry everything was fine, all the time. How to make Barry trust him. How to keep him happy.

Once a week Barry called Kevin's mother from his

office, and the two of them talked with her on speaker. During these calls Barry complimented Kevin; he told his mother how Kevin was dependable, agreeable, very capable. That the life up here suited him. That she should not worry.

"Are you really liking it?" she'd ask Kevin, and Barry would roll his eyes, and Kevin would tell her the truth.

"I'm having a blast, Mom. This is working out really well."

And it was. He'd met Denise. He'd hiked to the top of a nearby mountain with Luis and Paulie and smoked an excellent joint with them at the summit. He'd made a lot of money, though he had nothing to spend it on—he ate for free at the restaurant, and paid no rent for his cabin—so he wrapped all his cash in rubber bands and kept it in a tackle box left in the cabin.

He liked the lodge, and the job, enough that he began to fantasize about staying here. About asking Barry if he could, somehow, be a part of Pine Bough in a more permanent way.

His hair grew out, long and blonding, until Denise finally cut it one morning while the two of them sat on a boulder beside the shore. Her mother was a stylist, and Denise had learned a lot from her, despite—she said—trying not to. She ran her fingers through it, asked if he was sure he wanted it cut.

"I love your hair," she said, and it was all he could do not to turn around and pull off her clothes in front of god and everyone.

Denise spent two or three nights a week at his cabin. On her days off she sometimes came by and sometimes didn't.

He liked it when she did.

He liked that she knew how to talk about sex: what she wanted, what she was willing to try. (He liked that she liked to try a lot of things.) He liked that she talked like a boy. He liked her enough that he started seeking her out in the restaurant.

"We're just letting off steam," he heard her say once to one of the other waitresses—this was the day after they'd all gone again to swim beside the firepit, and Denise had spent the evening curled beside him in full view of the others. No one at the lodge could keep a secret, so why try? "He's a sweet guy," Denise told her friend. "And cute! But it's only a summer thing."

She'd said as much to him. Even so, overhearing this saddened him.

He still hadn't broken up with Monica, and Denise hadn't asked him to. In fact, she hadn't brought up Monica at all after that first night. This seemed to be important, though Kevin didn't know yet how to interpret the information. He spent most of his days thinking and feeling as though he *already had* broken up with Monica.

This feeling was disrupted only by the texts Monica sent him every day and night. He always answered them, becoming, for a few minutes at a time, the man who wanted to. But that man was set easily aside, like a shirt stripped off before a swim.

He told himself he would break up with Monica in person, when both of them returned to school. She was having a hard enough time this summer, he thought—why make it harder?

Breaking up with her in person, he told himself, was the honorable thing. The right thing.

He *would* do the right thing, he told himself. When the time came, he really would.

• • •

Gene Mathers continued to arrive every other weekend. Each time he was accompanied by a different woman, and driving a different luxury rental car. He introduced Barry and Kevin to them all:

Andi, who was redheaded and freckled and loud, and who liked to paddle the canoes around and around the lake;

Lynne, who was slim, Latina, and who spent most of her time reading on a deck chair on the shore;

Ingrid, who was blond and had some kind of European accent and wore a lot of dark makeup around her eyes and didn't seem to like the sun, or Kevin, or anyone but Gene, to whose arm she clung when they walked together around the lodge.

Gene acted as though he adored each of them–and maybe he did. He doted on them, told them jokes (the ones Kevin overheard never seemed to be funny, but the women laughed at them all the same), and seemed to be heartened by their company.

Kevin, talking to them, meeting them on the path, helping them into canoes, kept in mind Barry's talk about being a mirror. He'd learned how to read the other guests, and was–he thought–getting good at it. Gene, for instance, was easy: He wanted to be a rich playboy, a total boss, and as long as you seemed a little in awe of him, he'd tip in kind.

But what did the women he brought with him want? Who did they want to be, when they were at the Pine Bough Lodge? Kevin saw them so little–and almost always in Gene's company, close to Cabin 12–that he couldn't guess.

Midway through the summer a possible answer came to him. He thought they didn't mind being looked at—they were beautiful, all of them, or they wouldn't be here—but none of them seemed to want to be *seen.*

Here at the lodge, they didn't seem to want to *be* anybody.

• • •

Kevin came to understand this fully one Saturday night in mid-July. As he walked back from the parking lot—he'd been saying goodnight to Denise, which meant he'd made out with her for several minutes in the shadow of a cluster of pines, before she climbed in her little Subaru and drove home—he encountered the woman staying with Gene that weekend. She was smoking on one of the docks, and if not for the cherry of her cigarette, he might not have seen her at all. He struggled to remember her name. Linda? Melinda? She was tall, and had glossy black hair and severe cheekbones. He lifted a hand to wave, but she turned her head away, toward the water. Kevin thought he heard her sniffling.

Barry probably would have wanted him to keep walking, to be discreet. The woman was out here in the dark, trying to be invisible, and crying. It wasn't the lodge's business.

Kevin did not stop because he was curious about Gene. He stopped, he told himself, because she might be in trouble. Because it was the decent thing to do.

"Are you all right over there?" he called.

For a moment she didn't answer, and he had decided to leave well enough alone when she said, "Wait."

He walked closer.

"You're Barry's kid?"

"Nephew."

"And you what, run the place?"

"I do whatever."

"Uh-huh. I bet you do."

She was drunk, he realized, a lot drunk.

She said, "Do you know Gene? Like, have you known him awhile?"

"Not really. I just met him this summer."

She took a long drag on her cigarette. "So you don't know his wife?"

This was the first time anyone had confirmed aloud for him what he had always suspected. What he had sensed he was never supposed to ask.

"No."

She shook her head, as though he'd lied. She looked out over the lake. "All of you here judge me. You're not supposed to, but you do. I can feel it."

"I don't judge anyone," Kevin said.

"Jesus, maybe you should." She threw her cigarette into the lake and walked unsteadily past him, back up the walk to the door of Cabin 12.

• • •

In the morning she was gone. Gene, Kevin heard—the news ran quickly through the staff—let her take the rental car back to wherever it was she'd come from. She'd been crying, shouting, as she loaded her bag into the back. Gene would stay the rest of the weekend by himself.

The surprising thing Gene did, in the wake of the woman's departure, was invite Barry and Kevin and Denise to have dinner with him in his cabin. When he told Kevin this, he didn't say Denise's name. "Bring your girlfriend," he said to Kevin. "The brunette, the one I see you with."

Kevin was not only surprised by this; he was surprised by Barry's reaction, when he told him: "Denise? I like that girl," he said. "I'll get someone to cover her shift." He fist-bumped Kevin. "Nice work."

Denise made a face when he told her—leaving out the part about Gene calling her his girlfriend. He expected her to say no anyway, but then she shrugged. "Sure. Might as well get a meal out of that douchebag."

She dressed up for dinner, in a white sundress and leather sandals. She always wore a little makeup to work, but tonight she'd put on dark red lipstick, and painted her nails, and added a few curls to her hair. "Wow," Kevin said, when she knocked on his door.

"Good answer," she told him, and left a lipstick smudge on his cheek, then made him put on a button-down shirt and long pants.

Gene and Barry were already drinking when they arrived. Gene greeted them—"Madam," he said to Denise, and bowed a little, "It's lovely to make your acquaintance. That's a gorgeous dress"—and then sat back down, his tanned legs stretched out to the side of the table. (He and Barry were dressed in shorts and T-shirts and flip-flops.)

Gene ordered them steaks from the restaurant, and several bottles of wine. Luis delivered it all to the cabin, and gave Kevin a look through the open door that seemed equal parts envy and rage.

Gene was himself: Magnanimous. Charming. He poured drinks, then spent a long time asking Denise about herself, about her time in college, about her family; she answered him at length, telling sarcastic jokes, seemingly at ease.

But then Gene asked, "So! How long have you been seeing our boy here?"

Kevin winced, but Denise only smiled. "Since about the minute he got here," she said. "He was too cute to wait on."

Maybe it was the wine, but Denise reached under the table and held Kevin's hand.

Gene and Barry then began telling stories about college, genuinely funny ones. Gene had once been the singer in a wannabe grunge band, and had grown a ponytail; Barry had broken his wrist falling drunkenly out of a tree, trying to trespass at a zoo; the two of them had once dated twin sisters.

They learned that Gene had, in college, been nervous around women.

"Like with your mother, for instance," he said, winking at Kevin. He had drunk quite a lot of the scotch by now. "She used to come visit Barry. Such a sweet girl. But she would have nothing to do with me. I couldn't figure out how to talk to her."

"Good thing, too," Barry said, maybe with a hint of warning.

"Oh, I know. She had to marry Chuck, and I had to marry Renee."

Kevin tensed, hearing his father's name spoken like this, hearing his mother mentioned in such a way—and by Gene, who seemed to live on another world entirely than the one his mother and father occupied. And then he realized they'd just heard the name of Gene's wife.

Barry said, "You know, Gene, Kevin could use a little advice about school." He gave Kevin a look, one that said, *Play along.* "His grades aren't so good. Probably destined for failure."

"Probably," Denise agreed.

Gene grabbed Kevin's shoulder, a little too firmly. "What your uncle wants me to say is that I nearly flunked out of college."

"Really?"

"Oh, sure. I didn't even want to go! And then I had no idea what to do when I got there."

Kevin was delighted to hear it—and that the subject had successfully changed. "That's my situation, for sure."

"You think I grew up wanting to *sell pharmaceuticals?* No. When I was your age, I wanted to be a rock star. A professional pilot. I wanted to play shortstop for the Giants." He laughed at himself, and Kevin thought he could understand, then, why so many women came here with him: his laugh was kind, almost sweet, and made him even more handsome. "I only went to school because my father told me he'd write me out of his will if I didn't. Then I ended up taking business classes—I have your uncle to thank for that idea—and I found what I was good at. You might give it a shot, Kevin. Business. You can listen, and you're good with people. You could do my job. You could do Barry's job."

Kevin decided to risk a personal question. "But it makes you happy?" He added, quickly: "Sales?"

Denise squeezed his hand.

Gene took a drink and said to Barry, "See? He can read people. He can see that no matter what I say, I'm secretly melancholy." To Kevin, he said, "What you just did is, you asked me to double down on myself. To reveal myself fully. That's the essence of sales, Kevin. That's *seduction.*"

He winked at Denise. Kevin waited, trying not to feel her disgust.

"And *of course* you don't ruin it by talking next. You wait me out, so I lose the transaction. Now I owe you information. Okay. I'm unhappy, Kevin. I'm a sad old bastard."

Kevin looked at his half-eaten steak.

"But it's not because of my job. Not because of that."

Barry cleared his throat. He quickly began telling another story about college, and then another, and Gene cheered up again, and the evening went on like that for a while. Gene ordered a second bottle of scotch, and when he did, Barry stretched and asked if maybe Kevin and Denise could take their empty dishes back to the kitchen.

Kevin had the definite feeling he was being punished, that he'd crossed a line he shouldn't have.

Or maybe it was that Gene couldn't be trusted to talk in front of them about happiness.

• • •

When they were inside his cabin again, Denise kicked off her shoes and sat heavily on his little loveseat, her cheeks flushed pink with wine.

"Thanks for going," he said.

"Yeah," she said. "Your frat brothers are really charming."

"Come on."

"Come on," she said, in her dumb-Kevin voice. "Gene's so fucking shady."

"He's nice enough."

"Tell that to his wife."

He sat next to her and put his arm around her shoulders, but she was stiff.

"Did you tell them I was your girlfriend?"

"No." He wondered if she was about to end this thing between them, whatever it was, and he felt a sudden lurching nausea, like seasickness. "They just assumed."

She snorted. "Yeah. They assumed. I *assume* you haven't broken up with Monica?"

He didn't answer.

"I should go," she said.

"You don't have to." He put his hand on the back of her neck, under the soft sheaf of her hair. "I don't want you to."

She surprised him. Her posture softened, and after a long moment she let out a breath, then leaned her cheek against his shoulder.

"We're the worst," she said.

"Stay here," he said. "Just stay with me."

"I'm on my period."

He told her he didn't care. And he didn't. He rolled them a joint, and they smoked it, and then she lay with her head on his lap while he rubbed knots out of her shoulders. He was happy to do these things, happy to be with her. Happy she'd stayed. Happy she climbed into his loft with him, and snored beside him, breathing out wine, her skin smelling of perfume, their bare feet intertwined while they fell asleep.

● ● ●

Monica texted him in the morning:

I feel like I'm losing you. I feel like you're trying to break up with me, and you're just too lazy to do it.

He wrote back, *You're imagining things.*

It would be cruel to leave me hanging all summer.

You should just do it and get it over with.

I'm not going to, he wrote.

I don't know why I am the way I am. I don't know why people won't love me.

Denise was peeing in his little bathroom, and humming to herself.

But I do. He hit send, his throat tight. *I do love you.*

Then he turned off the phone, but not before Denise came out of the bathroom and saw him do it.

V.

For nearly a month, Gene stayed away from the lodge.

Barry didn't want to talk about it, when Kevin asked. He did not, it seemed, want Kevin to ask at all. "Gene's business is his own," he said. "We'll see him when we see him." His uncle looked worried, though; he'd been bleary-eyed of late, distracted, and Kevin couldn't help but think that Gene's last visit had gone more poorly, somehow, than their dinner had let on.

"It's not your business," Denise told him, when he asked her. "And would it really be that terrible if Gene takes the rest of the summer off?"

Kevin knew he was supposed to agree. Yet Gene was a mystery to him. Gene was a piece of work, sure—but then, so was he. So were *they.* How could he judge? How could Denise?

Melancholy, Gene had said, and Kevin had found something familiar in that word. He was happy at the lodge, but not at home, not at school, not with Monica. Why was that?

He wondered if Gene's wife was like Monica. If she

was the source of *his* sadness. He wondered how a marriage like that had come to be in the first place. Why it had lasted so long.

He imagined taking Gene a bottle of Macallan 12 one night—buying it with his own money—and asking him. He thought about the two of them talking it over, man to man. Kevin was good with people. He could find the right way to ask, if Gene ever came back.

• • •

During this time Kevin and Denise spent almost every night together—mostly in bed, but sometimes they watched movies on his laptop, or played checkers. Sometimes they walked around the lake, hand in hand.

Sometimes, during a movie, he'd realize she was watching him. Sometimes he'd realize that he was watching her, the line of her neck, the fall of her hair onto her shoulders, the way she chewed her bottom lip.

With three weeks left before the start of the school year, Monica texted him: *I'm going to see you soon!!! Almost out of jail!!!*

She wrote: *Tell me what you're going to do with me when I see you.*

Whatever you want, he wrote back, queasy.

• • •

Then, in mid-August, on a Tuesday, Barry texted Kevin, summoning him to his office: *Urgent.*

On his way there Kevin saw why: A station wagon was parked in front of Cabin 12. As Kevin watched, Gene climbed out of the driver's seat and walked to the trunk.

He opened it, and then took something out, and then unfolded that something into a wheelchair. He opened the passenger door and bent down, and then straightened— and when he did, he was holding a person, someone tiny: an old woman, maybe, or a child. He set the person into the wheelchair, very gently. Then he slowly pushed the wheelchair up the long access ramp into the cabin and shut the door.

When Kevin entered Barry's office, his uncle looked as though he had been crying.

"Gene needs privacy this weekend," he said, not lifting his eyes from the desk. "I'll handle everything he needs. Make sure the rest of the staff knows to stay away from him. Cabins 10 and 11 are empty, but keep the noise down everywhere else. And keep your distance. It's not personal."

All the cabins but 12 were booked solid through the end of summer. If 10 and 11 were empty, that meant Barry had canceled their reservations. That would have cost him a lot of money.

"I saw the wheelchair," Kevin said. "Who is it?" Thinking: Gene's mother.

"Renee," Barry said, after a moment. "His wife. She's very sick. She wanted some time at the lake. And we're giving her that."

"Sick? How sick?"

"No questions." Barry let his gaze drop. "I mean it. Not from you, not from anyone."

• • •

Kevin found Denise on shift in the restaurant, and motioned her into the dry storage pantry.

"I can't talk now," she said, but she moved closer to him, smiling and slinky, in a way that he liked.

He didn't want to say it, but he knew he had to. He told her what he'd just heard: That Renee Mathers was in a wheelchair, had had to be carried from the car into her cabin. That Barry had been crying in his office.

Denise had pressed herself against the wall of the pantry while he spoke. On the other side of the wall, in the restaurant, the sounds of eating and clinking and tinny pop music seemed far too loud.

"Do you think that makes him okay?" she asked, finally. "That he cried?"

"I—no."

"Is she *dying?*"

"I don't know."

But he did know, and he could see Denise knew, too.

"Come find me later, okay?" he asked.

"Sure," she said, and then, "Jesus Christ." She shook her head, as though clearing her mind after a blow, and returned to work without saying goodbye.

• • •

Kevin did what Barry had asked; he moved among the staff, telling them to stay away from Cabin 12, that Gene needed quiet. He told them he had no idea why.

Afterward he stuck close to the main building, instead of retreating to his cabin to wait for calls. It was a sleepy night; after he emptied the trash cans, his evening stretched in front of him without obligation. He waited for Denise to come out the rear door for a smoke, but she didn't, and when her shift ended, he never saw her. He walked to the parking lot and found her Subaru had gone. He texted her, standing near the highway, looking toward town, but she didn't answer.

The lights glowed in the windows of Cabin 12.

Kevin went finally to his own cabin. He climbed onto the roof and waited for Denise to return. The night air was cold, this late in the season. He wore a fleece and jeans, and closed his eyes and listened to the treetops bend and straighten in the wind.

• • •

Not long after midnight Barry texted him: *Gene's cabin. Now.*

Barry met him on the path. He was sweating, wild-eyed, and the neck of his T-shirt was torn. He pointed behind him at Gene's cabin, the windows of which were still dimly lit.

She's dead. That was Kevin's first thought.

He did not want to see a dead body. He did not want to be in the cabin with a dead woman and her grieving husband. He thought again—as he had for the past several hours—that he might not ever want to be in the same room with Gene Mathers again. Or with his uncle, for that matter. He wondered if someone like Gene was even capable of grief.

Barry said, "We have a situation. Gene's really drunk, and he just ran off. I have to go get him back. He'll listen to me. So I need you to sit with Renee for a while."

"Barry, no—"

"She's sleeping," Barry said. "Just go sit with her. She's on a lot of medication. If she wakes up, she won't make any sense. Just tell her to go back to sleep."

When Kevin still hesitated, Barry told him, "Ten

minutes. That's all. I'll make this right tomorrow. But someone has to be with her now. This is important. So man up and do it."

• • •

The inside of Cabin 12 was warm, a fire roaring in the fireplace. Kevin immediately began to sweat. He stood just inside the door. He did not want to look at the bed in the corner of the room, but he made himself.

Renee lay there, propped up by pillows. She was thin—desperately, hurtfully so—her head a bald white skull sketched onto the pillowcase, her cheekbones shadowed charcoal smudges. Her eyes were closed; her lids were waxy and pulsing. Her mouth hung slightly slack, her lips thin and colorless.

Kevin sat down in one of the pine-log chairs by the fireplace; it was hotter there, but he didn't want to be any closer to the bed. A smell hung in the room, both stale and sweet, that reminded him of baby food. Two bottles of scotch were open on the table in front of him. One was completely empty. The other was half full. He drank a couple of swallows. He didn't think Gene would mind. Then he told himself he didn't care what Gene minded.

He kept his phone in his hands, hoping for a text from Barry or Denise. He wanted Denise here with him—the want was sudden and total and draining. He stood and went to the window.

"Gene?"

The voice a soft, warm whisper.

Kevin turned from the window. Renee was looking at him, her eyes startlingly wide and gleaming, all the more frightful for being so suddenly alive.

"Gene?" she said, panicky; she tried to lift her head

from the pillow. "Gene, it hurts."

"Hey, no," he said. He took two steps closer. "I'm . . . a friend of his. He'll be right back."

Was he even telling the truth?

"Is this . . . are we in the hospital . . . ?"

Her voice was murmurous, the words themselves barely holding together.

"No. This is the lodge. Barry's lodge."

She pursed her lips suspiciously. "Gene."

"He's coming right back," Kevin said. "I promise."

"You always say that," she said. Her eyelids blinked languorously down and then up. "You always say you promise and, and you promise and you . . ."

Please don't, he thought.

She stopped talking. Her eyelids closed. He walked carefully closer to her. He was not sure why. Maybe to make sure her chest rose and fell—which it did, too quickly, too shallowly, as though she were panting.

On the nightstand by the bed was a picture in a frame. A wedding photo, he saw: Gene in his tuxedo, standing next to a slim blond woman in a long, long dress, both of them young and smiling in the sunlight. Behind them was the lake.

"That's my favorite," she said, in a murmur, startling him again. "You brought it." Her voice was kind. "You're so so so sweet. My sweet husband. My sweet..."

"It's . . . I'm not Gene, remember? I'm just a friend."

She lifted a hand from the bedcovers and gestured to the picture. Her face crumpled when she couldn't reach it.

He lifted the picture and held it closer to her. She gripped it with both hands.

"You were so handsome," she said. "We were so happy."

"You were beautiful."

The words came quickly and clearly from him. She smiled, then frowned, as though trying to locate him in a mist.

Maybe, he thought, that was exactly what it was like.

"You're not him," she said.

"I'm Kevin," he said, but she'd closed her eyes. Her hands lifted from atop the covers, thin and corded. She scratched the air in front of her throat and then dropped them, her lips working. "Thirsty."

A water bottle with a plastic straw was on the bedside table. "Here," he said, and held it out to her.

He realized she might not be able to hold it. He tipped the straw closer to her lips, which pursed as though she were taking a drag from a cigarette. She drank, pulling gently. His hands shook when he returned the bottle to the table.

"I have been trying to think of what to say," she said, her eyes half-lidded, her voice breathy and singsong. He thought about dandelion fluff, floating in a breeze. "I know about them, Gene."

Kevin held very still.

"I know you don't love them," she said. "I know who you love because you, because you love . . ."

Her hand seized at his. Her palm was hot and damp, but her grip was very weak. She gave out a cry of dismay.

"Where's your ring?" she asked. "Did you lose it, or did you—did you give it someone else? Did you get married to someone else, to—"

"No," he said. "It's around here somewhere. I'll find it. It's okay."

"Please stop lying."

"I—"

"Because, because as I have mentioned, I—we don't have much time. Not very much time. Not much."

She was asleep for a while, drifting, and he watched her while his face burned.

She opened her eyes, and smiled. "You're here."

"I'm here," he said.

"It hurts. It *hurts*. I feel like something is—like something is going to—"

"Shh," he said. "It won't."

"Don't lie," she said, almost fondly.

Her eyes moved past him, to the corners of the room. "Is this where you brought them?"

"I don't—"

"Don't lie."

"Yes," he said.

She seemed to sink into the pillows, as though the bed was a pool of water, and she was drowning.

"It really hurts, Gene. It hurts so much."

"Do you want more water?"

She held his wrists with both hands as she drank.

"We're at the lodge," she said when she'd finished. She stroked the back of his hand. Her eyes were a deep green.

"Yes."

"And when it's light, you'll take me down to see the water."

"I will."

"Like when we were married."

He said, "We still are."

She took his hand.

"Tell me you love me," she said.

He was crying. "I love you."

"Tell me I'm your wife."

He could barely say the words, but she did not seem

to mind. She smiled and touched his cheek, then took his hands in hers.

"I forgive you," she said.

"I don't deserve it."

She touched her hot fingers to his cheek. "There's no time for that."

She drifted off. Her eyes moved back and forth behind her lids. Her hands lifted off the covers, as though reaching again for the picture. She even smiled a little, as though her eyes were open, and seeing it.

• • •

A few minutes later Barry knocked softly on the door. Kevin opened it. Barry stood beside Gene, whose head lolled on his shoulders; his eyes had barely more consciousness behind them than Renee's.

"Help me get him to the couch," Barry said.

Gene was muscular and tall, and this drunk he weighed as much as two men, but they managed to arrange him on the couch cushions. He smelled of vomit. Barry looked at Renee, whose hands plucked at the air. He told Kevin, "Go."

Kevin knew he should have taken another look at Renee. That he would never see her again if he did not.

He walked quickly outside; the rush of cold air against his skin made him gasp.

• • •

In his cabin he texted Denise, over and over again. *I need you to be with me,* he wrote. *Please?*

She did not answer.

• • •

Kevin must have slept; one moment the sun wasn't up, and the next it was.

He checked his phone; no one had texted him while he slept.

He climbed onto the roof of his cabin and sat cross-legged in the sun. He could see all of the Pine Bough Lodge from here. Wednesday mornings were sleepy, but breakfast was being served at the restaurant; he could see guests at the tables inside. Two children were playing with a corgi dog outside Cabin 8.

Denise texted him then. He read what she'd sent and then turned off the phone for a little while. The sky above was deep and flawless.

He turned the phone back on, and then dialed his mother's number.

• • •

Half an hour later Barry and Gene came out of Cabin 12. Barry pushed the wheelchair; Renee's small shape was in it. Together they carried her down the steps to the dock, then set the chair down and pushed her to the end. Slowly she began to gesture at the water. Barry and Gene lifted her out of the chair and sat her carefully on the boards at the end of the dock. Barry stood behind her with his hands on her shoulders; Gene knelt and took off her socks, then lowered her feet into the water.

Kevin heard her voice, then, a slippery fluty thing, skipping across the waves to him. It sounded like bird-call. It maybe sounded happy.

• • •

On the drive out of the mountains Kevin's mother told him, at length, how disappointed she was.

Her brother was the kindest man she knew, maybe the only kind man she could name. He'd been so generous, so goddamned generous—was Kevin listening?—and whatever Kevin had done to betray Barry's generosity, to screw up the opportunity he'd provided, she couldn't imagine.

Was he listening to her? Or was she just talking to a goddamned wall?

"I'm listening," he said.

He was lying in the back seat, exhausted. He wanted to sleep, needed to, but couldn't.

He thought about Gene and Renee, who were, right now, sitting together in their little cabin. He thought about what Renee might be trying to say to Gene. What she had probably been saying for a while, now, over and over again.

He thought about what Barry had tried to tell him this morning, in his own cabin, while he packed, after turning in his resignation: how Gene had helped Barry buy the lodge; how Gene had bailed him out a couple of times during the recession; how, if you looked at it a certain way, the giant wad of cash Kevin had just packed into his bag had been paid by Gene.

How he hoped Kevin would understand someday that when you really knew and loved someone, when someone was like your brother, you had to help them try to be happy, in whatever way you could.

He thought about what Denise had texted:

I'm sorry. I can't even look at myself.

I like you, I do, but what about Monica?

I'm going to miss us, but I just think we need to try to be different people now.

Halfway to Sacramento his mother stopped at a rest area. In the bathroom he sat for a long time on a cold metal toilet, not needing to go so much as needing to be alone, apart from his mother's bitter anger.

His phone buzzed. Monica, texting *What's going on??? How's your day?*

He thought about what he might write back. About how he would see her again, in a couple of weeks. About how happy she would be, seeing him again. He wondered, not for the first time, why.

Then he thought about how he'd felt, when Renee had taken his hands the night before.

About what had moved inside him when she'd told him he was forgiven, in a voice so soft and whispery that—if you closed your eyes—you could imagine it coming from just about anybody.

Big Guy

I. Big

Can't

Doug Ritchie had heard the nickname for years, and he'd never allowed himself to mind it. He had no right to mind—he was, after all, a fat man: six-foot-two, and somewhere to the north of 300 pounds. He saw what he saw in the mirror; what use was pretending others couldn't?

Big guy, people called him. *Big man. Big fella.*

On the last day of school every May, before his senior high school students left him for the world beyond, he delivered a farewell speech to his last class. Doing so was corny, but he believed in what he told them, and each graduating class of students had come to expect it from him. In the speech he urged them to follow their dreams—as he had his—and reminded them they had all the tools within them to do so. He told them that he wished for them to keep reading and researching and writing, and by doing this to seek out ways to know themselves better. He knew they would come through any crisis just fine, as long as they kept remembering to seek their best selves.

You have to know who you are, he'd say, *in order to be happy in this world.*

Doug would say, if he was asked, that he was happy with his life. He was married to a woman he loved–Wendy Spaulding, whom he'd met in college–and he had a job he liked, and which he did well: teaching junior and senior English and journalism at Hunter High School in suburban Reno. He'd learned enough about the world's horrors (he taught *Beloved, Fahrenheit 451, The Handmaid's Tale*) not to complain about his place. He was a white, middle-class (upper-middle, if he was being honest, given Wendy's salary) male, which made him one of the luckiest people who'd ever lived.

He knew all of this about himself. And if what he told his students was to mean anything–that you had to see yourself clearly and without self-deception–then he had to acknowledge that he was fat.

Even so, the nicknames could rankle him. The way people felt comfortable, labeling him. Assuming his own comfort with himself. People from whom he needed repairs were especially fond of doing so. He'd pull up to the body shop and a mechanic would happily cry out, *Watcha need, big man?* A plumber would emerge from the hall bathroom, wiping his hands on a rag: *All done, big fella.*

(These people were always men, always smaller, stronger: people from whom he needed work that he could not, himself, do.)

He heard the nicknames most often from servers at restaurants–those people from whom, especially, he could keep no secrets. They'd appear toward the end of his meals out with Wendy and ask, *Any dessert for you folks? How about you, big guy?*

The server would raise an eyebrow, and even though inwardly Doug cringed, he would laugh–because it helped to be in on the joke, didn't it?—and take a menu.

After it was set in motion, Doug came to believe his divorce had begun with that very question, and his answer. Wendy claimed to have been planning on telling him she wanted out of the marriage for a long time, but Doug was unable, in those sleepless hours just afterward, to ignore the circumstances during which she finally had.

He and Wendy had been out to dinner, in May of 2013, a little past fourteen years into their marriage; he'd been gaining weight steadily almost the entire time. That weight gain had happened for many reasons, but the most basic among them was that Doug was almost never in the habit of turning down dessert.

He and Wendy were finishing up a meal at a nice restaurant buried deep within a casino in downtown Reno, where they'd lived since just after their marriage. His school year had just ended—he had given his final speech to his students just hours before—and the two of them were ostensibly celebrating the onset of summer. Even so, dinner had been quiet—ominously so, in retrospect, but at the time Wendy had only claimed she was working through a headache. She had still put on a nice dress, had done her makeup and put up her auburn hair away from her neck, as she knew he liked; she had still managed to tell him the latest news about the politics of her law office, had listened to him update her on the politics of the teachers' lounge, had laughed and grimaced at the points he expected she might. He ordered steak frites, and she had a beet salad. He cleaned his plate; Wendy, as was her habit, pushed around her salad and drank two glasses of wine. At the end of the meal the server appeared—a tanned, fit, snowboarder type, his hair pulled into a topknot—and asked the magic words: "Did we save any room for dessert? 'Bout you, big guy?"

Doug smiled and played his part; he ordered a slice of key lime cheesecake. "You?" he asked Wendy—he always asked her, even though she was thin, could still fit into her college clothes, because she nearly always turned down dessert.

She shook her head, and he thought then, for the first time, that she seemed troubled. Maybe her headache had gotten worse; maybe her dinner had made her sick.

When the server had left, Doug asked, "What's wrong?"

She withdrew her hand from underneath his and said, "I can't do this anymore."

Though she went on immediately (her voice taking on speed and force), to tell him what she meant—that she wanted a divorce, that she'd fallen in love with one of her fellow attorneys (Ed? Ed *Panecki?*) that she had known for a long time that their marriage had failed—she spoke those first words—*I can't do this anymore*—with a kind of awe, as though she was revealing the truth to herself for the first time . . . and though they would experience a great deal of ugliness in the coming two years, Doug was always able to recall that when she said those words, before she went on, his first thought was to offer her his help. Whatever "this" was, his urge was to take it on himself.

She talked to him for several more minutes, stopping only when the waiter dropped off Doug's cheesecake. It sat untouched between them as she continued to speak.

This was when the import of what she was saying sank in, and he began to cry, with the helplessness of a small child.

"Why don't you go to the car," Wendy said, not unkindly. "I'll pay up."

He wanted the memory to be different, later, but he could not make it so: He walked quickly out of the restaurant, shoulders hunched, then hurried through the clamor of the casino floor to the elevators. He then wept behind the wheel of their car until Wendy arrived, a few minutes later. He saw her approach in the side mirror, her slim bare arms hanging at her sides, her steps measured, calm. He noticed—part of him noticed right away—that she was carrying only her purse. She had not gotten a box for his cheesecake. He noticed himself noticing, and then an abyss opened, and he knew he was never going to undo this. They were really and truly done.

Later during that long night, after hours of trying to undo it anyway, he said to her, "It's because I got fat, isn't it? Say it! Have the courage to say it!"

She shook her head, wearily. "No, Doug, it's not that."

She said, "It's that you stopped trying a long time ago."

Though he could have interpreted that answer in a number of ways, he heard what he thought he needed to: Wendy did not love him anymore, and that was because he had stopped trying to be lovable, because he stopped trying to be desirable. Because he was too big, too ugly, too far gone. Too *fat*.

There was nothing more to say. When dawn broke, he loaded two suitcases and several bags of books into his car and drove to a motel, and there he began his new life alone.

Solitude

The following week, a divorced friend who called Doug to commiserate told him, *When my wife left me, it was like a bad dream.* Doug was envious, honestly. He could have handled a bad dream. A bad dream was a thing from which one woke.

There was no waking from what had become of his life. Wendy had planned the delivery of her news so that he wouldn't be devastated during the whirl of the semester; that had been a small kindness. The downside was that Doug now had three months to spend by and with himself: time that moved too slowly, the hours grinding by with a troubling illogic. Time in which to examine all that had happened, and to loathe himself in conclusion.

Immediately after Wendy told him the news, Doug went to stay with his parents for a week in their small Minneapolis condo. They were in their early seventies, and happy with one another, and they loved him, but even so the fact of their marriage, their long, comfortable stability, was painful every day he beheld it. (So, too, was the fact that his father was a big man, and his mother a small woman—that their happiness had, for all these years, accommodated the disparity in size.) Every night Doug watched his father move hugely, passively, through the house; he watched his mother cook for him, clean behind him, and he began to wonder if in fact she secretly hated his father, wondered if she had sex with him anymore, wondered what there was in him to love.

But then every evening they sat down to dinner together, and his mother fed Doug his favorite meals, and sometimes while he ate them (ham, mashed potatoes, clam chowder), his mother sobbed, reached for his hands, asked, *How could she do this to you?*

He asked Wendy that, too, late one night, a little drunk on his dad's pissy beer, crouched over the pale pink handheld telephone in his parents' guest room.

"I don't want to talk about this," she told him. "I don't want to split hairs. What good would it do?"

"You have a responsibility to," he said, tears already in his eyes.

"Okay," she said, after a long silence. "If you really want to know. I don't know *who you are* anymore. The guy I met in college had all this ambition."

As she spoke, her voice took on a little more force; here, he realized—finally—was her anger. He hated it, but nevertheless felt some satisfaction, having rooted it out.

She said, "He wanted to write, or to get into politics. The guy you are now doesn't want to do *anything*. He goes to work and comes home and that's it. He plays a lot of board games and reads novels and keeps to himself."

Doug said, "I make a difference for the kids I teach. And I was happy."

"Well, I wasn't, even if that's true, which I don't really believe." Her voice had suddenly become clipped, lawyerly, as though playing for a jury. She was in control again. He wondered if Ed Panecki—slim, corded, bald—was sitting within earshot. "You haven't been happy in a long time. And I got really tired of hoping the guy I met was still in there."

She kept talking, doing as he'd asked, laying out the case. She'd tried to involve him in the parts of her life that meant the most to her. She tried to follow him into his own interests. He used to listen to her, and she used to listen to him, but somewhere along the line they'd stopped. They'd been hiding from each other. She'd felt like she was living with a roommate, rather than someone who could offer her love. Didn't he feel the same?

But she'd already slipped. *In there,* she'd said. The words repeated themselves in his head long after he'd thanked her, bitterly, for her honesty, and hung up.

When Doug returned to Reno, he rented an apartment just south of downtown: a small one-bedroom, upstairs from a bar and around the corner from his favorite coffee shop. His new neighborhood was trendy; the bar served mostly hipsters and young professionals who lived in the old, wealthy brick neighborhoods nearby. To reach his front door he had to climb a narrow wooden staircase that kinked in the center; sometimes his elbows brushed the paneled walls, and—sweating and panting— he imagined himself one of his own blood cells, trying to navigate an artery.

And, living alone for the first time in twenty years, almost all of his possessions in storage, facing a summer mostly devoid of work and an empty bed every night, he began eating more poorly than he ever had. Why shouldn't he? No one and nothing could prevent him from eating a plate of pizza rolls, or ice cream from the carton, or ordering a tub of hot wings to go from the bar downstairs and carrying them, too eagerly, upstairs to his table. No one would be disappointed; there was no one, now, who could leave him.

He was getting bigger, he knew, though he could not say how much. Wendy had kept a scale in the bathroom, but he did not, and he had no inclination to buy one.

When he thought—and he often did—that he might be trying to eat himself into a heart attack, a voice within him would sometimes answer: *Good.*

Single

In August, just before the start of his new school year, the divorce was finalized. The process had been quick—Reno could be a backward, stubborn place, but it had always done right by those wanting a divorce. He and Wendy had no children, and though they'd both hired lawyers, Wendy had been accommodating throughout, more than fair, in splitting their assets. They would sell their house and split the profits (selling that house now, post-recession, prices skyrocketing, they'd each clear six figures), and their savings. She'd made a lot more money than he did; financially he would be fine. He was miserable, fat, and alone, but he could quit his job and go be miserable and fat and alone on a beach in Central America for years, if he wanted to.

Doug had told himself he would not spend his first day as a single man brooding, and for the most part he had not; he'd gone out that night with friends. That evening he stood in the kitchen in his boxer shorts, eating a slice of pizza he'd brought home, trying not to think about it, knowing he was going to fail, now that he was, truly, alone.

Music from the bar below thumped into the soles of his feet.

He lay down on the couch, stomach aching. As though probing a wound, he remembered a night in Wendy's apartment, when they'd both been sophomores at Pitt, not long after they'd begun dating. He'd been studying on her couch, and Wendy had been cleaning, when without preamble she walked into the room completely naked. She opened the louvered doors that hid her washer and dryer, and began to scrub cleaner into a blouse. They'd only slept together a few times, and though he'd examined it closely, he was not yet used to the sight of her naked body, slim and tall, unadorned except for red polish on her finger- and toenails. She said nothing to him, asked nothing of him; she started her washer and then returned to her room. He'd been stunned. She'd had a small, fading bruise the size of a quarter on the curve of her right buttock. The little bruise—minor, for all these years unexplained—had broken his heart.

On that evening in her apartment, he probably weighed 175 pounds. He'd run cross-country in high school, and all through college played intramural basketball. (Though, even then, his weight was creeping up.) Wendy liked his body, wanted his body. Despite that encouragement, he'd never had anything like Wendy's comfort with her own. He was tall, but knobby; his face was pleasant at best, wide and smooth and Midwestern; his hair was a color equidistant from brown and blond, lank and characterless. When he'd been in top running shape, he'd been able to see the muscles in his abdomen. By his sophomore year in college, though, his stomach had already started to protrude. It was widely known among his friends that in dating Wendy, he was—as the phrase went—punching above his weight.

(Why are you with me? he asked her once. He winced to remember, now, her answer: *Because your mind is always on. You see the world like it is. You want to fix it.* This was in a hotel room in Washington, DC, which they'd shared after riding a bus to take place in a pro-choice march, after he'd followed her through the crowd, ever more impressed by the fearlessness with which she chant-

ed and sang. They'd stayed up late, talking, making love.)

He'd slowly grown bigger ever since. (He remembered his desperate panic, in a Pittsburgh hotel room, when the trousers of the tuxedo in which he was about to be married had barely fastened.) He'd gone through periods of exercise and diet, but always halfheartedly. When they first had moved to Reno, they'd hiked and swum and biked—Lake Tahoe and the Sierra Nevada peaks and the dry desert air and nearly unrelenting sunshine demanded it. Doing so had been easy when he was unemployed. But then, six months after moving, he'd gotten the job at Hunter High, which cut into his evenings and weekends far more than he'd ever dreamed. His job did indeed let him make a difference, but doing so required him to spend hours every day sitting in a chair, turning pages, making marks. Learning the job, how best to manage the grading, took him two years, and by then he was forty pounds heavier.

Five years after moving to town they'd abandoned birth control, but Wendy never got pregnant. After a year of trying and waiting, they'd gotten drunk together on their couch and talked it over. Should they see a fertility doctor? Try IVF?

It's okay like this, isn't it? Wendy asked him, cheek resting on his thigh. *Just us? Is it okay if I admit that I'm relieved?*

He'd been touched, if a little disappointed. *Of course it is, love,* he'd said. His belly rounded, his jowls filling in. His lovely wife still wanted him, only him. Of course it was okay.

During the last five years of their marriage—well after he'd passed the 250-pound mark—they'd barely touched. Doug had told himself that this was natural—

just the way things went, as married people grew older, busier. When he'd felt lonely, or sorry for himself, he'd never talked with Wendy about it; he'd gone instead to the kitchen and melted shredded cheese over tortilla chips and eaten the result by the plateful. Or he'd heated up a pizza. After she'd gone to sleep, or whenever he found himself alone, he'd watched pornography on the computer in his den. Taking care of himself instead of bothering Wendy was, he'd somehow managed to convince himself, merely an act of consideration.

He remembered this, too: overhearing Wendy and one of her colleagues talking, maybe seven years ago, in the kitchen, when they thought he was outside. *Don't you mind?* the friend asked. *Doug's a sweetheart, but he's getting so big these days—*

Wendy had been sharp. *I appreciate your concern,* she said, *but he's my husband, and I love him.*

A shaky embarrassment had filled him the rest of that evening. The next day he'd stopped and bought Wendy flowers, awed by her love. He'd vowed to do better, to eat less, and had spent six months dieting; he'd lost twenty pounds. But then he'd agreed to head up the language arts department at the high school, and soon the extra workload had undone his diet.

Everything would be all right, he'd told himself. Wendy loved him, no matter what. One of these days, he'd told himself, he would get serious about losing weight. He'd fix the problem, in time.

Now Doug understood: he had been a lazy coward, and this new life was a coward's reward.

He went to his bathroom, where he took off his boxer shorts and stood naked in front of the long mirror the previous tenant had left behind, and which Doug usually kept covered with a bathrobe.

Look, he commanded himself.

He was a fat, forty-year-old man. He had sagging breasts and a vast quaking belly and too-round cheeks and gray in his hair and beard. His penis was a shameful, half-hidden nub. He looked like a statue of a man that had been left in the sun and had begun to melt.

This was what Wendy had seen, all these years. This was what had dressed itself next to her in the mornings, this was what had slept snoring beside her at night. This was what had assumed itself wanted.

He'd spent all summer trying not to think about his future, but here it was. Wendy was thin and beautiful and unmarried, and—right now—asleep (or, worse, not) in bed with Ed Panecki. And this was him. This body. This apartment.

He thought about the ways one could end oneself. Pills. A razor in the bath.

Or, rather: a heart attack. This body slumped gray and gape-mouthed in a chair, in an apartment like this one, where no one would find it for days.

Doug looked at himself, large, dumbstruck, naked. Alive, in a manner of speaking. He hated himself with a vehemence that left him dizzy.

For the first time, he asked himself, truly, what he intended to do about it.

Lifestyle

Two weeks later his doctor told him—gently, sorrowfully, as though he were about to give him a terminal diagnosis—"Well, Doug, I don't see much wrong with you that losing weight won't fix."

Doug was surprised. He had done everything he could to avoid the doctor, these last ten years, and especially the doctor's scale—which, just a few moments ago, had confirmed his worst fears: he weighed 336 pounds.

"Your cholesterol isn't awful," the doctor said, sitting across from him on a stool, "and your blood pressure could be better, but both could also be a lot worse. You're prediabetic. But you're not in terrible danger of a heart attack. Not yet."

The doctor was a white man older than Doug, but he was skinny, a runner, as lithe and quick in his movements as a Jack Russell terrier. He said, "Your heartburn we can fight back with pills, but if you can lose weight—if—you'll be doing yourself so many favors. These numbers aren't going to stay this way forever."

"I'll be totally honest," Doug said, and then, to his surprise, he was: "I'm depressed. I have a lot of bad habits."

"I've been there," the doctor said, though Doug thought that was probably a lie. "A lot of people have been there. Have you been seeing someone about it?"

"I've been thinking about getting a bicycle," Doug said, which had once or twice been technically true.

"Okay," the doctor said, as though Doug had just asked Santa for a pony. "That's great. I encourage it. You might get a bike, you might like it. But I need you to hear this: Nothing is going to change for you in any serious way unless you eat less. A lot less."

And there it was.

"If you want to change," the doctor said, "you have to dedicate yourself to an entirely new way of living."

"Tell me what I have to do," Doug said.

At home he looked at himself naked in the mirror

again. Soaking in the vision. Then he downloaded an app for his phone, and—as the doctor had made him promise—he began to enter everything he ate into it, so he could track his calories against a daily limit.

He walked three blocks across town to a bike shop afterward, and—conscious of the stares of the pipe-cleaner people inside of it—bought a thousand-dollar road bike, and a helmet, and three pairs of the shop's largest Lycra shorts. He even endured it when the woman behind the counter—his age, made entirely of blond hair and sinew—told him he was probably too big for a carbon-fiber frame.

She was gentle, saying it. Everyone was so gentle. "It's just that big guys like you, the bike frame won't hold up—"

"It's okay," he told her, tasting coppered rage. "Show me one that will."

In my experience, the doctor had said, *people change a lot less than they want to. Doing this is going to be very difficult. Everyone can feel inspired for a day, or a week, or a month—*

You watch, Doug had told him, his heart swelling. *You just watch me.*

• • •

The first month—just as the doctor had warned—was terrible. Doug diligently entered his calories into the phone. He filled his refrigerator with bags of carrots and portions of sliced turkey and diet sodas, and his pantry with power bars. He ate what he was supposed to eat, and always, if he could, aimed for a little less—

—and all the while, he felt as though he were dying.

Which, he supposed, he technically was. Even mild starvation impelled his body toward panic.

Which was why, sometimes, he felt *like* dying: overcome by a despair that was tangible and shaming and left him wrung out, so tired he could barely hold a pen in his hands. This was natural, he knew; and yet he fantasized about going to sleep and never waking up. Better a quick death than this slow one.

He hated himself for thinking so, hated his own weak brain and body every time he walked past a homeless man sitting on a bench mumbling for change; every time he saw men and women who were even bigger than he was—the morbidly obese, the poor bastards—every time he read the news; every time he was reminded that his problem—the reason for this pain, the necessity of it— existed solely and wholly within himself.

• • •

Meanwhile, the school year had begun again. Walking into Hunter High, seeing again his colleagues and his students, left Doug terribly self-conscious; though everyone greeted him kindly, the news of his divorce had clearly spread; he felt and sometimes caught the pitying glances, the comments whispered behind hands and with lowered voices. And he was aware, as he had never been before, of his size. For years he'd known the students had mocked his weight, but he'd learned to treat that mockery as insignificant—you had to, in this job; even the students who loved you would make fun of your weaknesses. But now? Now he had no armor.

He'd lost fifteen pounds by the start of the semester, but he was still a fat man, teaching; he was a fat man

whose lovely, skinny wife (many of the students had met
Wendy, who sometimes helped him chaperone dances,
who sometimes visited school during career day to talk
about practicing law–who was, indisputably, *hot*) had
divorced him, and he could already hear the students'
judgment, rippling among them. The greatest danger in
this job, he thought, was letting the students make a kid
out of you, and here he was, forty years old but tender as
a seventh-grader, walking the halls and worrying about
the timbre of a sudden burst of laughter.

One day, two weeks into the semester, standing by
the blackboard and talking to the journalism students—
all of them juniors and seniors, and more jaded than their
peers; they were his favorites without question–he grew
light-headed. The classroom filled with cascading lights,
and he had to stop speaking and brace himself against
the chalk tray, then drop heavily into his desk chair.

"Are you okay, Mr. Ritchie?" asked tiny, birdlike junior Inez Ochoa, the newspaper editor, president of the
creative writing club, and his undisputed pet.

He felt anything but okay, and he couldn't bear to
lie to her, to any of them. "I skipped lunch," he said, his
vision clearing. "I'm on a diet. I'm sorry."

This admission was met by the students' immediate
interest and joy.

"Don't be sorry," several said. A couple of them actually shouted, "Yes!"

"No, no," he said, reddening. "Look, guys. If you
really want to help me, don't make a big deal about it. I'm
doing this for my health, not for vanity."

"Um, it's not healthy if you pass out, dude," said
Lawrence Happ.

"Is this because you got divorced?" asked Javier

Mendez, who liked to think he was edgy.

"We all heard," said Rachel Perth.

"Javier, god!" cried Inez. "You're terrible."

"It's hard to lose weight," Sam Irving said. "My mom lost a hundred pounds last year; she used to pass out all the time."

"Thanks for sharing, Sam."

"No! I'm saying it with respect, Mr. Ritchie. We got your back."

This was new, this way of talking: the way the students looked at him, bright and excited and concerned. It was a dangerous feeling, he knew it; they did not really need to see his personal problems on display, and he did not need to want them to. Even so.

Inez dug in her bag, and produced a bag of baby carrots. "Would one of these help?"

He took, very solemnly, her solemnly offered carrot. He bit into it. It was, simultaneously, the best and worst food he'd ever eaten. This must have shown on his face, because the room filled with laughter.

"You *got* this," Sam said.

They all beamed at him, the day's lesson forgotten.

"All right," he told them. "Here's the deal. If I show up here with M&Ms, or Mountain Dew, you get to call me on it. And you can ask me once every two weeks how much I've lost. Deal?"

They loved this deal. They *adored* this deal. Maddie Fuller, who enjoyed making spreadsheets, shot up her hand and asked if she could make a weight-loss spreadsheet that they could hang on the wall beside the desk. "It's good to write down goals and progress," she said, and the class laughed, because this was advice he gave them all the time about reading and writing and putting together the yearbook. He waved her on. Maddie and Inez worked on the chart, then handed it to him just before the bell rang. Inez had drawn a crude picture of his face at the top, smiling and bearded and perfectly round. When class was over, he retreated to his office, where he was wracked by sudden sobs. He had not known how hard this would be, had not known how much the kids—bless them—had been concerned, had not known how they'd assumed him to be weak, unhealthy.

But god, he had been. He still was.

Lonely

When Doug went home from work that afternoon, his apartment—small, cluttered, humid with the smell of him—seemed especially empty. He'd embarrassed himself in front of his class, had wanted to get away from them, but now that he was here, the quiet cut at him. He wanted, now, to tell someone about the day he'd had, how the students had cared for him. Someone he could tell about his weeping, afterward, and his shame. Someone whose presence, here, now, would head off the need to weep at all.

Someone he could hold, and kiss. Someone who would slide between the sheets with him.

And there it was: he was lonely, yes; he missed living with someone, and all its casual intimacies.

But he also, very badly, wanted someone to make love to.

He had not had sex with anyone but himself for nine months, now (and those last few times with Wendy, they both might as well have been alone). He wanted to have sex like he and Wendy had when they were twenty, and small, and young. He wanted to go back in time and shake himself, slap his dumb, younger self across the face, and shout at him: *You're going to lose it all!*

And when he thought of sex—the sex he was not having and was unlikely to have anytime soon—he felt the pull of despair, and when he felt despair, then he wanted to *eat*. In lieu of sex, this kind of pleasure was far more plausible: potato chips splintering between his teeth. A hamburger releasing its juices onto his tongue.

Why shouldn't he? He was still fat. No woman would be coming here. No one would see.

And sometimes, thinking this way, he had weakened; once or twice he'd ordered a hamburger, wings, a pizza; he'd stopped at a gas station and bought a bag of Reese's Cups. And then despair took him anyway, and he'd sat alone and ashamed, his belly taut beneath its fat, sated and often in pain.

He'd learned tricks to head off these moments of weakness. He'd go to a movie; once he was past the concession counter he'd be isolated, distracted. (But of course going to a movie alone, at his size, was an act accompanied by considerable shame.) Or—if weakness came over him late at night—he'd take several diet sodas out of the pantry and chug them, warm, one after the other, until he felt like vomiting.

He'd take his clothes off in front of the mirror. Yes, he was smaller—almost exactly twenty pounds smaller by the end of September. Even so he told himself: *You're fat, fat, fat.* Because it was still true. Because he needed to hear it. Because, now that he understood Wendy was not coming back—now that he had to think about his future—his loneliness was less about nostalgia and more about hope, and he had tried living without hope. He'd barely survived that.

Today he told himself to put on shorts and sneakers and go for a walk, away from his refrigerator and cupboards. He walked, hands jammed in his pockets—he took no money, so he wouldn't be tempted to stop at the 7-Eleven for chips—through his neighborhood, until he was lightheaded and sweating.

While he walked, he imagined women, seeing him, wanting him. Beautiful women. Some of them looked like Wendy. Some of them looked like movie stars, like colleagues, like the gorgeous girls from the college who wore nice dresses and makeup and complicated shoes to the bar below his apartment and ordered drinks and smiled at trim, handsome men; women who—he saw them do it—appraised the bodies of these men, wanted those men, went home with those men, and even though once he had been that age, imagining this happening was like watching a movie, like watching impossible people do impossible things.

He walked until he had punished himself sufficiently for being a man who had, however briefly, confused the pleasure of sex with the pleasure of eating.

Fuck you, he thought, with every footstep.

Go to hell, he thought, at home, standing in front of the mirror.

You're weak, he told himself, looking down at his disused genitals, trying not to feel hungry.

Shopping

Nine weeks into his diet, he weighed 295 pounds.

The number surprised him, appearing on the scale; even though he'd been pursuing it relentlessly, he'd been doubtful he could ever say the words: *I've lost forty pounds*. But he had. He was losing weight; he was actually doing it. He loaded a cardboard box with books until he'd gathered forty pounds' worth. He lifted it, straining. Astonishing, that this much of him could be gone, that he'd ever carried it on his frame.

Astonishing, that he could lose so much and still be fat.

He'd developed another trick: he was now riding his bike to the grocery store. The store he liked was two and a half miles away, and up a small hill from his apartment, in a pleasant, tree-shaded suburb where he knew Wendy and Ed would never shop. He rode there wearing a backpack, and only allowed himself to buy what fit into it; when he ran out of groceries, he had to ride his bike to the store again, immediately. The last ten pounds had come off faster, even, than he'd planned.

People were noticing. *Man, you're really losing weight,* they'd say, and, *Am I imagining it, or is there less of you around these days?* And though they could sound patronizing, god—hearing all this felt better than *Big guy;* it definitely felt better than *Jeez, Doug, I heard about Wendy—I'm so sorry, man.*

His students had begun to look at him with conspiratorial smiles. When he put a bottle of soda on the top of his desk at the beginning of the hour, Inez would frown and twirl a finger in the air until he turned the label so that the class could see it was a diet. Every other Friday he told the class his weight, and Inez would mark it down on the chart, and since the numbers were slowly, consistently dropping, the class would always applaud.

He was able to cinch his belt closed one more notch. The face suggested by his nipples and navel seemed, marginally, less depressed, and perhaps even registered faint surprise.

He sometimes—sometimes—didn't feel hungry in the evenings.

And he began, for the most part, to leave behind the pools of despair that had so threatened him. He'd begun seeing a therapist, finally, which helped. But losing weight—the result of so many years of accumulated immediate gratification—required immediate, urgent tactics, too. When he felt bad, he made himself climb on the bicycle. This was the answer for everything: Ride. Or walk. Or even jog. Burn calories. Take a hit of endorphins. Grow smaller still.

"Watch it, fatass!" cried someone in a pickup truck one Saturday morning, swerving in dramatic, aggrieved fashion to avoid him when he was wobbling uphill on the bicycle.

"I'm losing weight, motherfucker!" he'd gasped back, pedaling steadily, feeling his breath, his blood, the ripples in the road. In his backpack was a bunch of bananas, chicken breasts, bags of prewashed kale. When he had reached his apartment, he was seeing stars, and laughing.

• • •

He liked going to the grocery store. That was because one of the checkout staff had grown friendly with him. A woman. Veronica.

She was thirty-eight, and looked younger. She was not fat, but she wasn't skinny, either, and Doug found her almost unbearably lovely, her cheeks curved and smooth, her eyes large and brown and grave. Her voice was ever so faintly tinged with her first language, Spanish. He knew a little Spanish, and they talked several

times a week when he bought his groceries, and she test-
ed him—especially after she learned he was a teacher—on
the Spanish names for the things he purchased: *Pláta-
nos. Pechugas de pollo. Papel higiénico.*

She was divorced, too—they had found this out about
one another—and she had a young girl, three years old,
she was raising on her own. Her ex-husband had given
them up for methamphetamine. She was direct and dis-
arming in what she was able to say to him. She told jokes,
said occasionally cutting things about her coworkers, or
the angry old white people who—she said—always gave
her extra trouble.

"Who could ever give you trouble?" he asked her.

"Not *you*," she said, and gave him a smile that broke
his heart.

He'd begun using her lane weeks before, because of
her kind eyes, and then she began to remember him, and
once she commented on his food, and he told her, wearily, sadly, "I'm dieting."

She said, "That's hard, I've done it before," and then,
"But you have to make sure you get your proteins." She
smiled the whole time, and seemed at ease with him. *How
nice*, he'd thought. Once she told him, "I work every
Tuesday," in an inviting sort of way—why would you tell
a customer this?—so Doug made sure to drive to the store
on Tuesday evenings when he was done with school, his
exception to the bicycle rule, so that at least one day every
week he would not go through Veronica's lane bedrag-
gled and sweat-dampened. He couldn't hide a lack of dignity from her, but at least he could show her he cleaned up
nicely. He figured that this regular visit was good for his
diet, too; he wouldn't be able to stand himself if he weakened and sent bags of candy across her scanner.

He had begun to wonder if he could ask her out.

She would say no, of course. Veronica was a pretty woman, and she wouldn't lack for interested men. (Younger men, smaller men.) He was a customer, someone she found sympathetic, and that was that. He said *please* and *thank you* and asked after her daughter; he was a pleasant man, he'd always been pleasant, but pleasant was not the same as desirable.

And yet: She smiled happily when she saw him. She knew his name. He knew her daughter's—Erica, maybe. How many men her age, after all, wanted to date a single mother? Who, in the end, could explain attraction? Veronica might appreciate his wit, his steady job, his devotion to self-improvement, even if he was still, very obviously, a fat man with an unconvincing beard. (She could always tell herself, *He's trying, he's changing himself, he's really doing it.*)

His therapist told him the same thing. "Would it be so very strange," he asked Doug, "if she liked you? Full stop?"

"Yes," Doug said. "I think it would be very strange."

The therapist—thin, like his doctor, a younger black man who preferred bow ties—looked at him for a long time over his steepled fingers, then said, "Well, Doug, maybe next time let's dig into that."

Whenever Doug thought he should invite Veronica out to dinner, he made himself strip naked in front of his bathroom mirror. He had seventy-five, eighty pounds yet to go. He was smaller, but he was not small. He imagined undressing in front of her, her face watching him expose this body, and that was that. She could be a fantasy—and what was the harm?—but he could never reveal his attraction to her.

His body, though, was coming to life after a long dormancy. Outside it was fall, turning into winter, one of his favorite times of year; in the cooler air he was less oppressed and languid, and he felt himself moving more quickly, with a new and surprising vigor. He thought of Veronica constantly; he caught himself daydreaming about their conversations during his last-period Tuesday class.

He imagined her naked, touching the curves of her body, caressing her face.

Doug told himself he must never flirt with her while she was behind the register, must never make her feel trapped there, must never force her to be nice to him when he was being awful, *must never must never must never,* and each time she rang him through and said her traditional sendoff—"Okay, sweetie, adiós"—and turned her attention to the person in line behind him, he took his bags and went outside, and there he deflated, there he hated his cowardice, and felt, despite his shrinking size, everything he shouldn't: old, unlovable, fat.

Then one evening in November, as Veronica rang up his salad fixings, she said, "How much have you lost? It's got to be a lot."

"Forty-six pounds," he said, "give or take. A lot to go."

"You look great," she said, and beamed. "You're really doing it."

Don't, he told himself, but he was filled with such good cheer he said, "I know what the answer's going to be, but I'd take you to a movie sometime. If you wanted."

The way her smile died was exquisitely, slowly painful, like a needle sliding under his skin.

"Oh sweetie," she said. "I've got a boyfriend."

Even though she was obviously lying, even though

she had mentioned before how hard it was to meet people, even though her face had closed off from him, become wary and older and sad, he said, "That is a lucky man, Veronica."

"Hey—"

"It's okay. Forget I asked, please." He hefted his bags and went quickly to the car.

He made himself a salad for dinner that night, but could not eat it. He threw it in the trash, ate a power bar, then went to bed hungry, his eyes stinging. He told himself to be kind to Veronica, not to be weird about it, to go back to the store and act like nothing had happened—but the next afternoon he rode his bicycle to another grocery, one a mile farther away, pedaling harder, so hard he made himself dizzy. He did not go back to her store again.

That weekend he bought a pair of running shoes. He began going to the high school early in the mornings and running a lap or two on the asphalt track that ringed the football field, in the cold shadows of the foothills against which the school was nestled.

The members of the football team were often practicing on the field before classes, and they began to shout in welcome when they saw him stretching—he taught only a couple of them, but they all seemed to know about his quest, the spreadsheet on the wall of his classroom. They began to shout when he slowed down: "One more, Mr. Ritchie! Do it!"

He'd do it.

"Go!" they'd shout. "Go!" And then he'd do another, his lungs burning his big body from the inside out, and he always wondered if these handsome, laughing athletes egging him on—half of them dating cheerleaders—understood even a fraction of what kept him moving forward.

II. Nancy

Company

One morning at the end of November, a month into his devotion to running, Doug arrived at the track and found one of his fellow teachers already running laps.

Her name was Nancy Dreyfus—she preferred Nan—but he did not know her well. She had only been at the school two years; she taught sophomore mathematics. She'd taught in Los Angeles for a few years before coming to Reno, where her father had been living alone and terminally ill. After he passed, there had been a collection; the faculty had bought her a spa weekend at a hot springs in California. Everyone was happy she'd chosen to stay in town after her father's death. She was younger than Doug, by almost a decade; he liked her, everyone on the faculty liked her. Doug didn't interact that much with the math faculty, but he and Nancy had been on an assessment working group the prior semester, and that had been fun; Nan was sensible, funny, competent. She had glossy black hair and a wide, infectious smile.

And she was fat.

New forms of shame came to Doug nearly every day, and this was a bad one, as he sat in his car and watched her slow, lumbering progress around the track: Nan Dreyfus was no more overweight than he was. He found it harder to tell with women, but he guessed she was at least seventy pounds too heavy, and the sight of her made him want to slam his car into gear and drive away from school as quickly as he could, never to return.

He didn't, though. This was his penance.

Because even though Nan Dreyfus was single, even though she was smart and funny and told jokes in the teachers' lounge that made everyone cackle, even though his Facebook feed sometimes showed her out on the town—surrounded by her pretty friends, dolled up in dresses and heels, at concerts and at weddings in brides-maid gowns and clustered around long tables in hipster bars—he had always seen her and dismissed her: *fat.* Since she'd come to work at the school, she'd been as invisible to him as he was sure she'd been to the hordes of hipster bros populating the same downtown bars as Nancy and her friends.

And therefore as invisible, as irrelevant, as Doug had been, too.

That morning at the track she was dressed in blue shorts and a white T-shirt, and had her hair pulled back in a bouncing ponytail, and her cheeks and arms were blotched pink with exertion. But she smiled and slowed when she saw him approach, then jogged to his side.

"Hey, Doug," she said, breathless but sly—she always spoke as though each sentence were the middle step in a long, elaborate joke. "Hope you don't mind the company."

"Of course not," he said, trying to smile.

"I've seen you out here a bunch. You inspired me."

"God help us both," he said.

She laughed and wiped her brow. "I know, right? It feels like dying."

And just like that, they were comrades, their weight a commonality.

"I used to like this," he said. "I was a runner in high school, believe it or not."

"I believe it. You have *good form.*"

While he tried to make heads or tails of what she meant by this, she went on: "I myself was a swimmer. Third all-state in the backstroke, once."

"Good for us," he said, as something like a place-holder. He had *good form*. How long had it been since a woman had complimented him on anything to do with his body?

A long, long time—which might have been why, when she asked, "Mind if I run with you? I won't hold you back," he said, "Sure!"

So they ran, side by side, chatting companionably, for a half hour. She did not hold him back at all; if anything she was a little faster. She pushed him. His breath rasped and smoked in the cold, and his feet were aflame.

Nan was, he learned, forty pounds lighter than she'd been at the beginning of the year. (He hadn't noticed!) He learned she had a cat named Fancy, and that she collected and played vintage synthesizers, and that she'd promised herself a tattoo if she could lose all the weight she wanted. She wanted all eighty-eight piano keys running from her left shoulder to her elbow. She and Serena Maple (who also taught math) wanted to start a punk band, whenever they could find a drummer.

Did he drum? He didn't? Too bad.

She slowed. "One more!" he told her, gasping, and picked up the pace, his lungs ripping, and she cursed him and laughed and followed.

They left the track together, and on the way they passed the principal: slim, bald Bob Burroughs, and Bob smiled and waved in a way Doug recognized: as though trying not to intrude.

Had he mistaken them for a couple? Doug's face burned.

He hated himself for this embarrassment, though,

so he turned to Nancy and said, "Hey, same time tomorrow?" before they split for the locker rooms.

She smiled at this, a happy, uncomplicated smile, a lovely smile, her cheeks rosy—her eyes a bright green, he'd never noticed—and reached out a fist and bumped it against his.

• • •

They ran together for three months, even over the holiday break, even when the weather grew warmer. He was grateful for Nan's company, as his efforts to motivate himself had begun to flag; his numbers on the scale had remained constantly between 275 and 280. "You're replacing fat with muscle," his doctor told him, happily—but Doug had gotten used to those numbers shrinking. He found himself grateful for the company of someone who cared, someone who was also trying, someone who would forgive him for his occasional trespasses—but who was also capable of policing him.

I don't wanna! he texted her from his apartment, one shoelace still untied, just before the dawn.

Pussy, she texted back. *I will literally kill you if I have to run alone.*

Though at first he was shocked, he came to like her cheerful profanity, her immediate assumption that she could speak to him like that. That he was cool enough to be spoken to like that.

He felt competitive with her. Nan was, if anything, losing weight faster than he was, and he was astonished and amused by her willingness to talk numbers—no woman in his experience had ever wanted to broach that topic. She had started at 225, and wanted to lose eighty.

She would hit her goal, she told him, a year from March, if she kept it up. He would hit his target later, maybe that April or May. Maybe. Maybe, he thought, he could match her pace.

He told her about his divorce, about Wendy, about his lowest points. She told him she'd had a bad breakup, too: her boyfriend had chosen not to come with her to Reno when her father had taken ill. She told Doug, frankly, that she'd hated her father, and that caring for him had not only kept her inactive, but isolated and sad. She'd already gotten big—that was why the man in Los Angeles hadn't come with her, she was pretty sure, even though he was a coward and wouldn't admit it—but sitting with her sick dad—who never missed a chance to criticize her for her weight—had put on another forty pounds.

She'd always used food as an escape, she told him. She was a good cook, and liked to cook for herself. Even so, she'd surprised herself, that she could let herself grow so big. She didn't want to be the sort of woman who needed to be skinny to be happy about herself, but she also didn't want to be this size. She wanted to prove to herself that she could be healthy about food. Healthy in life, without her father.

Food as a substitute for happiness. Doug's therapist had been talking about this very topic quite a lot.

"I'm giving myself permission to be shallow," she said. "I'm getting older. I want to be hot, you know? Like, okay, I'm hot anyway? And no one had better say otherwise? But when I was in college? Damn."

Doug had, by now, looked through her old Facebook photos, and he agreed with her on this point. He said, "You're doing all right for yourself."

She'd told him, earlier that morning, about meeting a man over the weekend. She was frank about these things, and to hear her speak about sex made him feel . . . a pang. The man who'd stayed over, she told him, was good-looking and quite stupid. He'd been in town visiting the boyfriend of one of her friends. He had big muscles, she'd said.

"Yeah," she said, a note of caution in her voice. "But still. I want to like myself, you know?"

He knew.

"I definitely don't like myself," he said. He thought of Veronica turning him down, the embarrassment in her face. He hadn't told Nan about her. "But I don't want to spend the rest of my life single. So here I am."

Her reply was immediate, concerned. "You won't."

"Thanks," he said, "And back atcha."

She pulled even with him. The track rolled by underneath their shoes. "Listen to us," she said, and now her voice was acidic. He'd heard this tone before, recognized it from his own worst moments. "You know you don't have to be skinny to get laid, right?"

She was right, of course, but he could not make himself agree, could not tell her, *It's different for me than it is for you.* If he did, he'd have to try and explain why.

"You haven't dated anyone?" she asked. "Since?"

He shook his head, pretended to be out of breath. He felt her eyes on him, lingering. Then her hand, resting briefly on his shoulder, a little touch, before she passed him by.

Closer

Of course he thought about dating Nan. Asking her out. Kissing her. Having sex with her.

She was a beautiful woman. She had been when she was skinny, and she still was, now, despite her weight—the added clause he could never snip from his thoughts. She would go out with him, he was pretty sure. She would sleep with him. Those events might not even have to happen in that order.

Nan wasn't leaving him much room for doubt. They had begun meeting before their runs for a cup of coffee at a Starbucks around the corner from school. They enjoyed each other's company in that time, unshowered and grumpy and wearing sweatpants. When he saw Nan in the hallways of the school during the day, after she'd showered and put on her nice clothes and makeup and had done her hair, he almost didn't recognize her; then she looked older, more severe—but she was stylish, pretty, and he liked the conspiratorial smiles she gave him, simple references to their private times. He liked the way she'd stop by his classroom between periods to tell him a joke, even though doing so was out of her way. They texted each other jokes, too, after work, and sometimes those exchanges turned into long, serious conversations. Twice they'd watched movies at the same time on Netflix while texting commentary back and forth.

During runs she'd bump his shoulder with her own, or give his ankle a friendly kick. She found excuses to hug him in greeting and in goodbye. He knew, already, something of the curves and the softness of her body. She made a point of complimenting him—his clothes, his hair.

His friend Jerry Rupp, who taught civics, had asked him point blank: *So what's happening with you and Dreyfus?* When Doug told him, *Nothing,* Jerry had shaken his head and grinned. *Sure, buddy.*

The students, of course, had noticed Doug and Nan's

friendship, their mutual weight loss, that they'd run together in the early mornings, and a couple had asked
him questions about her, fishing. Inez Ochoa in partic-
ular wouldn't let the subject drop; she was a lot more interested in it than in reading through *Gatsby* in AP Lit
these days, and would smirk to herself after Nan waggled
her fingers at Doug through the classroom door.

And yet. Doug did not ask Nan out. They had a good
friendship, one he quite liked. He'd joined her and some
of her friends for drinks a couple of times after work, but
that was as close as he'd gotten to expanding their time
together beyond their running—and when she was with
her friends, he was reminded that she was younger, that
she had a younger woman's attitudes and brashness and
sense of humor. Listening to her and her single friends
complain about the profiles of men on Bumble, he felt
every second of his age: shy, cautious, terminally square.
He felt, in fact, as though he were still married, as though
the wall that separated him from signing up with dating
apps still existed.

And if they hit their weight targets, then what? If,
when, they did what they'd set out to do, Nan would be
thirty-two and single and shapely, and even if he was
skinny, he'd remain a middle-aged man with a salt-and-
pepper beard and a receding hairline. How could he
date, think of dating, someone who would know how
to navigate the downtown bars filled by muscled dudes
sporting bowling shirts and full-sleeve tattoos and tan-
gles of lumberjack beard? (She found such qualities
attractive, he knew; what on earth was she doing, then,
flirting with him?)

His therapist asked Doug whether he was denying
himself an opportunity. Wasn't he cutting off the pos-

sibility of optimism at its root? *If you're attracted to this woman, and she to you, why not act?* What was he losing weight for, if not for confidence to act? *Who would understand you better than someone*—god, he hated his therapist sometimes—*who was taking the same journey?*

Once, in April, he nearly talked himself into it; before running, as they warmed up, he was close to saying, as casually as he could—which was not casually at all—*You know what? Let's get a drink after work tonight, it's Friday*—but, as it happened, Nan beat him to it.

"Hey, so," she said, lifting herself from a butterfly stretch, "I've got this wedding coming up I have to go to, my cousin's. It's gonna be a real hippie shitshow out in the desert. I was going to go stag, but I don't think I can handle it alone. Want to come with me?"

He was stunned—not only that she'd asked, but that her voice held a nervous quiver. She was, he realized, afraid he'd say no.

"Sure," he said. "Be happy to."

"Would you? I haven't been able to tell."

He was sitting opposite her on the cool springy surface of the school track, legs splayed. She put the soles of her sneakers against his, and pushed.

He said, "I'm older than you. I didn't want to assume."

This made him sound noble.

"You're not that much older. And come on—I *like* you. You're decent. You're cute. That combo doesn't appear as much in the field as I was led to believe."

Cute! "I have nothing to wear," he said, stupidly.

She brightened. "Me neither. Nothing I have fits anymore! Let's go shopping."

"Seriously?"

"Sure. I need a good set of eyes. And you, my friend, definitely need a woman to help you dress."

"Okay," he said, hoping he hadn't winced. "Thank you for asking me."

"Just so you know," she said, "it's gonna be an overnight thing. But no expectations, okay? We can get two beds in the room."

"Okay," he said, which was the least committal word he could produce.

"But it's a date," she said. "Right?"

"It's a date," he said.

They stood to begin running. He extended a hand and she took it to haul herself upright. She kept hold of his hand. "Okay," she said, as though answering an unspoken question, and pulled him closer and kissed him, briefly, with closed lips.

Then she ran ahead of him down the track, laughing.

• • •

That Saturday they went to the Macy's in the mall and shopped for clothes. Doug had not thought about clothing in any hopeful way since he'd been in college, back when he'd been flying flannel and sporting a goatee like every other white guy on campus. In his adult life he mostly only bought clothes for work, the office-casual menswear most of the male teachers favored: khakis, button-down shirts, loafers or white sneakers. He owned a single sport coat and a suit that no longer fit him, purchased to attend his mother-in-law's funeral. He owned a fistful of ties and kept them in the back of his sock drawer. He had two pairs of jeans at any one time, and they never fit him right. In the summertime he wore cargo shorts and sneakers and sacklike XXXL T-shirts, all in some variation of gray, green, or brown. Colors, patterns—he didn't dare drape such things on his body.

Shopping with Nan was a revelation. She liked colors; she seemed—far more than he could—to view her progress toward her target weight as a cause for celebration, as a reason to try on dresses in bright reds and blues and dark, shimmering greens, to perch atop the highest heels. Doug sat outside the women's dressing room, waiting for her to emerge and model each dress, and whatever embarrassment he was tempted to feel was swept away by Nan's pleasure in the clothing, in dressing up. In being *seen*.

The fifth dress was red and featured a slit up to mid-thigh, and though it didn't work—Nan didn't like the color—she twirled in it anyway, and let him see the way the fabric split, let him see her creamy thigh. When she spun away, he realized: she wasn't simply enjoying the clothes, the game. She didn't like being seen so much as she liked being seen by *him*.

In his fantasies about her, when he imagined them sleeping together, they were both smaller. Nan, however, did not want him later, thinner; she might want him *now*.

She reemerged from the dressing room then, in an electric-blue gown, cut irregularly, hanging above her knees in front and behind them in the back. Its neckline plunged appealingly.

"You're beautiful," he told her.

He told her this because it was true, and because she wanted to hear it, and he wanted to give her what she wanted. Because he wanted her to say the same of him.

She gave him a look he could never have misinterpreted. "Thank you, kind sir," she said, and curtsied. Then she bought the dress.

They went to the men's department, and on the way she slipped her hand into his. They walked across the store floor together, and he felt sure they were being watched, commented upon, by everyone they passed. In a sudden terror he wondered whether they were sharing the store with any of their students.

She told him to try on a tweedy olive suit with a vest, and when he emerged from the dressing room her eyes gleamed. When he beheld himself in the mirror, Nan standing behind him, he looked both smaller and younger; the suit did not make him look silly or severe, but, rather, confident, knowingly hip. He seemed a man who liked himself, who was comfortable with himself, who knew how to make himself look good.

Was this because of the suit, or because of Nan, standing behind him, smiling, her face near his in the glass, her hands sliding around his belly to clasp each other, her breath warm against his cheek?

• • •

When Doug parked in front of her apartment, Nan said, "You can come up, if you want."

He almost said, *I know,* but stopped himself. With her he was a boy again, hopeless and stuttering.

He said, "I'm a little scared."

"Of me?"

"No," he said. "Of everything. Being with someone."

The worst euphemism he could think of for the act, but the more he thought about it later, the more apt it probably was.

She looked directly, sadly, into his eyes, then leaned across the space between the seats and kissed him, open-mouthed. She flicked her tongue against his. Her breath was sweet, her mouth soft.

When she withdrew, she said, "There's no rush. I just like you, is all."

"You're very patient with me."

"I know what I want," she said. She squeezed his thigh. "Don't make me wait forever, though? Okay?"

Wedding

The following Saturday they drove together out of the city, several hours deep into the desert to the southeast, to the lodge where the wedding was to be held. Nan was nervous, he thought—a little manic, a little breathless. She kept up a constant stream of conversation as he drove, telling him every story she could think of about her cousin, the bride. She played him music from her phone, electronic stuff he didn't know, and some of which he liked. "I will make you cool, Doug Ritchie," she said, and then tapped out a beat on the back of his hand with her fingernail. He had his doubts, but laughed.

They stopped to take pictures of a wide, empty desert basin between two craggy mountain ranges. Nan made him pose for a selfie in front of the vista, and squeezed his side. When she lowered the camera, Doug, not thinking too much about it, turned Nan's face to his and kissed her, deeply, pressing her back against the side of his Subaru.

She touched his cheek, then leaned her forehead against his. "That's what I'm talking about."

• • •

Nan's cousin had decided she would be married barefoot at the edge of the same desert hot spring where
she and her fiancé had first gone camping together.
The spring had, over the millennia, extruded a slick,
multicolored, house-sized nipple around its vent,
and the air near it smelled of sulfur and swarmed with
gnats. The vows contained references, he was pretty
sure, to tripping on acid at Burning Man. Yet the couple seemed happy, and kissed each other lustily at sunset, the bride rising onto her toes while everyone woo-
hooed and the desert fell into sudden chill shadow.

At the reception in the lodge, Doug drank a lot of
wine. He hadn't been drunk since he'd begun his diet,
and he was conscious, now, of the calories in every
glass—the wine seemed too thick on his tongue, more
like food than drink. The ceremony involved only a small
gathering of the bride's and groom's friends and family,
but even so, Nancy knew few people there, and she began drinking hard, too. The wedding guests were mostly
young people, outdoorsy people, and he and Nan, while
not the fattest people in the room, were nowhere near
the thinnest.

Nan introduced Doug to everyone as her friend, but
the tone of her voice implied *boyfriend*, as did the way
she kept her arm looped through his. Nan's aunt, the
bride's mother, was the first to ask the follow-up: "And
how did you meet?"

Doug took over, hastily: "We teach at the same
school. We ran together in the mornings before classes,
and things just . . . kind of developed from there."

The aunt beamed. "Nancy is such a wonderful girl,"

she said. "She's always been so full of life."

Nan slipped her hand into his, and he knew why, and felt their solidarity flicker into something more powerful.

The reception was in a room with floor-to-ceiling windows that looked out onto the desert, now lit blue by moonlight. Even indoors the smell of sulfur lingered, somehow more obscene in the air-conditioned chill; it smelled as though someone had been sick in the next room. A friend of the bride's was the deejay, and he played moody electronic dance music from his laptop between hits on a vaporizer, and the middle-aged guests looked on, concerned, trying to catch the rhythm, wondering when they'd do the Electric Slide. Doug felt very much like an alien being, landed on a strange world and trying to learn the customs. He tried not to remember his own wedding, the happy drunken whirl of it all, the look on Wendy's face as he knelt in front of her to remove her garter.

Nancy leaned into him during a rare slow song. "Um, do you get high?"

"Not since college."

She said, "One of the groomsmen has brownies. Want to split one?"

They ate it together, laughing, outside the lodge in the darkening evening, and he wondered what was more of a thrill—knowing he was about to have sex? Or eating more marijuana than he'd likely ever been exposed to in his life? Or was it that he was eating a for-fuck's-sake *brownie*? The sugar prickled on his tongue.

At one in the morning they said their goodbyes and retreated to their room. He was moving like a vapor. When the door was shut, Nan sighed and put her arms around his neck and said, "Doug, please please please fuck me."

She straddled him still wearing her dress; he'd brought a condom, but she told him it wasn't necessary, and that was unexpected, a little dangerous—and then he was gone; he couldn't remember an experience like this one, burrowed so intimately into a woman while she still wore her clothes, her lipstick barely smudged. She dug her nails into his palms, his shoulders. She made a lot of noise, and much to his surprise, he did, too.

Later they undressed and lay drowsing beneath a blanket, and then sometime before dawn they did it again, slower and more fumbling; Doug was aware of his winey breath, and hers, and the faint sulfur stink, and their sobriety circling the lodge like the coyotes that had woken them twice with their liquid, urgent yelps. He felt the weight and heft and pillowy fat on their bodies.

As the sun came up, they sat in the private hot spring on their patio, naked and sweating in the water, even though the nighttime air was nearly wintry. His head throbbed. Nan tipped her cheek against his chest and slipped her hand around his penis, companionably.

"Wanna be my boyfriend?" she asked.

He remembered the sight of her lowering herself, the body he'd just made love to, into the water. How large and pale she was, how her body was folded and shadowed.

"Yes," he said, and they held each other and watched the desert and said nothing.

Girlfriend

Having a girlfriend, after over a year of loneliness

and celibacy, was far stranger than Doug had expected. He had spent so much of that year cursing his loneliness, trying desperately to end it, that he was now surprised to find how deeply its habits, its rhythms, had become ingrained in him. Nan had already found a place in his life, but they'd gotten to know each other after he'd already left for work, on the grounds of the school, or not far away. Now Nan was in his apartment several nights a week, and vice versa. Until the semester ended, they both had papers to grade and lesson plans to prep, so it became natural to spend that time sitting beside one another on the couch, doing their work together. And when the semester ended (which, suddenly, it did; Doug's final speech to his seniors that year was especially emotional, as he had lost, by then, sixty-eight pounds; when he was done, the students cheered him and high-fived him before walking out). Nancy kept coming by. He rarely if ever had an evening alone anymore.

They took turns cooking dinner for one another; but this was fraught, too, since each of them had a diet they'd been strictly following, and Doug had more calories daily to spend. Nan liked to cook, and taught him new recipes, techniques. She also liked a glass of wine after her meal, and planned for it; he almost never did, but began to partake when Nan was over, and this threw him off—nothing could make him grumpier these days (or, more accurately, panicked) than discovering his calorie counts were off.

(When he told Nan this, she asked, *Are you factoring in all the sex?* He laughed, but yes, he *had* been—according to the app on his phone, sex burned three and one-half calories per minute, and he suspected that was a measure of people more athletic in the act than he and Nan.)

His bed was the bigger of the two, so she slept over at his apartment more often than he went to hers. No matter the grind of the semester; on nights Nan stayed, she pounced on him the moment they'd both finished their work. Not since college had he been so sexually active, and maybe not even then.

Their sex was—well, it was different than what he'd been used to, before (if indeed he'd ever been used to sex at all). Nan's frankness was an adjustment. She liked to send him flirty texts, to talk about what she wanted him to do in advance, to shout her pleasure to the corners of the room, during.

And he liked it! He liked it fine. He'd been worried he wouldn't, after all—that for all their work together they'd be hindered by the bodies that so dissatisfied them. But they pleased each other. "You're good at this," Nan told him, one night not long after they'd begun dating, and he was amazed to hear it. Amazed to understand that he'd never before believed this to be true of himself.

Wendy had been gone from his life for a barely a year, and here he was, dating.

And for a time, three or four months, he was happy.

This was what other people told him, anyway. *You seem so happy now,* his friends told him, when he and Nancy went out to dinner or for drinks, when she excused herself to the restroom. *You've really gotten to a good place, man.*

And he was happy to hear it. To agree with them. He was happy to have someone to call, someone to whom he could tell jokes, to whom he could read sentences from books he enjoyed. He liked introducing her to his gaming group. He liked to sit next to Nancy as part of a couple, among other couples, to remember the rhythms of conversations involving four people.

He liked how she told the story of their meeting. Hearing it aloud, the back and forth between the two of them as they told it, the characters each of them had become within their couplehood: Doug as quiet and skittish, needing to be wooed—but a man with hidden depths, a drive that drew Nancy to him.

"I couldn't stop noticing him," Nancy said, her hand resting lightly atop his. "One morning I parked my car in a rainstorm and I looked over to the track, and I remember I was thinking, *Not even Doug Ritchie would run in this*—and there he was, running in the rain."

They were at a Midtown bar, with college friends of Nancy's from Portland, visiting her for the weekend. Nancy's old roommate Darcy (a tall, beautiful black woman, foul-mouthed and flirtatious) kept grinning at Doug as Nancy talked, and Doug tried not to wilt under the attention.

Of course he remembered that rainy morning, how cold and awful it had been, and he remembered how he'd yelled at himself for an hour to go out and run, remembered all the anguish and despair that had driven him to open the door.

"I sat in my car for a long time and watched you," Nancy said. "I was feeling pretty bad about myself then. I needed some inspiration. And there you were, really doing it. I went out that night and bought running shoes."

"I didn't know that."

"You're inspiring," she said, and squeezed his hand. "You don't know how the kids talk about you."

She *believed* in him. Her confidence in him boosted his own.

He'd wanted this feeling. Hadn't he?

He said, "Your students quote you, too, you know. They love you."

"They tolerate me. I'm a big weirdo."

He squeezed her hand.

"You guys are too cute," Darcy said. "Oh my god."

Darcy took him aside as dinner ended, as they were gathering their coats. She said, "I can't remember a time I've seen her this happy."

Doug didn't know what to say.

"She's had such a hard time of it," Darcy said. And by that he was sure—because Darcy was thin—that she meant, *since she got fat.* "I'm really so glad you're in her life."

"Me, too," Doug told her, and Darcy hugged him, and for a moment his hand brushed her slender bare back, her muscles and curves tight from yoga and running, and that memory did not leave him for a long while.

Plateau

When he returned to school after summer vacation, down eighty-four pounds, the reaction from the students was immediate. Walking the hallway between the lounge and his classroom, he heard cries of amazement: *What? That's Mr. Ritchie?* Inez popped into the doorway of his classroom moments before the first bell, and he nearly laughed: she was risking being late in order to see for herself what others had reported.

"Oh my god," she said, in a single breath, and he shooed her away, but she said, "You did so good," over her shoulder, and he said, "Thank you, Inez," while his classroom full of new junior lit students watched her in bafflement. (He tried not to notice that Inez herself had changed over the summer; it was best never to see that the students had bodies, unless those bodies were fighting or visibly bleeding or expelling some noxious substance. But she had changed: she was taller, curvier; her voice was huskier. She'd graduate in May, and go off to college, busy herself in being a woman, and the thought made him unutterably sad.)

Word of his and Nan's relationship got around the school quickly, too, once the new year began. Doug and Nan walked out of the building together every evening, and she was not shy about kissing him goodbye. One time, as she did this, they heard a whoop from the corner of the parking lot, and they turned, embarrassed, to discover they were being watched by a group of students, too far away to identify, though Doug was pretty sure Inez was one of them.

"Christ," Doug said, but Nan laughed.

"Such sweethearts. They're happy for us."

And that, he supposed, was Nan at her essence: Always seeing the best in people. She was as much a sweetheart as they were.

He was shamed by such optimism. Where had his own gone? Killed with overuse, he supposed. Only an optimist, after all, could grow as fat as he'd gotten. Only an optimist could eat another bite, order another dessert, avoid taking the stairs, watch his wife retreat to the far side of the bed, and still think, *Everything's fine!*

Now that he was losing weight, though, he was suspicious of optimism. He was all about finite quantities right now. Restriction. Knowing that he could not be trusted with any urge.

He'd spent a long time over the past fourteen months looking at his old pictures, at his face in the mirror, saying, *I will not backslide. I can't be like I was.* Imagining his fatter self as a creature to be slain, eradicated, buried.

He thought this, sometimes, when he was with Nan: his former self had, for all his maddening laziness, been a sweetheart. An open-hearted fool.

Sweethearts, he thought, tended to be children. People whose hearts had not yet been broken.

• • •

He rose early, still, every morning, with Nan, in order to run or to take a long ride on his bicycle. In the evenings, before he'd read or eaten or watched television or all three at once (and especially on those rare nights when Nan wasn't around), he made himself go for a night ride. He tracked his calories. He gave himself one day out of every week during which he could eat as he wished, but more often than not he kept to his diet on that day, too; he'd become superstitious about falling away from any of his patterns, even as a reward. He took a perverse joy in hitting his diet, on those cheat days, with extra force.

The clothes he'd bought for his wedding date with Nan had already become relics by the end of summer, too big for use. He used to resent having to buy clothes, but now he savored shopping, enjoyed letting Nan dress him for the new semester, turn him in circles, tell him he was handsome.

Even so, his weight loss was slowing down. *To plateau is natural,* his doctor told him. *Don't let it get you down.*

Was it, though? Or was he slowing down because of his relationship?

Because, for all their effort, he and Nan could and did sometimes cheat. After sex, both of them giddy and oftentimes a little drunk (Nan drank a lot; she could demolish a bottle of wine with little excuse; every once in a while this made him uneasy, even though, when drunk, she was often ferociously horny), they'd laugh and give themselves a treat: ice cream eaten out of the container, a delivered pizza, another bottle of wine or beer. And even though he was with Nan, laughing, he could sometimes see their old selves emerge—the silence that would fall over the room after the pizza arrived, the hesitation in the other when one of them would stand and hold out a hand for the bag of potato chips, the ice cream carton, the rapidly dwindling bag of peanut M&Ms. The sigh of recognition. The danger in continuing. *Yep,* Nan would say, chagrined, and hand it over. *Yep,* Doug would say, and they'd put the ice cream into the freezer or the chips into the pantry, or even the trash, and as he walked or let Nan lead him to bed, he'd feel the mass of what he'd eaten in his belly, a coagulation of shame. The strange and hesitant denial hovering in the space between them, after.

• • •

Doug did not see Wendy anymore. They traded emails and texts every now and again, mostly in regard to niggling financial issues related to the divorce, bills for the one that had been mailed to the other.

In mid-September, though, she wrote him an email to tell him she was leaving town, with Ed Panecki, for New Mexico; they'd both taken jobs in Santa Fe. Ed had asked her to marry him, and she'd said yes. She wanted Doug to find out from her directly, she wrote, and wished him well. She hoped he was doing all right.

Doug thanked her for telling him, and wished her well, too.

He went for a long run that night—ten additional miles, his calves and lungs screaming—and demurred when Nan asked him what was wrong. The feelings would pass, he thought, and keeping them out of her view was a kindness.

He'd not expected Wendy to stick around Reno, he supposed, but he had been constantly aware of her, living her life in their small city, and in a strange way he depended on her gravity, near but far. Once or twice he thought he'd seen her, at a distance, through the windows of restaurants, walking out of a Starbucks in the morning while he drove through downtown; once she was in a photo gallery on the *Gazette-Journal's* webpage, wearing a little black dress at a mayoral fundraiser, her hair up, a wide smile on her face, her arm linked through Ed's, and for a while, without knowing why, he'd saved the picture on his laptop (he opened it when he was alone, stunned by Wendy's face, her happiness, how little—apart from the happiness—she had changed), but that night, after coming home from his run, after showering and weighing himself—250 on the nose—he deleted it, and went to his bed, where Nancy was napping, and he roused her for sex, which made her murmur happily, even when he went at her roughly, and then afterward he sat in the living room while Nan hummed in the shower, remembering how all of this had started, all that happened in the past year, and he told himself, over and over, *You've made it to the other side. You're your own man.*

You can do whatever you want, now.

Nan emerged from the shower, wrapped in a towel. "Hey," she said, "Wanna cheat? Let's get a pizza."

But even though he was ravenous, and even though he was free, he thought of Wendy, wearing her wedding dress; he thought of thin, bald Ed Panecki and his sculpted forearms, and he said, sharply, "No, we need to be good."

He felt her startle at his tone, but he didn't apologize, didn't bend. "Sure, okay," Nancy said, and then sat down on the couch beside him. He put his arm around her, his stomach gurgling, and tried his best to ignore her hurt.

Sprain

And then, that fall, Nan stopped losing weight.

At the end of September a calamity struck her: she turned her ankle badly on the sidewalk outside of school. A freak thing; she could have fallen one hundred times and come away with skinned palms the other ninety-nine, but this once, her heel caught in a crack and sent a twist up her leg, and then she was in the nurse's office, her ankle swollen and already wreathed in deep, multicolored bruises. She was sentenced to a walking boot for a month, and banned from running for six weeks.

She was depressed afterward, deeply so, her ankle propped up on her coffee table. "Goddamnit," she said, crying. "I've worked so *hard*."

He gripped her hand. "I know."

"I really liked doing this together," she said.

"It's going to be okay."

Doug meant this. He meant to help her, to support

her. He imagined how much an injury right now would panic *him*.

He went to her apartment most nights of the week and cooked soups for her. He shopped for groceries so she wouldn't have to. When she could, she walked up and down the sidewalk with him, struggling on her crutches. "I'm sweating," she'd say. "Gotta be burning *something*."

For a while this worked. Within a couple of weeks, however, she began to backslide. She hid this from him for a while, but Doug took out her garbage for her, and he noticed the empty candy wrappers.

Should he say something? How? Nan was so dejected these days, he decided to let it go.

Then one night she admitted it to him, after they watched a movie. "I've been sneaking candy," she said. "I'm *hiding* it from you. I'm so weak. I don't know how I can do this—"

"I know you can do it—"

"But I'm not doing it! I've gained *five pounds.*"

Doug tried to joke with her. To help her think it through. The walking boot alone weighed a couple pounds, didn't it? He tried to remind her that the scale could vary widely from day to day. She might be retaining water. He held her hand, tried to be positive, but inside he was seized by fear. He had nightmares about going off his diet, dreams in which he was at a restaurant, brought plate after plate of food, and sometimes it was the same restaurant, the same waiter, as on the night Wendy had told him she wanted the divorce.

"My body wants to be bigger," she said, crying. "It feels like some monster in a fucking horror movie. I let my guard down for a second, and boom, I'm big again.

And I see how you work at it, and it makes me feel even worse that I can't—"

"Come on."

"Just tell me you'll still be here for me," she said. "Please?"

"Jesus," he said. "Of course."

• • •

Then one day, three weeks after the sprain, Doug noticed that Nan was right. She was, indeed, getting bigger. He tried not to see it, the new roundness in her face, her rear; he tried to look past the change, to look at her with the love he wanted to feel; because if he saw it, Nan surely did, and whatever he felt about it, it was surely horrifying *her*. And he tried not to see because, too, he could remember those long years at the end of his marriage when he'd inhabited his swelling body, believing that his wife loved him regardless of it.

He and Nancy were a good fit. Weren't they? She understood him. She was intelligent, funny; they liked the same movies and books. They'd even joked a couple times about finding a place together. (Down the road. Maybe.) If what they had was permanent, they'd see each other age, see their bodies change; if they loved each other, this would not make a difference.

But he noticed her size anyway.

And god, how he hated himself for noticing, for his mind's insistence on searching for clues. Not only in the way Nan's body looked and felt, but here: in the wadded-up bag of chips in the trash. The new clothes in Macy's bags on the couch that she'd gone to buy without him. The way she averted her eyes when he told her he was going for a run—even after her boot came off, and then again in October, when the doctor cleared her to run, too.

"You can come along," he said, lacing his shoes.

"I need to work back into it by myself," she said. "You're in far better shape than me right now."

"It doesn't matter. I can keep your pace."

"You'll just get frustrated with me," she said. "You're already frustrated. I can see it in your face."

He wanted to turn those words around on her. *She* would be the one suffering frustration, not him. That was simple psychology. But then he heard himself growing short with her, heard his own angry sighs—the ones he'd spent all those years telling himself Wendy was making because of her work, and not because of him.

Nancy had told him that she was prone to depression, and that depression made her want to eat. They had this in common. So he recognized the way she was sinking into her gloom. He felt helpless, watching her eyes turn inward, more so because he understood.

But she'd also told him, hadn't she, that he was an inspiration to her? If he was frustrated (not that he was!), well—couldn't he be hurt that he wasn't rousing her, anymore, to follow him?

He tried to be positive, measured; he tried not to push her, but to remind her that he was there to help her if she wanted. She'd gained only what, ten pounds? Twelve? In the grand scheme of things, twelve pounds wasn't all that much. She'd be back on track in a month of work.

"It's *fifteen*," she snapped, one morning. "I know, just quit badgering me, okay? Don't you think I feel bad enough?"

Later that day she apologized. "I love you," she told

him, curling beside him on the couch, after he'd come back from a run, and weighed himself and showered.

"I love you, too," he told her, and apologized as well, stroking her hair as she began to weep against his chest. The blouse she wore had a tag at the back of the neck that she'd forgotten to remove.

Flunking

He did love her. He did want to help her.

And yet.

He began to think of Nancy—not all the time, but sometimes—in a particularly insidious way: as a *failure.* As someone who had set out to do a difficult task, and who had not succeeded—not in the way he was succeeding, at least.

As someone who was *weak.*

Of course this was wrong of him. To think of someone as a failure was to think of them as someone who not only hadn't succeeded, but who *wouldn't* succeed. Not simply as someone experiencing a setback while losing weight, but someone who would never lose weight, someone who would *always* be fat.

His mind went to the topic unbidden—such as when he was at the track, alone, running, pushing himself angry and bored through the turns. Missing her. Missing the two of them in those early days—how happy and giddy and proud they'd been, running, doing the hard thing that neither of them had done before. (And—wasn't it true?—running faster, harder, because of how they knew they must look, trudging slowly beside each other; he'd run, some mornings, as though he hoped he might actually outpace his own body.) And here he was, running, aching, while she was at her apartment, putting it off, drinking coffee in front of the internet, and maybe, probably, sneaking a croissant.

Doug told himself not to be unfair. He had done the same thing, been exactly the same way, for over ten years, a lot longer than her; he knew what it was like to get big, how his mind had worked to keep him big. He'd never thought of *himself* as a failure. Even when Wendy had left him, even when he realized how sour and slothful he had become, even when he agreed with her that he had been unlovable, he'd never been able to pin the word *failure* to himself, had never been able to lose the promise of hope.

Yet he had failed far more than Nan had—hadn't he? And for longer.

If his younger self, the college boy who'd wanted to write novels, or be an investigative journalist, saw him now—thudding around a high school track, divorced from Wendy, seventy-five pounds lighter and *still* sheathed in fat—would he be anything but bitterly disappointed?

His younger self would have thought of the weight loss as a corrective measure, akin to a medical procedure. Of course you'd have to lose the weight; of course you'd undergo any amount of suffering to do it. To his younger self, the one who had proposed to Wendy, who had been allowed to see the small bruise on her flank, he could be nothing but a horrible, devastating failure.

He might weigh 215 someday, but he would still be Doug Ritchie, the man who had let himself top 330. The man who'd *had* to get smaller. A man who'd failed his way to success. It would always mark him.

No, he thought—and he loved the part of him that

said this. *No. Lose the weight, and then it will be better. Lose the weight, and all is forgiven.*

You'll have succeeded. You'll be happy again.

He pumped his arms, focused past a stitch in his side, huffed out steam. He imagined himself smaller, faster, muscular.

He imagined living in a house, not an apartment; he imagined, in that house, a beautiful, slender woman standing in a doorway and smiling at him, wearing one of his shirts over her lithe, naked body. She wasn't Wendy.

She wasn't Nancy, either. She reached out her arms to him anyway.

• • •

Nan gained another five pounds.

They had sex less and less. This was a thing that happened, of course, to any couple, but Doug knew what was happening, though he denied the truth of it for a long while.

Nan was too tired, after a long day? Well, okay, that was fine, because he'd wanted to open up a new novel anyway, so he read in the living room after she'd gone to bed, content in his privacy.

He was going to be out late with a friend, so maybe they'd have sex tomorrow? And in the meantime, out with his very single friend, watching a movie and turning down offered popcorn, having drinks at a bar, he felt himself enjoying a guilty, subversive freedom, found himself flirting with his waitress, watching with tipsy joy the bouncing retreat of her ass.

Nan's period had started, so they'd have to wait a few more days—and Doug felt his shoulders loosen. It was all right, he told her. He went out for a run, alone.

Then one night, all the stars aligned. She kissed him, he kissed her back, felt the new fat at her hip, felt the beating of his own heart, and finally admitted it: he didn't want to have sex with her. He didn't want to make love to his own girlfriend, the woman with whom he was practically living.

He did it anyway—the flesh was willing, and for that he was grateful, because he had nightmares about impotence, about seeing Nancy's body (always bigger, in his dreams, than in reality) and going soft in turn, insulting her with his instinct, showing her the truth, which was—

She sighed, bit at his shoulder, told him his name.

Doug allowed the word to form in his mind when they were finished, and she slept beside him, her breath soft on his neck: Maybe he did not love her. Not anymore. And maybe he hadn't, ever.

Curb

Doug tried not to end things—he tried first to find again the joy he'd once felt with her, the happiness that he was sure had been there for the both of them. The love.

For a week he was solicitous to her; he took her out to dinner and to a movie; they had sex several more times. He reminded himself of things he had loved about her: the way she'd modeled her dress for him at the department store (when she'd been bigger than she was now); the way they'd laughed, eating pot brownies and watching the desert night as she squeezed his hand. The way she believed in him. Her happy brashness, when she wasn't caught in the grip of her sadness.

But even as he did all of this, he knew that Nancy suspected the truth. She was tender around him, these days: skittish, too loud, too quick to ask him his mood.

And she was eating more and more; she was sneaking more candy, taking second helpings at dinner, and in these actions he saw a kind of relief, a surrender, and he ached for her, and wished he could help her, and he thought that to stay with her like this was probably crueler, in its way, than leaving would be.

Was this, he wondered, how Wendy had felt, at the end? Sitting in her office, or in their bed, sick to her stomach with guilt and anger, listening to the creaking footfalls of the man she'd loved move heavily across the kitchen, and then to the opening of the refrigerator door?

Was this why Doug had hidden himself, more and more, from his wife? Why he'd waited until she'd gone to sleep before going to the kitchen to eat leftovers in front of the open refrigerator? Had he known, all along?

And if he had, why hadn't he *done* something?

• • •

In the end, the words came out of him without premeditation. They were sitting in Nancy's car at a stoplight, on their way to see a movie. They'd argued about what to see, and he'd grown sullen, and she'd pressed him on his sullenness, and then finally she snapped– "Doug, just tell me what's wrong!"–and he realized as she spoke that all he wanted was to be home, alone, and then he told her:

"I don't think this is working, Nan."

"Please don't," she said. But she wasn't the sort of person who would beg for anything, so she switched, as he'd known she would, to anger. "Okay. Okay. I knew this was coming. Jesus. Jesus."

"Nan—"

She swung the car to the side of the road; one of its wheels popped over the curb and he lurched against the seatbelt.

"Get out of my car, please."

"I'll get a cab."

"So cold," she said, and then she screamed it: "Get out of my fucking car!"

He did, numbly. The moment he shut the door. she screeched away. A block down the street she pulled over again to the curb. He waited for her to put the car in reverse, to come back and yell or beg, but she didn't; the two of them remained separate, a block apart, for a long minute, and then finally she drove away for good.

He ended up walking along the back streets; he didn't mind the three miles, and had often run this same stretch. It was late October, and very cold, so he moved briskly, and his feet shushed through fallen leaves. He kept his phone in his pocket, turned off. He did not know how to feel. He had never broken up with anyone in his life before. He felt sorrow; he felt guilt; he felt, too, a wild, happy freedom, an understanding that he was, again, the master of himself.

He wondered whether Wendy had felt like this, after he left their house for the motel.

When he walked inside his apartment, he turned on his phone again. He'd gotten many calls from Nancy. Even as he was scrolling through them, his phone buzzed.

"Why are you doing this?" Nancy asked him, when he answered. She was, he could tell, trying hard not to cry; yet she was, clearly, crying.

He said, "I'm doing this because it isn't working."

"You're not making it work. It *could* work, but you're not doing your part."

"I know you're mad."

"I'm not mad, Doug, I'm heartbroken."

"I'm sorry."

"It's because I'm still big. I gained weight and you fucking bailed."

"No," he said, wincing.

"You're a shitty liar," she said. "You love me as long as I'm getting small, but not when I struggle. Don't you remember what this feels like?"

"Of course I remember."

"Well, then, that's even worse. I thought you were different. I thought you'd understand."

"Nan, this is different—"

She laughed, derisively, as though she could hear his thoughts. "You know what, Doug? If our positions were reversed, I would still have loved you. I don't care if you're big. I don't care if you're old, I don't care if you're sad. I never did. But you do, and that's the difference."

"Nan, that isn't—"

The phone went dead against his ear.

III. Smaller

House

After he called it quits with Nan, Doug was surprised by how hard it was, being alone again.

Of course this new loneliness was different; it was, after all, one he had chosen. Now his mornings and evenings were his own again—but they were often painful, intolerably lonely. (*See?*—he'd say to Nan in his head, when he was struck by the onset of sudden tears, when he imagined her screaming in the car as she drove away, when he watched a television show he knew she'd find funny—*this hurts me, too.*)

When he felt this way, he found a kind of solace in returning, without her, to his best habits. In the mornings he went for runs—though now he chose to run through neighborhoods, or on trails winding through the dry, scrubby foothills above the city bowl, rather than to return to the track at school. (He tried it, once, but spent the entire time in fear that Nan would show up as well, that they would have a confrontation in front of the football team's practice.) In the evenings he would read and grade, and practice the guitar, or watch old films, or go downstairs to the bar. He tried his hand at writing poems and short stories; they were terrible, but he liked the idea that he was making them, as he once had. He kept a journal. He would often take a second run of a few miles through his neighborhood just before dark. On the weekends he began each day with a long bike ride into the old ranchland and rolling foothills to the south of the city loop.

He dreamed of Nan sometimes, crying, angry. He would run from her, but slowly, as though he were big again, bigger than he'd ever been before, and when he woke, he was ashamed at the emptiness he felt, upon finding himself alone in his bed.

He began to drop weight again almost immediately; the slothfulness that had been creeping over him the last several months was quickly replaced by a steely, nervous energy. His clothes loosened. He walked around his apartment snapping his fingers, humming.

Not long after the breakup, restless, he called a realtor. Three weeks later he'd closed on a small brick bungalow just south of downtown, in the city's oldest and leafiest neighborhood.

Here, finally, he began to feel at ease. The process of buying and then furnishing the house consumed him, and though he spent too much of his savings in the process, he loved the house, the way it fit him, and he it. He now had an office, and a small backyard with a tall fence and two mature maple trees that were already shedding their leaves into a lovely carpet. The house's glass windowpanes were rippled by age, and its hardwood floors were warped and creaking. Best of all, he had built-in bookshelves in his living room and in his office. He loved having all his books arrayed in neat rows, instead of hiding in storage. He had a finished basement, too, and he put in a weight bench and a training stand for his bike.

He felt an occasional twinge of sadness, moving in, that Nan would not see any of it.

While shopping in an antiques mall he found an old, brass-framed mirror; he took it home and hung it at the end of the house's central hallway. He liked the continual surprise of spotting himself in it: smaller than he'd ever been, muscled in ways he'd never been muscled, his salt-and-pepper beard trimmed and neat. An entirely new life, in a new body; a new body in a new house.

It had taken work. The mirror was a reminder of this, too. He had made hard decisions, had denied himself small pleasures to gain greater ones. He had hurt someone who certainly did not deserve to be hurt. But here, framed in the mirror, he could see the reasons why. And now he could work on himself again. It would be easier, now that he was alone for a while.

He tried sometimes to see the outline of his old self

in the glass: a ghostly cloud surrounding his new form. As motivation, and out of pride, he hung a photo of himself at his heaviest beside the mirror. That Doug Ritchie looked jolly, bloated, insulated. Stupidly unaware of all that was coming for him. Dead, now, he thought. A memory.

That was what he came to love most about his house, perhaps: for now, at least, it contained memories of no one but him.

Time

Nan had texted and emailed him angrily for weeks after their breakup. He understood. He supposed he owed it to her to read every word, so he did, even though every outburst cut him as deeply as he was sure she intended. He almost never replied, letting her vent—but then, finally (he'd gotten a long text while lacing up his shoes one morning) he succumbed to irritation, and answered: *Enough. You hate me. I get it. That doesn't change anything.*

They avoided one another at work; Doug was aware of her friends on the faculty having closed ranks around her, saw their stares when he entered the lounge, but what could he do? He sat on the other side of the room at meetings (though he could feel Nan's hurt radiating out from her, a subtle heat) and kept out of her way when he could. His own longtime friends on the faculty buffered him, ran interference for him. When they had to attend meetings together, he and Nan spoke civilly, professionally. And in time he grew used to it, as his therapist told him he would.

The students found out, of course. After he dismissed his senior lit class, a week after the breakup, he saw Inez lingering in front of his desk, looking sad and doubtful. He knew what she was going to say before she opened her mouth: "I heard about you and Ms. Dreyfus. We all did."

He did not want to talk about it, or discover where, exactly, Inez had learned such information. "It's all right," he said. "She's a great person. This is for the best."

"But it's so *sad*."

As though he and Nan were somehow fated for one another, such that their breakup was only to be mourned.

"It is," he said, anyway.

"Are *you* okay?"

"I'm fine, Inez. I—"

He wasn't sure what he'd been about to say. Despite her concern, the entire conversation was making his skin crawl; he had broken up with Nan, and he didn't want to explain the details to anyone who didn't need to know, let alone a moony high school senior, and he especially didn't want to do anything—such as being mysterious—that would cause her and the students she told to infuse the situation with more drama than they already would.

He said, "You know, it's inappropriate to discuss this."

Inez looked hurt. "Ms. Tanner talks about her and Mr. Gavin all the time."

The upcoming wedding between Gail Tanner and Zach Gavin was preoccupying the entire school body. Doug loathed the two of them, not only because they were young and thin and classically beautiful, but because they clearly reveled in the attention—especially

Gail, whose ninth-grade girls were constantly bringing her playlists and clippings of dresses for something called her *vision board.* That they both taught the same subject depressed him.

"We're all different people, Inez," he said. "And we need to do things different ways. I'll be fine. Ms. Dreyfus will be, too. I promise."

Inez looked doubtful, the way she did when he disagreed with her interpretation of a sonnet, but she left the classroom without further comment.

• • •

And Nan *was*, in the end, okay. She told him so. Three months after the breakup she slipped a letter, handwritten, into his mailbox at work.

She had, she claimed, written the entire thing while camping by herself high in the Sierra. She wrote that she had learned to enjoy her own company again. She still was hurt by the breakup, and what she suspected his true reasons for ending things had been. But in the end, what could she do? He did not love her anymore (*and you did love me once*, she told him—*I know you did, Doug*) and that was his right, anyone's right. She was learning how to be happy, and she was hoping that he would someday learn to be happy, too. Because—and she wasn't saying this to be hurtful, but because she had loved him more than anyone else she'd ever been with, and so had come to know him well, maybe better even than he knew himself— he *wasn't happy*. She had almost never seen him happy. That, she wrote, had been her biggest mistake: trying to make things better for someone who was so unhappy.

I had a date, she wrote, near the end.

He didn't care what size I was.

When Doug saw her at school next, in the lounge be-fore their first classes, he thanked her for the letter. She was wary, and did not meet his eyes, but he was glad, at least, that they'd talked.

When she walked away to her classroom, he noticed: she looked good. Ten, fifteen pounds down since the breakup, he thought. At least.

Friend

Two months after Doug moved into the house, short-ly after his weight hit 230 pounds, he brought a woman home to it.

He hadn't intended to, not so soon. He'd imagined doing so, sure—but that it happened when it did was a complete surprise.

His house was a short walk from a Midtown bar, a new, darkly lit place with an excellent selection of whis-keys, and he'd taken to spending a couple of early eve-nings there each week, grading papers at the end of the bar while nursing a single drink, and leaving before the crowds came in. Before long he developed a rapport with one of the bartenders: Trace, who was in his late twen-ties, who wore suspenders and maintained an impressive beard. Trace liked that Doug liked good whiskey, and that he was an English teacher. They lent each other nov-els. Trace dated a lot (he told Doug one evening, mat-ter-of-factly, that he'd slept with over a hundred women, and Doug had spent the rest of the night fascinated and appalled, his own number—three!—lit shamefully in his head), and when he found out Doug was single, began pointing out women to him: "Check your six, Dougie," he'd say, *sotto voce.* "Brunette, very shapely, and I think she's getting stood up."

Doug would always laugh, and sometimes look, but—smaller body notwithstanding—he was terrible at meeting strangers, and always waved Trace away. Afterward he'd wonder what it would be like to have grown up looking like Trace looked, to know that, if you were forward with a pretty woman, she would not stammer out that she had a boyfriend, that she would almost certainly give you a few minutes' time.

One afternoon in late January, casually, Trace leaned across the bar and said, "Hey, Doug, I want you to meet a friend of mine."

The friend—standing right behind him—was a woman about Doug's age, tall and curvy and possessed of a long red ponytail. Her name was Paula. She owned a craft store on the south end of town, and she had employed Trace there, once. She smiled at Doug when she shook his hand, and her nose wrinkled cutely. "Why, hello, Doug," she said, as if she'd been looking high and low for him. He blushed, and he thought she might have noticed, but she kept smiling.

They chatted first with Trace, then with each other, as the bar filled around them. Doug could feel what was about to happen long before it happened. Paula liked him. She liked the looks of him. He liked the looks of her: she wore bangles on her wrists and tight jeans and glossy black boots, and she jogged her knee up and down, tapped her nails on the bar. She had a quick wit, and seemed to enjoy his; she had a loud, rich laugh. She liked to have the last word, too, and he let her, enjoying her energy, basking in it, maintaining a crooked smile that he'd practiced, which he hoped made him seem rakish.

Paula told him she had been divorced twice over. He told her he was a year and a half past a divorce himself. She nodded sympathetically. She wasn't looking, she told him offhandedly, for anything serious these days.

"It is possible"—she winked at him over the rim of her glass—"that I maybe am not super good at monogamy."

He wondered if she actually *was* married. Or seeing someone seriously.

"But is anyone?" she asked, and laughed lightly, and touched his forearm.

He thought: *I was.*

When she was in the restroom, Trace came over to him. "She's into you," he said. "Don't fuck up."

The bar had become crowded. When Paula returned, Doug took a deep breath and asked her if she'd like to take a walk through the nearby neighborhoods. So they could talk without shouting, he said. She smiled. "Sure. That sounds nice." He paid the tab. Outside it was cold and dry, but the air was still and the quiet, after the chaos of the bar, was pleasant. Paula put her arm through his as they walked. She was a reader, kind of, she said, though she demurred when he asked her what books she liked. She had recently gone back to school for an MBA. She had done CrossFit for a year, but those people were crazy, so now she was addicted to spin.

Doug told her about running, biking. He swallowed hard and told her how he'd lost a lot of weight. Paula exclaimed and told him she would never have been able to tell, and even if she was lying, the thought filled him with a fizzy joy.

She told him she was looking at buying a house. He told her about the house he'd just bought, and how reassuring it was, to have a space like that to himself.

"Sounds nice," she said. She slid her hand down his forearm. "Is it close by?"

In his bedroom she was eager, assertive. Her body was trim and firm. She was shaved bare. She complimented his body, which made him happy, though he was too aware of the little bit of loose skin at his hips, and kept his T-shirt on. At one point he lifted her and turned her to a new position, and she laughed and said, "Oh! You're a strong one!"—and though she sounded like a bad actress, no one had ever told him this before, and it invigorated him. He went at it, at her, harder, and she kept laughing and exclaiming. Afterward she wore one of his hoodies and explored his house, and he followed her from room to room, explaining its amenities.

In the morning, just before dawn, he walked her back to her SUV. He buzzed with a lack of sleep, bemused by the idea that he'd have to appear in front of his students in three hours. The beep of her car door opening was shockingly loud. Everyone was asleep, he thought, and here he was, awake and alive.

"Did we have fun?" Paula asked him.

"We did," he said. He almost asked for her number, but she was already moving on, moving forward; he could see it in the set of her shoulders, the wincing look she gave herself in the mirror behind her sunshade, and anyway, she said, "Good night, Doug, or good morning. See you around."

She squeezed his fingers and then shut her door and drove away.

He went home and poured himself a glass of water, and then another. He ate a power bar. The sun was just coming up. No time to sleep, he thought, so he changed into running clothes and pounded off down the sidewalk, as fast as he could manage, trying to outrun the hangover he guessed was coming for him.

Later, just before showering, he logged the run into his phone, as well as sixty-five calories for sex.

Unserious

Over the next several months, as winter sharpened and then dulled, Doug slept with three other women. Each of these relationships was, for all intents and purposes, a one-night stand.

Living this way was new—but it was easier than he'd ever expected. All he had to do was be thin. (And he was, still, growing thinner all the time: 229, 225, 220, 215, 210.) To trim his beard and dress in nice clothes and listen and laugh and say gentle, funny things. To act like nothing was that big a deal. All his life he'd assumed it was difficult, to date casually, *unseriously*, but it really wasn't—especially with dating sites to help make introductions, and armed with the proper attitude.

He'd never been *un*serious, before. Never before had he approached women without wanting, *longing*, for seriousness: a relationship, a commitment, a marriage. He had wanted—desperately—for the women he pursued to love the idea of his future, his potential. To love him wholly and forever.

Now he realized how exhausting that was. Sometimes it was all right to want someone to desire you in the here and now. Sometimes it was easier not to worry about potential at all.

• • •

First was Tina, who was small and wiry and tattooed, and

who—even though he'd met her on Tinder (Trace had shown him how to make an account), and even though they went to bed not even eight hours after meeting in person—was strangely intimate with him, insisting on looking into his eyes, on breathing plaintive dirty talk into his ear. She'd left him stunned, and then went home and texted him: *hey man that was rad—take care of yr-self!*

Then there was Jessie, whom he met one night at Whole Foods; the two of them struck up a conversation while deciding whether to buy starfruit. Jessie dressed in slouchy sweaters and yoga pants and had drawn, tired features, but she had a quiet, fierce intelligence. They saw a couple movies together before she spent the night at his house—but their lovemaking was, in the end, perfunctory. Jessie had recently gotten divorced, and he felt for her, wouldn't have minded being her friend, or more, but she stopped texting him after they slept together, and he could only wish her well.

Then, finally, there was Hanna, whom he'd met on-line, who was married.

She told him so via text as they set up a date: *I'm not looking for anything serious. And I have to be discreet. I just want to be clear up front about what I need.* He could have said no, but he did not; Hanna's picture was too alluring. She was young, younger than Nan. Just twenty-nine.

I just have this fantasy, she'd written.

Hanna met him at his bar. She was half Chinese, half white, slim and boyishly angled, her hair chopped short, her cheeks downy, her arms and long neck smooth. Her voice shook and she seemed not to know whether to meet his eyes. When he told her he was having a bourbon, she asked if he'd order her one, and he said, *Okay*, and asked Trace to bring them two Blantons, neat. She told him, hesitantly, that she was acting on something she'd wanted to do for a long time. For a long half hour, as they talked, she seemed to be on the verge, any moment, of gathering up her purse and leaving without a word. And wouldn't that be for the best, really? She was married, after all, and he tried to imagine the man who was her husband. (He traveled a lot, Hanna told him; she was alone so much more than she ever thought she'd be.) Doug could only picture someone like his old self, kind and oblivious and fat, and he thought, again, about how Wendy and Ed must have begun things, the words Wendy might have said, whether she'd been nervous, whether she'd been eager, whether she'd met Ed one night for drinks like this, whether she'd struggled to return Ed's gaze, and he realized she probably had been the one to start things; he could blame Ed all he wanted, but Wendy–well, Wendy was the strong one, Wendy always had been.

But then Hanna seemed to warm to him; she began to laugh at his jokes, his inquiries into her tastes; and here was a flash of her gaze, accepted, held; she told him, laughing, a little glittery with drink, how she'd been so nervous, sending him a message, and he said–he meant it–*I'm nervous too*, and she said, *Oh god this is nuts*, and he thought that what he ought to do was send her home, call this off for her, but then he told himself they were each adults, they could each make their own decisions. She was so lovely; he wanted her more and more as she talked, and bent conspiratorially toward him. He could not imagine why she wanted him, but that she could was one of the reasons he'd lost so much weight, had undergone so much struggle–wasn't it? And shortly afterward she accepted an invitation to his house. *Your call,* he said, softly. *It's okay either way.* She seemed to vibrate when she said, *Sure, okay,* and in his house she said, *This place is really nice,* and there, in the doorway to his bedroom, he pulled her to him and kissed her, and she said *Oh,* and then began to tug at his clothing, and later she scratched him with her nails.

Afterward she drowsed under his arm, or seemed to, and it was in this quiet time that the thought came to him: she was just young enough that she could have attended Hunter High during his tenure there. His eyes might have passed her over at a convocation in the gymnasium; she might have stood in line in front of him in the cafeteria; he might once have scolded her in the hall. He thought of a girl some years ago he'd marched to the office, after he'd caught her outside, just finishing a cigarette; he hadn't been terribly cruel, but he'd been stern and angry, and that girl had sobbed as he pulled her along by her wrist; *Please don't tell my parents, please,* she'd said, and he did not remember her name, though wherever she was, she surely must remember his, and then he thought that if she saw him now, she might not recognize him, because he'd been fat when this had happened; now they could see each other, pass each other by, and never know.

He thought of Inez Ochoa, a decade hence, meeting a man like him, making the decisions Hanna had made, laughing and sighing.

Before leaving, Hanna said, "Thanks," and hugged him on his porch; in this light she looked wan, and even younger. He wondered what his neighbors would think, if they saw. She stood on tiptoe, kissed his cheek. "This was fun," she said, though she already seemed to doubt it, and then the Uber he'd called for her stopped, and she got in and was gone.

He would never see her again. That was the deal—she needed no attachment, and he'd expected none. But as she left him he felt, again, what he'd felt when Paula and Tina and Jessie had left his bed, his house—an old and nagging worry, and a door opening onto a deep and unsettling shadow. And a sudden desire to call after them, to ask:

But don't you really want to stay?

Message

Not long after that evening with Hanna, Wendy emailed him.

The email came as a surprise; he and Wendy had had almost no communication in over a year—they'd only traded messages about various nagging bills and financial records. Doug did not blame her for the silence; he had behaved during the divorce in ways that veered between the cruel and the pathetic, and when he remembered those times—especially after all the texts and emails Nan had sent him, after their breakup—he understood all too well why Wendy had kept her distance.

Wendy had a Facebook account, and he'd followed it—pathetically—for longer than he should have. He did not stop himself from clicking through her public photos, even after she took down all the old ones of the two of them. She seemed to live a good life in Santa Fe, and often posted pictures of herself and Ed doing beautiful, athletic things: she was a member of a climbing gym for a while; she ran a marathon; she went on a weekend climbing trip at Red Rocks in Vegas. A photo from that trip finally caused him to unfollow her. She was smiling up at the camera, her skin tanned and her grin wide and white, and her limbs were splayed across the rock, and far below were the tops of pinyon pines, and he ached to see her so far away from him. He wanted to tell her, *Be careful.*

Wendy had come back to Reno once or twice since then—someone always told him when she did—but she never lingered, and they never met. Even their mutual friends admitted she was different, now, distant.

Hey Doug, her email read. *I am going to be back in Reno from June 2–6 (old case finally going to trial). I hope this offer doesn't upset you—that is not my intent—but I was wondering if you would like to get a drink and catch up one evening while I'm there.*

I understand if it isn't possible, but I would like us to find a way to be friends, or at least acquaintances. People who sometimes talk. For my part I know I've kept you distant, which I think was necessary for my own well-being (please take that in the proper context), and for that I'm sorry, and have been sorry for a while. I can well imagine that you want nothing to do with me right now and maybe in the future, and if this isn't the right thing for you to do, I will absolutely understand if you say no.

But I hope you don't. I want to say that too. I would like to see if we could sit together and catch up, and not wonder if we can.

Please take all the time you need to answer. I hope you're well, regardless of what you think of this or me. —W

The message caught him off guard. It sounded odd, he thought. Strangely, uncharacteristically hesitant. Not fussed over with her usual lawyerly vigor. He went to her Facebook page—his first trip there in a couple of months—and found her account shut down. He felt guilty, as though she'd caught him looking in her window, and had shut the blinds.

Doug didn't answer her right away. He wasn't angry—he could always make himself angry about Wendy if he wanted, but more often than not, these days, he had to work at it. He read and reread her message, and the feelings that came to him were like old song lyrics in a high school notebook: written in tears, remembered with embarrassment. But still powerful, nevertheless.

He missed her. That was what it boiled down to. And from the tone of her letter, she missed him, too, at least a little.

The adult thing to do—what he had been doing for a while, he realized, pleasantly—was to admit that this didn't matter. Their marriage had been a failure, and both he and Wendy were in a better place, now. And, further: he had to admit—he made himself admit—that all the hard work he'd done on himself might never have occurred unless Wendy had pulled the plug. That, for all the pain she'd caused him, they had both come to benefit from her leaving.

There's almost never a happy divorce, his therapist had told him, more than once. *But I have seen a lot of divorces that produce happy survivors. It is possible.*

When Doug reminded himself of these words, he thought not only of Wendy, but of Nan. Would he have the courage to write her an email like Wendy's, a year from now? To ask her for friendship?

After a night's sleep he emailed a reply: *Thanks for suggesting this. I think it would be good for both of us, honestly, and I'm not sure I could have asked. I'll keep those nights free, and you can let me know when you get to town what works for you.*

After he hit send, he stood and he weighed himself—he did so every morning—and came in at 211: one hundred and twenty-five pounds down from his high point after the divorce.

He pulled on his running clothes and went out for a five-miler, and as he ran he told himself he had a little over a month before his meeting with Wendy; he could lose even more weight, by then. (All along he'd been hoping to reach 220, but now that he'd sunk below that target, he'd been recalibrating. Should he try for 199? He felt so good these days, why not keep it going? And why not make his meeting with Wendy the deadline? It would be hard, but he thought he could just manage to do it.)

He breathed deeply through his nose and thought about being 199, and walking into a bar where Wendy was already waiting. The look on her face when she saw his size, the shape of his body. He imagined her leaning toward him, the way the other women had. He did not want Wendy back—but he imagined her asking him to take her back. Wanting him. Leaving Ed for him. He thought about telling her no.

Or maybe even saying *yes.*

Preparation

The rest of the time before Wendy's visit passed quickly. Doug had a routine he liked, and his job had its own rhythms and marks to hit, especially in spring semester, when his journalism students had to ready the yearbook for print.

All the while, as he worked and dieted and ran, the idea of Wendy's visit hung in the background of his mind.

He was not nervous, or anxious, but he used the fact of her to push himself, to motivate himself. If he thought about ordering too much food at a restaurant, he remembered the way he'd felt when she told him she was leaving him; if he did not want to lace up his running shoes, he thought about Ed, how the man's shirt fronts fell in a clean line from his pectorals to his waist, how his face seemed to be made of right angles. If he wanted to break away early from a run, he imagined Wendy's face, seeing his new body.

He dropped more weight: 208, 206.

He went to Macy's a week before Wendy's visit and bought himself a new wardrobe. The salesman who helped him with his measurements—a young white man, college-aged, and very gay—asked, "And what's the occasion?"

"Well," Doug said, "I'm having drinks next week with my ex-wife, and I've lost over a hundred pounds since she saw me last."

The salesman straightened and put a hand over his mouth. "Oh my god."

"So I need to look really good," Doug said.

"Oh, you will," the man said, chuckling.

Wendy emailed him a week out from her trip: Was a Thursday evening a bad night to meet? He told her that was fine, and that he was looking forward to it. He felt a certain symmetry; they were going to talk on the night before the last day of his semester—one day shy of two years since they'd split.

The next morning when he weighed himself, he came in at 202.

He spent that last week in a frenzy of exercise and starvation. He had to drop two pounds in six days: hard work, but it could be done. Thirty-five hundred calories went into a pound, so he had to come in 7,000 short on the week. Every day he got up early, then put on his bike togs and went on a long ride–twenty to thirty miles each day, pushing himself on flats and uphills alike, arriving home trembling and dizzy, with barely enough time to eat a power bar (begrudgingly) and drive to school. In the evenings he made himself run. He ate protein shakes and fruit. Once or twice he grew dizzy in class, but he hid it from the students, pushed through, his voice at a far remove speaking about themes, about the proper use of a semicolon.

On the night before he was to meet Wendy, after a three-mile run, the scale told him he weighed 199. He sank to the tiles beside it, laughing.

He was, of course, back over 200 the next morning. You could never trust the first low point.

So the day of their meeting he restricted his calories even further. He went for a long ride again in the morning, and ate little afterward. After school he ran five miles. He'd hoped the run would calm him, wring his nerves dry, but he shook as he put on his new clothes, his empty stomach a clenched fist.

Was he afraid? Anxious? He couldn't rightly say.

Before he left, he thought about eating a full meal, but as he'd put on the new corduroy pants he'd purchased, they seemed–was he insane, imagining it?–not to fit as well as they had in the store. He told himself to take deep breaths, to be calm, to remember how far he'd come. That, in a way, all his hard work these past two years had gone toward making this evening possible. That he had come a long, long way; that, because he had, everything was going to be fine. Wendy would see him, what he'd become, and be astonished.

Wendy

Wendy had asked to meet him at a casino bar, downtown, a place they'd had drinks before, after shows, tucked just outside of the main floor of the Silver Legacy. She was already sitting at the bar when he arrived. He took a moment to watch her from the entryway. She was peering at her phone, texting with someone, frowning. Ed, probably. He recognized her posture even before he saw her face; he told himself he could not actually smell her perfume, but who knew—maybe he really could. Maybe if you lived that long with someone, you were attuned to her at the level of the subconscious.

Wendy had not changed. She was long, slender, wearing a sweater dress and glasses, tights, and low heels, her hair falling in a clean line to the tops of her shoulders. She'd darkened its shade, he thought. She was a beautiful woman, even more so here in the dim, cinematic light. In a different bar, Trace would have pointed her out to him. Or maybe approached her himself.

Doug pushed back a surge of fear and walked toward her.

Wendy did not recognize him at first, and only when Doug smiled and waved did she react, and then it was as he hoped:

"Jesus. Is that *you?*"

He was, to his surprise, suddenly, sharply angry—because only a person used to him being fat would be so shocked; only someone who had vanished entirely from his life would have to struggle to recognize him; she had been his wife, he thought, his *wife*; she had told him his weight did not matter to her, but now look at her amazement, look at her face, her eyes taking him in—

"It's me," he said.

She stood but she did not hug him, and he did not offer to hug her, though he wanted to—and then his anger was gone. He was surprised by how much he wanted, then, to feel the familiar curve of her hip, to smell her hair.

"I mean," she said, waving her hands at him, "I heard you lost some weight. But—you're not sick, are you? I mean, are you okay?"

"I'm just fine," he said, and laughed. "I've lost one hundred and thirty-six pounds."

She shook her head. "Wow."

"Hardest thing I've ever done," he said and, as he said it, knew it was true. "I'm a new man," he said—and that was where his confidence failed him, that was when he thought of Hanna, turning off her phone and tucking it in her purse; of Nancy's letter in his mailbox.

Wendy was looking inward, now, frowning, rifling through her mental files, her prepared statements. "Thank you for meeting," she said finally.

"Thanks for asking."

"We're okay with this?" she asked, hurriedly.

"Yeah. This is necessary. Like you said."

They sat across from one another in a corner booth. He asked the hostess for one on purpose; when he'd been big, he'd not been able to fit in booth seats. Wendy ordered a complicated, flavored martini. He drank a bourbon, neat, and after the first sip knew it was a mistake—he'd barely had anything to eat, after all, and he only got a few sips in before he began to hear the sounds around him, the words coming from his mouth, at a muffled remove.

Wendy said, "I don't suppose there's any way to keep this from being awkward."

"Maybe not," he said. "But here we are, doing it."

"Here we are," she said, musingly. "Okay. So. Doug. How are you?"

He told her he was fine. Better than fine. He'd bought a house, he told her. (She'd heard, but she was happy for him.) He described the house to her, the decor, the furnishings, the maple trees in back. He did not tell her about the women who had been there with him, the things he'd done inside of it. She asked him how work was, and he told her all was well—but not about Nancy. He told her cheerful anecdotes.

He could only really tell Wendy about the surface of his new life. He wondered if she wondered about the other, more private parts. What she would say if she knew.

He told her about running, about biking. He told her he was thinking about a dog. He did not mean to say that; it wasn't really true. Wendy liked dogs; Nan liked dogs. He didn't know if he could take care of a dog. He trailed off.

She said, "I don't know if I can ask this. It's all right if you don't want to talk about it. But I heard you were dating someone for a while?"

She smiled as she asked, but he thought he felt sadness in it. Even a little fear.

"Yes," he said. "Her name was—is—Nancy. We broke up a few months back."

"I'm sorry."

"I was the one who ended things. That was . . . hard."

She gave a thin-lipped smile. "My friend Muriel knows her a little. She said she's nice."

That Wendy knew anything about Nancy at all made him shift in his seat. "She *is* nice. Just—I didn't know what I wanted." He took a deep breath. "I still don't know what to think about it. She wanted it to be permanent, and . . ."

She was fat, he almost said, just to see the look on Wendy's face. *You know how it is.*

"She's a great person."

Wendy nodded, sympathetically.

He said, "Okay. So. How's Ed?"

Wendy made another complex face at the sound of Ed's name, and he nearly apologized—he'd not meant, really, ever to say Ed's name again, but there it was. Here they were.

"Edward and I split up," she said. "Just last month."

"I'm sorry to hear that," he said, though the shock of it ran through him to the tips of his fingers. "Wendy. I hadn't heard."

"I haven't told many people. And you don't have to be sympathetic. I would never expect that."

"Maybe not. But I'm sorry for you anyway."

She took a drink. "Thank you. I didn't want—it's hard to admit this to you."

"Well. I didn't want to tell you about—"

"About Nancy."

"No."

"That's the reason to do this, though," she said, carefully. "So we can say these things. We have lives. It doesn't seem right to act like we don't." She finished her martini.

"You want another one?" he asked. "On me."

She nodded, a little embarrassed, maybe. Lawyer Wendy was gone. The Wendy he'd been afraid of, mad at, was gone. She seemed smaller, more fragile—more *there.* He was reminded of buying her drinks in college, when they were dating, the way she'd let him order for her. *Surprise me.*

When he returned with their drinks, she straightened and said, as though she'd been rehearsing it, "Thank you for listening just now. That means a lot to me, Doug. You'd have been within your rights to . . . to gloat."

For the past two years he might very well have gloated, had the news come then. Now, though, sitting with her, he felt a surprising tenderness. He didn't think it was because of the drinks. "No," he said. "I'm not like that, Wendy."

"Well," she said. "I appreciate it."

He said, "Tell me what happened."

She told him that the story was entirely undramatic, banal, in a way that embarrassed her. She had fallen for Ed when she was upset and trying to split from the marriage, and she'd made him into someone and something he couldn't be: the partner she needed the world to give her, at a time when she felt unhappy. ("Sorry," she told Doug, wincing, but he motioned for her to go on, his head cottony, his hands seeming to float.) Ed, for his part, had loved her genuinely. He had been her friend for years, all the while nursing a private longing. She'd always known about it, and (as Doug had suspected) she'd been the one to make the first moves. When she'd broken it off, Ed had said unkind things, words she deserved, given that he'd uprooted his entire life for her. (Doug could guess what those words were—but screw Ed Panecki, anyway.)

"I've been trying to understand it," she said. "And I think I'm learning more about who I am. I've needed— no. I *expect* people to be what I want, and I maybe don't come and find them where they *are.*"

Her second drink was almost gone. Her eyes were glistening. Doug could not imagine what it had cost her to say this. That the woman who had lived in his imagination as she had these last two years could become the person sitting across from him now, admitting such things.

"I didn't know if I could say all that to you. But I think I owed it to you." She straightened. "And I want to say I'm sorry for the pain I caused you, Doug. I'm still trying to figure this all out, but I want you to know that I know I hurt you, trying to get to the place I need to be. To be a better person. I don't know if it helps to hear. It doesn't erase any hurt. I know that."

He'd imagined many outcomes to this meeting, but not this one, not Wendy struggling, Wendy so clearly lost and questioning. Wendy apologizing.

She said, suddenly, "Are you all right?"

He thought he knew what she meant. How she wanted him to answer. Just weeks ago he might have answered, *No. I will never be all right. I cannot be all right. Not after what you did.*

And yet, sitting here, he didn't feel that anger overwhelming him. Not at all.

"You're thinking about it too long," Wendy said. "I shouldn't have asked."

She was near tears. She really did want him to be all right. She wanted him to tell her that he'd survived. And though he'd spent two years wanting to show her exactly that—to survive and then thrive, to create an entire new self—her face and her wet eyes stopped him. To tell her he was fine was to tell her he had learned to live without her.

But here they were, sitting opposite one another; their hands were ringless, but not far from one another on the glass tabletop; they had both been through so much pain, and still he wanted to squeeze her fingers between his own, to forgive her anything.

"I'm trying to be all right," he said. "I know I wasn't, before. When we were married. You were right about that. I wasn't happy. I'm trying to get there, now."

She nodded, biting at her lip.

"I'm sorry, too," he said. He wished he'd eaten, wished he hadn't drunk two whiskeys so quickly. "I know I wasn't what you wanted me to be."

The words seemed to shake her.

He said, "I'm trying to be better, but I don't know if I'm succeeding at anything."

"No," she said. "Look at you. Look at how you've changed. That had to take so much work . . ."

Was it the tone of her voice? The care in it? All the memories it carried, of the years' worth of quiet conversations they'd had, the long accumulation of small comforts and assurances? How much else had he forgotten?

"I'm lonely," he said. "This has been hard."

She did not seem surprised to hear it.

"I am, too," she said. "And it is."

• • •

She finished her martini and excused herself to the restroom. He watched her go, the sway in her walk, the sadness in her shoulders. A waitress came by the table and asked if they wanted another. Doug ordered both of them another drink. Why not?

When Wendy returned, she saw the new martini. "Oh, that's one too many for me," she said. "I'm sorry. I have to be at trial tomorrow."

Of course, he thought, disappointed. He'd forgotten. He had to teach, too. To enter the world of his life again, even if, right now, it seemed impossibly distant.

Wendy was still kind, friendly, but she seemed to have pulled away, inside, from their earlier intimacy. She asked him about less weightier topics: about school, about why on earth he wanted a dog, about exercise. He took sips from his drink, even though his head swam. He wished that they could return to the earlier moment, the one that had so moved them both. He asked about her new job (she liked it); the case in town that had brought her back (they'd win it when it went to jury, she was sure). They talked about mutual friends, joking, filling in the gaps.

She laughed at something he said. And then, for a moment, she was at ease again; they were at ease with each other.

So many times, when they were married, when things between them had been good (or, perhaps, not so bad), he had loved sitting across from her, hearing her speak. Feeling the little thrill that passed through him when this woman met his eye, when she smiled. He had missed it.

"Do you want to stay in Santa Fe?" he asked.

"Actually," she said, "I think I'm going to be moving home."

For a moment he thought she meant Reno, but then she added, "To Pittsburgh. I've got an offer at a firm there."

"Oh," he said.

"Really," she said, "that's why I wanted to meet. If we didn't talk soon, we might never have gotten the chance."

He'd finished his drink. "Wendy—" he began to say, and leaned forward over the table, but she said, "I should really go to bed" at the same time. She laughed and rubbed the back of her neck. "Sorry. It's been a long week."

"Where are you staying?"

"With a friend," she said. She looked at his empty

glass. "Please tell me you didn't drive."

"I did," he said, "but I don't live far away. It's not a bad walk."

She smiled. "You've done this a few times."

He smiled back.

"Well," she said.

"Walk you to your car?" he said. "Just to be safe."

"I'm a big girl," she said. Then, "But sure."

Together they threaded a path through the casino floor, past the tired gamblers and the lost tourists (so many of them, he saw, were fat, sallow, plodding, unhappy), and as always it was a relief to leave the noise and the old-smoke smell and stand in the cool outside air, even if it was in the parking garage.

Wendy led the way to her car, a nondescript white rental sedan. Every step they took filled him with too much memory, too much feeling. He remembered the night she'd ended things. And yet he recognized so much of their marriage in her walk, the breeziness of her voice, the rocking of her hips, the click of her heels.

She said, "I'm really glad we could do this. It's been good to see you. And really. You've done all right." Her voice caught. "I—I'm glad you're all right."

"I wish we could do this again," he said.

Wendy hesitated, her lips parted, but she did not seem to know what to say, and he was sure—sure—that she was feeling what he felt, too; he reached out and took her hand, and she squeezed it, but he pulled her to him, and hugged her fiercely.

She hugged him back.

"Don't go," he said.

"I have to—"

And in that moment, the feel of her body against

his was so familiar, carried with it such intimacy, that he ran a hand down her back, in a way she'd always liked, to her hip, and as he did so he moved his mouth to hers as though by instinct, and their lips touched, and she pulled back, but he took her cheeks between his hands and kissed her, and then she pulled away with more force and said, "Doug! No—"

But he could not let her go; he still had her hand gripped in his, and she said "Doug," again, but warningly, and he said, "Don't go yet," and pulled her closer, and she said "You have the wrong idea," and he said, "I've *missed* you—" but now she shoved him, and then finally he was standing apart from her, his breath coming hard, and she was rubbing her wrist.

She said, "You *hurt* me."

"I'm sorry." His voice seemed rubbery in his mouth, not his own. He was dizzy.

"What the *hell*, Doug?"

The words jumped out of him: "I still love you. And I thought—"

She turned to her car, jamming a hand into her bag for her keys. "Unbelievable."

Her fury, finally, reached him. "Wendy, wait. I'm sorry—"

"Goodbye," she told him, and unlocked the door of her car and got quickly inside. He waited for her to climb back out, to come back to him, even as he knew she never would, even as the engine started up, and she pulled out of the space and drove past him, too quickly, and was gone.

Farewell

In the morning he woke in pain. After pounding his alarm clock into submission he sat for a long time rubbing the back of his neck. He did not remember much of the previous evening, except that he'd drunk a great deal, both at the casino with Wendy and then more, when he'd come home afterward. He'd eaten, too, he remembered—on the way home he'd stopped at a grocery and bought himself a steak and a tub of mashed potatoes. Thinking of this made his stomach turn over. He stumbled to the shower and stood under the water for a long while, debating whether he'd vomit, and tried as best he could to piece himself together, to clean himself, and it was there, bent forward, his head throbbing, that he remembered that he'd tried to force Wendy to kiss him.

When he was out of the shower, he sat in front of his computer and tried to compose an email to her. He put a few words into the empty text box, but none of them were the right ones, and finally he typed *I am so so sorry,* and hit send.

In the kitchen he saw evidence of the meal the night before, the dirty skillet furred with grease, the plate in the sink, a bottle of whiskey still open on the counter; he felt the meat in his stomach, heavy and unfamiliar, and went to weigh himself, and when the numbers on the scale read 198, he almost didn't believe his eyes.

He went to school because he had to; it was the last day of the semester. He took several Advil and drove carefully the two miles to campus, wondering if he was, in fact, still drunk, if despite his scrubbing he smelled too much of alcohol.

The school was too loud, too bright, the students buzzing and frantic, as they always were on the last day. Doug was sure, as he moved through the hallways, that people would know what he had done. That shame must be visible on his face. But his fellow teachers smiled at him, and greeted him, or didn't, as usual. The students were giddy with impending freedom and did not look at him at all; he was an obstacle to be moved around, a stone in a surging river.

In the bathroom he looked haggard—his skin sallow, his eyes red-rimmed and weepy; his hair especially gray and wild—but also *skinny*. Sunken. Not just thin, but *old*, as though he'd withered.

He let his classes do what they wanted all day; several of them had brought him gifts, cards, copies of their senior pictures. He handed back the final projects and portfolios he'd spent all week grading. He apologized to each class for feeling ill, and received sympathy; if any students recognized his hangover they kept the knowledge to themselves. (A lot of them were likely hung over, too.) He signed the yearbooks his journalism class had produced, laughed feebly at jokes; he posed alongside some of the students for selfies, trying not to wince.

Between his classes he checked his email; Wendy had not written him back. At lunchtime he did not eat, but sat at the desk in the antechamber off his classroom and wept piteously.

He decided to text her: *I'm sorry. That's not me.*

She texted back. *My wrist is bruised. You were the only one there. So it WAS you.*

His final class of the day was journalism, his last hour with his beloved seniors: Maddie, Lawrence, Javier, and especially Inez. In previous years he had put up streamers and bought small farewell cards for his editors, but he'd been too sick this time. He apologized to them, and they didn't seem to mind. He put out a plate of cookies

and thanked the class for their hard work. They set up
a camera on a timer and all posed together. Inez stood
next to him wearing her Northwestern sweatshirt—she
was headed there in the fall; he'd written her an enthu-
siastic recommendation—and together they held up a
copy of the yearbook, and when the picture was taken,
she cleared her throat and—tears in her eyes—presented
him a gift from the class: a fountain pen and a bottle of
red ink. "Thank you," she said, "For inspiring us." Then
she hugged him.

He hugged her back, tried not to feel the shape of
her body, tried not to hurt her.

When the period was nearly over, he called for their
attention. Half the students in the room had been here
with him when he first announced his diet. They turned
to him, leaned forward (though a few of them gave each
other side-eye looks or rolled their eyes)—all of them
knew about his traditional farewell speech to the seniors.
How he would tell them he loved them and believed in
them. How he knew they could do whatever they wanted,
as long as they kept looking inside. How they had to do
the hard work of knowing themselves. And they would
believe him even more, now that he was small, now that
he'd transformed himself, now that they could all see
by looking at him that he'd made his own dreams come
true—

And god, he couldn't do it, but they were still looking at him, Inez was looking at him, sweet and unsus-
pecting and small and human.

He stared at them. From the back of the room, a nervous titter.

The bell rang, earlier than he expected, and they all
waited a beat, then rose up. The moment had passed.

He said all he could think to say:

"Be good people."

"We will," they said, laughing, confused. "Goodbye, Mr. Ritchie," they said. Inez put a hand over her mouth, trying not to cry, but then freedom caught her, too, and she gave him one last finger-waggle and joined the others, gathering their bags and purses and pulling out their phones, high-fiving and cheering and then rushing from the room; not a single one of them turned back to see him standing there, trim and alone at the front of his classroom, having done all that he had set out to do, and shaking with hunger.

Acknowledgments

I am grateful to many people, without the help and faith of whom I'd not have made a book at all.

Huge thanks are due to early readers of these stories, as well as those who helped with research and/or advice: Erin Andersen, Casey Bell, Mignon Fogarty, Cameron Filipour, Joelle Fraser, Jack Fredericks, Cindie Geddes, Shari Goldhagen, Cyndy Cendagorta Gustafson, Don Hardy, Thomas Hertweck, Cindie Geddes, Jason Ludden, Ben Rogers, Amanda Rush, Amy Schnupp, Alissa Surges, Gabriel Urza, and Curtis Vickers. (If I missed anyone, it's my fault and not yours.) Special thanks go to my dear friends Michelle Herman and Michael P. Kardos, constant readers along the way.

Thanks to the journals and editors who published a few of these, especially Kelly Abbott and Matt Weiland.

Thanks to the students I've had the honor of teaching these last years at the University of Nevada, Reno, especially those with whom I've worked in the MFA program, and all of whom inspire me every day I walk through the doors.

Thanks to my terrific colleagues in the Department of English at UNR, who have been endlessly supportive of this project and my writing; I could name everyone in my department, but special shout-outs go to Michael Branch, Stacy Burton, Ian Clayton, Jane Detweiler, Katherine Fusco, James Mardock, Ashley Marshall, Lynda Olman, and Eric Rasmussen. And many thanks to my colleagues in the MFA program, all of them wonderful writers and humans: S.M. Hulse, David Anthony Durham, Ann Keniston, Steve Gehrke, Gailmarie Pahmeier, and Jared Stanley.

I finished this book with the help of a teaching release from the UNR College of Liberal Arts, for which I am deeply grateful.

Thanks, as always, to all my teachers. One of them, Lee K. Abbott, passed away while this book was being finished. I dearly wish I could send him a copy now.

Drs. Marvin Levenson and Lynda Ross: thank you most kindly for your help and guidance.

I am as always indebted to my agent, Marian Young— and to Joseph Olshan and Lori Milken of Delphinium Books for taking the collection on, and getting my best work out of me as we shaped the book.

Thanks to my mother, Jan Coake, and my sister, Whitney Coake, who both kick a lot of ass.

And finally, thanks to my wife, Stephanie Lauer, for sticking with me while I learned how to write all this.

About the Author

Christopher Coake is the author of the novel *You Came Back* (2012) and the story collection *We're in Trouble* (2005), which won the PEN/Robert Bingham Fellowship for a first work of fiction. In 2007 he was named one of Granta's *Best Young American Novelists*. His short fiction has been anthologized in collections such as *Best American Mystery Stories* 2004; *The Best American Noir of the Century*; and *Gutted: Beautiful Horror Stories*; and has been published in numerous literary journals. A native of Indiana, Coake received his MFA in fiction from the Ohio State University. He is an Associate Professor of English at the University of Nevada, Reno, where he directs the MFA program in creative writing. He lives in Reno with his wife, Stephanie Lauer, and their two dogs.